UNWITTING

ERICA ROSEN MD TRILOGY: BOOK 2

DEVEN GREENE

PANTHERA
PUBLISHING

ISBN: 978-1-964620-02-2
Published by Panthera Publishing

To my son Aaron, the inspiration for this book.
I hope you understand how smart, good, and special you are.

UNWITTING

Chapter 1

I remember that afternoon in August, the first time I saw the video of people walking slowly, talking, and laughing, as they entered San Francisco's Oracle Park baseball stadium. Then a fiery flash. I'll never forget the slender arm, a silver bracelet around the wrist, flying through the smoke and debris. This was followed by images of dead bodies, bloodied people crying, some being comforted, some comforting others. My assistant, Martha, showed it to me on her cell phone when I was between patients in the pediatrics clinic at UCSF, where I am director. Martha dabbed tears from her eyes as I watched.

Looking around, I noticed other doctors and staff studying their cell phones. Over the next few minutes, people spoke in hushed tones, put away their phones, then peeled away to finish the day's work.

I called Lim, my husband of two months, to make sure he was okay, even though he was at work miles away from the disaster. Then I called my best friend, Daisy Wong. I knew she wasn't a baseball fan, and the probability of her being at the game was close to zero, but during times of danger, one's mind can imagine all sorts of improbabilities. I was glad when she answered her phone and assured me she'd been home all day as usual, remotely working at her job as a computer programmer.

For the remainder of the day, the clinic atmosphere was subdued as gloom settled in the hallways, work areas, and exam rooms, stamping out the usual noisy cheerfulness exuded by the staff. When I'd finally seen my last patient, instead of catching up on paperwork as was my custom, I looked forward to spending a quiet night at home, finding solace with my new husband. After all, the explosion had taken place at the Willie Mays Gate of Oracle Park, only a few blocks from our third-floor condominium. Lim and I had chosen our unit in the new, modern building for its view of the San Francisco Bay, proximity to interesting shops and restaurants, and relatively low crime rate.

That evening, upon entering my building, I was doubly glad that a passcode was required to open the main door. Although that didn't ensure complete security, it gave me a modicum of peace of mind. In the lobby, a neighbor told me one of the residents, a young man I knew only enough to smile at and greet should our paths cross, had been injured in the blast. Fortunately he'd suffered only a laceration on his arm from flying debris and was expected to make a full recovery. As I took the stairs up to my unit, I imagined the horror he must have felt in the moments following the explosion. Although his arm would probably heal, I wondered if his psyche ever would.

For the rest of the evening, Lim and I were glued to the TV news as we commiserated over the disaster that had taken place in our neighborhood, thankful we had escaped unscathed. Like most others, we assumed that, like 9/11, it was the work of Islamic terrorists and awaited the announcement by a group proudly claiming responsibility.

*

Until I had moved into the condominium with Lim several months before our wedding, I lived with Daisy in a nearby apartment. I'd met Lim while Daisy and I were in China the previous year. We'd gone there at the urging of Ting Chen, an illegal immigrant from the People's Republic. Ting had escaped China with her two older children, Kang and Wang Shu, now four and six, respectively. After her children became my patients, I learned they were the products of embryonic stem cell gene editing at a secret facility in China. This had been a covert government operation, an operation aimed at producing super athletes to dominate the Olympic games. Those in charge of the program felt the risks of manipulating the DNA of unborn children were inconsequential compared to the benefit.

Ting was forced to participate in the program because she had been a Chinese Olympic track star. Her eggs were removed, fertilized, and edited. Three times one of the resulting embryos was implanted in her, and three times she gave birth to the resulting genetically engineered baby. She loved each child, one girl and two boys, with all her heart despite each pregnancy being involuntary on her part.

Wang Shu, one of the first products of the gene-editing experiments, had DNA edited to change her eye color to blue. Kang and his younger brother, Mingyu, grew from embryos whose hemoglobin DNA was edited to deliver more oxygen, giving them increased stamina. When I first met Ting, she hadn't seen Mingyu, still an infant, since being forced to leave him behind in the secret facility.

Daisy and I set off to China, intent on gathering evidence of the Chinese program and rescuing Mingyu. This required the help of Ting's twin brother, Lim, an anti-government activist who still lived in China. We were successful on all accounts. I recorded evidence of the gene editing taking place, and Daisy smuggled Mingyu out of the facility.

Although Daisy was able to return to the US immediately after our mission was complete, I was prevented from going back at first. As I waited for an opportunity to leave, I stayed with Lim and Mingyu, during which time Lim and I grew close. Eventually, I returned to San Francisco, followed by Lim, who escaped to the US with Mingyu on a cargo ship. With the information Daisy and I had gathered, world opinion forced the Chinese government to abandon its program, although one can never be entirely sure about such things. While meeting Lim was no accident, the falling in love part was.

What had started when I met Lim in China blossomed after we spent more time together in San Francisco. I had no job at first and helped Lim and his sister, Ting, gain asylum and secure the release of their parents, who were in a Chinese prison camp.

Like his sister, Lim had been a Chinese track Olympian. He knew a lot about the US already, having had a Chinese-American coach from Chicago who had told him much about this country and taught him to speak English almost as well as a native. That eased the transition to his new home.

Lim and I have our differences, sure, like where we squeeze the toothpaste tube and how to sort the laundry (he doesn't), but our general approach to life, our curiosity about the world, and interest in helping others are perfectly synced.

*

After I first saw the bombing video, I must have seen it fifty times on the various news channels. It was hard not to think about the haunting images. The recordings retrieved from security cameras aimed at the crowd, far enough away to escape being destroyed by the blast, had an eerie quality. The footage was silent and grainy, in black and white. People looked like they were screaming, but there was no sound. One could only imagine the cries.

Every time I watched the video on the news, I noticed something new. Uniformed officers standing off to the side before the explosion occurred were watching intently. A woman and four men in dark suits positioned around the crowd's perimeter appeared to study the people sauntering past. Two of the men each held the leash of a dog sitting at attention by their side, one a tan German Shepherd, the other a black Labrador Retriever. The man with the German Shepherd was speaking into his shoulder radio seconds before the blast. It struck me that the level of security exceeded the usual.

According to the initial reports, fifteen people had died, including the bomber, and thirty-two were injured, ten seriously. The dead included a father, his seven-year-old son and nine-year-old daughter, two off-duty firefighters, a retired Vietnam vet, and a Japanese engineer here on vacation. Among the more seriously injured, two lost an arm, and one lost most of a leg. Flying debris resulted in paralyzing spinal injuries to two victims and head injuries to three more, one the mother of four who was still comatose.

The last successful terrorist bombings in the San Francisco area had been perpetrated by the Unabomber in the 1980s, with two bomb explosions in Berkeley around the time I was born. None were in San

Francisco itself. Since then, a small number of attempted bombings in the city where Tony Bennet left his heart in 1962 had been foiled. Before the baseball game explosion, bombings weren't on the minds of people here. Gang shootings, home invasions, random acts of violence from muggings, and perceived microaggressions were more of a concern. The whole city was now on edge. We weren't used to this sort of thing. Not that I suppose any city ever is. Not even the Big Apple.

My neighborhood was flooded with police and the curious public for days after the bombing. I wondered about my own safety as I carried out my usual daily activities—walking to work, shopping in local stores, and meeting Daisy for coffee.

The stadium was cordoned off with crime scene tape and makeshift barriers. Walking by, I saw the ballpark was crawling with cops. A crowd of people stood by, apparently entertained by watching police officers walk in and out of the entry gate and up and down the stadium steps, while taking pictures and talking on their radios.

The death toll crept up, with three additional victims, including a mother of three, succumbing to their injuries. No information was forthcoming about the bomber's identity, what organization, if any, was responsible, or if another target was threatened. National and local news programs televised only a series of interviews with witnesses, relatives of victims, first responders, local residents, and members of the Giants team. I wasn't the only one surprised at the dearth of meaningful updates and the failure of any group to claim responsibility.

The lack of information proved to be fertile ground for the spread of baseless rumors. It became widely assumed the bombing was the result of a carefully planned Islamic terrorist attack. Whether this conclusion was promoted by Russian hackers or white supremacist groups, I don't know. However, the constant barrage of bombing coverage brought out the worst of humanity. Hate groups lashed out. In addition to verbal attacks against Muslims and people who looked like they might be Middle Eastern, several retaliatory murders at mosques and businesses were covered by the national news. In all, six such killings were reported—four Muslims, one Arab Christian, and one Hindu. I imagined there were other cowardly attacks, fatal and nonfatal, not reaching national attention.

Three days after the bombing, a stunning report made a news splash, with headlines plastered on the front page of newspapers across the country. An investigative journalist, through cunning, contacts, and, I suppose, some sort of sixth sense, penetrated the wall established by Major League Baseball (MLB) to prevent information on the case from leaking to the public. The journalist was intrigued when he studied tapes of the bombing and recognized a man he'd met in Israel several years earlier while doing a story about security at Ben Gurion Airport in Tel Aviv. The man had been a member of the Mossad, where he headed up the behavioral sciences department analyzing data on the conduct of suicide bombers. Those agents are the best in the world at studying people, looking for signs that reveal a nefarious purpose.

In retrospect, I realized I'd seen the Mossad agent's image countless times on TV in footage showing the crowd streaming through the entrance shortly before the explosion. Dressed in a suit, he was standing to one side, watching closely as fans, laughing and talking, walked past, never suspecting the horror that was only seconds away. The sight of the agent casually standing around the entrance to a baseball game here in San Francisco sparked the journalist to do a little digging. He knew where to poke with his shovel, and an Israeli buddy of his was able to fill in the blanks. The Mossad agent had retired a short time earlier and started his own security firm, based in Tel Aviv, which employed mainly ex-Mossad. The agency handling the Giants' security had recently hired that Israeli firm specifically to thwart a possible suicide bomber.

Armed with that information, the reporter coerced the management of MLB to divulge the truth about what had happened. He learned that one week ahead of the game, the top brass in the Giants' organization received a threatening email message. A suicide bomber would set off an explosion in the stadium unless a sum of five million dollars was deposited in a specified Cayman Islands bank account at least forty-eight hours before the game's opening pitch.

The alarming email was forwarded to the MLB administration, which in turn notified the FBI. They traced the email to an IP address out of the country and deemed the threat not credible. Most likely, they concluded, the threat came from a disgruntled MLB wannabe, someone who had dreamed of playing baseball professionally all his life but lacked the required ability. They advised the Giants not to pay the ransom and keep the threat under wraps to avoid scaring the public. Instead, on the off-chance there really would be a bombing attempt, the FBI offered to plant agents around the stadium and provide bomb-sniffing dogs. The Giants' top brass agreed but provided additional insurance of their own, arranging to have the crowd carefully monitored by behavioral experts trained by the anti-terror division of the Mossad.

Once this information was circulated, public sentiment was quick and unforgiving. Political pundits accused the MLB of behaving disgracefully, placing money ahead of people's safety. The SF Police Department and FBI were deemed worthless. Despite having the most state-of-the-art analytical tools available, neither DNA evidence nor fingerprint analysis (if there were fingerprints to analyze) had led to the identification of the bomber. If that didn't speak to incompetence, what did?

Then the Mossad bashing began. The agents were declared inept. The mystique behind the Mossad's reputation for quietly hunting down criminals, performing daring rescues, and warding off terrorist attacks was proclaimed by many to be fictitious. Instead, they were portrayed as incompetent hacks who had mounted an effective public relations campaign years ago to impress the public. The haranguing must have gotten under the skin of the former Mossad agent the journalist had identified. He flew from Tel Aviv to San Francisco to hold a press conference in front of City Hall on day five.

A tall, muscular man with thick white hair and a heavy Israeli accent, he described previous instances when, along with his colleagues, he had prevented attacks by suicide bombers. The FBI's assessment was reasonable, in his opinion. Before the attack at Oracle Park, he'd been confident he and his crew would be able to detect a bomber walking through the crowd. Then he described in detail the actions of the bomber captured on video from several angles before the explosion.

The bomber, a young man wearing an oversized T-shirt with the Giants logo, seemed alone, although a man whose head was down walked alongside him for a bit before moving to the side. The perpetrator didn't seem to notice, so it was unclear if the man was accompanying him. As the bomber walked on, he showed no signs of nervousness, agitation, or sweating. He appeared to be calmly looking ahead. Even in retrospect, after analyzing the video countless times, the agent could discern nothing out of the ordinary. Then, without making a motion, the young man's midsection exploded.

The agent said he had never seen anything like it. It was as if the bomber was unaware he was wearing a suicide vest. A vest weighing upwards of ten pounds, filled with plastic explosives and wires, probably with a heavy scent of flowers or something else innocuous to hide the smell from dogs. The bomber simply had to know what he was wearing. There would be no mistaking the gear for anything other than a heavy vest with pockets containing the clay-like substance C4. Favored by terrorists because it can be molded like clay, C4 is easily formed into shapes that can fit into pockets, like those found on fishing vests. The vest worn by the bomber would have been uncomfortable and inappropriate for a baseball game on a sunny day—even in San Francisco, which is cool most of the year.

Still more puzzling, there was no discernable political cause here. This wasn't the act of a zealot. Why would someone blow himself up so someone else could collect five million dollars? How did he manage to remain inhumanly calm and composed in the moments before the explosion? The agent said he'd thought long and hard about this. He wasn't making excuses for himself or his colleagues—this just didn't make sense.

The court of public opinion had already tried and convicted everyone connected with the incident. In my mind, it wasn't clear what should have been done. I thought maybe the Giants should have paid the ransom. On the other hand, if the organizers of the bombing had been paid off, there would be nothing to stop them from doing the same at the next game and the game after that. In the end, I concluded they should have canceled the game, and all the following games, until the criminals were busted.

At least they should have warned the public. And the players. None of them were told about the threat, and most were upset with the decision to leave them in the dark. Sure, they were paid big bucks to play, and the organization had some right to tell them what to do. But not to get blown up. There was nothing about that in their contracts. There was plenty of blame placed on the Giants organization and MLB. Of course, if the agency they'd hired to spot the bomber had been successful, we probably would have sung their praises, if we ever learned about it.

On day six, police distributed an artist's rendering of the bomber to news organizations. Suicide bombers are typically beheaded when the bomb they are wearing detonates. Their heads, parts of their arms, and legs can often be retrieved. As pictures of a detached head were deemed too disturbing to circulate publicly, a police artist sketched the bomber from a photograph of the face. To the surprise of many, the bomber didn't look anything like the typical Islamic Jihadist. Fifteen to twenty years old, he was blue-eyed, sandy-haired, and clean-shaven. Having no idea who this young man was, police asked for the public's help to identify him.

I was glad that even though the event took place close to my home, I wasn't directly affected. Nevertheless, I was nervous walking around my neighborhood and had become a bit obsessed, constantly scrolling through the news on my phone, looking for updates about the bombing. Although I knew people who knew people who were killed, I didn't personally know anyone who had suffered serious physical harm from the explosion. A few days after the incident, I'd spoken to my neighbor who had been injured and sensed he was deeply disturbed, much more so than he let on. Six days after the bombing, that was the extent of my thoughts about the subject. Until I received a phone call from Brandy Monroe.

Chapter 2

It was a Tuesday morning. I had just finished breakfast and was rushing around, getting ready to leave for a day at the clinic, when I heard a knock on the door. After all we'd gone through with the Chinese government, a visitor at the door always filled me with apprehension until I could confirm there was no danger at my threshold. Usually, an unexpected visitor arriving without being buzzed in at the front door by us was Ting, her daughter Wang Shu, or one of Lim's parents.

Lim's mother, Fung, and his father, Enlai, live one level below Lim and me, on the second floor of our building, next door to Ting and her three adorable children. Fung and Enlai were awaiting final processing of their asylum application, having been released from a Chinese prison camp in exchange for two Chinese spies imprisoned here. They arrived in San Francisco on an Air China flight two weeks before our wedding, which we'd postponed, hoping they could attend.

Aged beyond their years and in poor health, it was a happy, tearful reunion. Our wedding, where Daisy served as my maid of honor, and Ting was Lim's best woman, was a small affair. I kept my last name, Rosen. I didn't want my young patients to be confused by a change. I was told my in-laws were disappointed, but Lim led them to believe it was an American custom.

I doubted Lim heard the knock, as he was in the study on a conference call related to his position as a partner in a local start-up tech company which we anticipated would be bought by Google at some point. While he made a good living and stood to rake in a fortune from stock if and when the company was sold, his biggest income stream was the ongoing bitcoin operation he'd started before leaving China. Despite Lim leaving much of those proceeds in his native country to fund anti-government activities, we were able to provide for his parents. Ting, an engineer, landed a well-paying job at a local company several months earlier. She supported herself and her children but was unable to contribute to my in-laws' expenses. If it weren't for my income, Lim and I would be stretched pretty thin. My salary allowed all of us to live comfortably.

Shortly after we were married, my new in-laws underwent a battery of exams and began receiving treatment for vitamin and protein deficiency as well as parasitic infections. Having arrived with less than half their teeth, they each received a full set of temporary teeth, to be replaced by permanent implants in a few months. In the short time they'd been here, their health had improved remarkably. As early as a month after our wedding, they were more active than most people their age, taking long walks at a brisk pace almost daily. They seemed to get more vigorous each time I saw them. It's easy to see how Ting and Lim inherited their athletic ability.

My in-laws seem nice and smile a lot, especially now that they have new teeth, but they speak almost no English, and I never have any idea what they are saying. Although Lim's translations indicate they like me, for all I know Lim is hiding the truth from me, trying to spare my feelings. I made an attempt to learn some Mandarin, but my mispronunciations and, in particular, inability to capture the appropriate tonal qualities so important in the language, led to bouts of laughter shared by my dear husband and his relatives. Several times, Lim said, "We are laughing along with you, not right at you," but that didn't encourage me to keep trying.

Ting still got requests for interviews. The public sought details of her time spent at the human embryonic stem-cell gene editing facility and wanted to hear about her kids. Some reporters asked if they might time

Kang running the fifty-yard dash, curious to know if he is destined to be a super athlete. Ting refused all requests, making it clear she wanted to protect her children's privacy so they could have as normal a life as possible. Fortunately, public curiosity appeared to be waning. To those close to her, however, Ting confided she was worried about her children. The possibility of ill effects down the road from the gene editing loomed large in her mind.

The hours of Ting's employment were regular, and she worked from home on Fridays. The other days, her parents watched her kids. It was an ideal set-up for a single mom. Wang Shu had attended several months of kindergarten in public school before the term ended and was planning to start first grade in the fall. Both she and her brother Kang were picking up English. I hoped they would continue to speak to their grandparents in Chinese so they wouldn't forget their native tongue.

Looking through the peephole, I was relieved to see Ting. I opened the door and saw she was holding her older boy, Kang. She explained he had been seated at his child-sized table doing a puzzle when, at Wang Shu's urging, he started to pull the chair apart. While an impossible task for most kids, he succeeded in yanking off one of the wooden legs. In doing so, the jagged exposed surface left a nasty cut on his arm. Ting had wrapped his wound in a white towel, which was now stained with blood.

I examined Ting's children regularly, looking for signs of adverse consequences of gene editing. So far, they seemed healthy and happy. I couldn't help but notice that Kang ran faster and had more stamina than any kid I'd seen before. I was happy for him, I suppose. What kid wouldn't want to be a super athlete? Yet, I had mixed feelings about it.

I was disturbed the abominable gene-editing experiment appeared to have been successful, while at the same time worried Kang's future might hold something disastrous, an unforeseen result of the procedure. I wondered if he and Mingyu would be able to participate on the US Olympic team if they remained healthy, provided elite athletic competition was something they wanted to pursue. After all, it wasn't our government that tried to rig the system. Such questions wouldn't need to be answered for fifteen years or so. I told myself not to worry about it now. For all I knew, I might be demented or dead by then. But, of course, I wanted the best for them.

"I'm just about to leave for work. Why don't you come with me and bring Kang? I can clean out his wound and bandage him up before I see my first patient," I said. "He'll be as good as new."

"He'll be new?"

Ting and Lim still had problems with American idioms. They were both smart, so they were learning quickly. But each new phrase had to be separately taught. "I know, another one of our strange expressions. It means he'll be fine," I said, chuckling. "He won't be damaged anymore. Like he's new."

"I think I get it now. Very funny. Yes, he be like new baby. But with teeth."

We both laughed. I went into the study and waved at Lim. He looked up from his desk, his cell phone to his ear, and I motioned I was going to work. I blew him a kiss, and he reciprocated, still listening intently to the call as he took notes. Looking at him, I found it hard to believe it had taken him less than a year to transform from a streetwise Chinese political activist living in poverty to an upper-middle-class American entrepreneur. He seemed completely at ease in his new identity. The old Lim was still there—gorgeous on the outside as well as the inside.

I ordered an Uber on the way down in the elevator. On rainless days like that one, I usually walked to work, but at the moment, with blood seeping through the white towel around Kang's arm, I thought it best not to walk on the street with him.

We entered the clinic building through a back door, avoiding the parents and crying children in the waiting room. I'd become clinic director a few weeks following my return from China. The former director had been fired after breaking the nose of a pediatric cardiologist he was dating when he got into a physical altercation with her. San Francisco, in the midst of the #MeToo movement, was not a good place and time to abuse women. After his termination, I was hired to replace him. It was an easy transition for me, as I had worked there previously and knew most of the personnel. I was glad to be working again with Martha, my trusted medical assistant.

The staff would be calling for the first patients of the day in five minutes. Martha was waiting for me.

"Dr. Rosen, what have we here?" she asked, smiling as she looked at Kang in Ting's arms.

"Just a little accident. You remember my sister-in-law, Ting, and her son Kang, don't you?" I asked as I donned my white coat and affixed my nametag.

"Certainly. I've seen Ting here in the clinic with her kids several times. And, of course, at your wedding."

I was thankful she didn't mention she'd also seen them on TV when news of the Chinese genetic engineering program broke. Ting didn't need another reminder of that unpleasantness. "Kang had a little accident while dismembering his chair," I said, pointing to the red splotch on the towel encircling his arm. "I'm afraid I'm going to be a little late seeing my first patient. I've got to take care of this first."

"Why don't you go into Room One? I'll bring you everything you need to clean him up. I'll even throw in a suture kit in case you need it."

"Thanks. You're the best."

I doubt Martha heard my last comment, as she was already halfway down the hall headed to the supply room when I said it. I ushered Ting, still holding Kang, into Room One and was shortly joined by Martha, carrying all the supplies I needed. "I can't believe someone his age could break a kiddie chair like that," she said. "Sounds like an unsafe product to me. I'd suggest finding out the brand and getting that crap off the market."

"Good thinking," I said. I took Kang from Ting's arms, placed him on the exam table, and unwrapped the towel around his arm. As I washed his laceration and examined it, he began to squirm despite Ting's effort to comfort him. The wound was jagged, almost two inches long, and fairly deep. *Damn. It needs stitches. Now I'm really going to be late for my first patient. I'll never catch up unless I skip lunch.*

I injected the area with lidocaine as Kang whimpered, and started the first of four stitches. As I concentrated on what I was doing, a disturbing thought intruded. *Maybe there was nothing wrong with the chair. Perhaps Kang is stronger than any kid his age should be. Why would that be? His genetically engineered hemoglobin gives him unusual stamina, but I don't expect his altered hemoglobin to make him abnormally strong. But what if . . . Oh, damn. I hope not. Nonetheless,*

I can't help but wonder. What if they did to him what Ting told me they were going to do in the future, what I'd seen evidence they were working on when I visited the facility? What if, besides altering Kang's hemoglobin DNA, they also destroyed his ability to make myostatin, the protein that regulates muscle development? Without it, muscles develop incredible strength, so-called double-muscling. I needed to hold off on complaining to the chair manufacturer until I had more information.

In addition to examining Ting's kids regularly, I'd been drawing blood from each of them every two months. They didn't like it, but I felt it was necessary. I wanted to catch anything abnormal before it became serious. I made a mental note—find out how to test for myostatin before the next time I collected the kids' blood. As I finished bandaging Kang, I noticed the beginning of well-defined muscles in his arm. Unusual for a four-year-old. Without mentioning my concern, I instructed Ting on how to care for the wound.

"Good as new," Ting said, smiling before she thanked me. She whispered something to Kang, who looked at me and said, "Thank you." I didn't believe he was sincere, but his improved pronunciation pleased me. After they left, I sat in front of the computer to enter my notes in Kang's chart. Martha rushed in to remind me I was running late.

"Your first patient is a new one. Four-year-old with diarrhea for two days. Room Seven. But before that, there's a person who's called twice already this morning. Says she needs to speak to you right away."

"Name?"

"Brandy Monroe."

"Never heard of her. Probably a drug rep."

"I don't think so. She sounds legit. Really worried about something."

"If she calls back, ask her what she wants."

"I've asked her several times already. She won't tell me. Insists on speaking to you and only you. Says it's vital. Her word, not mine. Here's her number. Please call her. I know you're behind and all that, but I can tell it's very important. At least to her. She sounds desperate."

I took the number from Martha while swearing under my breath. I didn't have time for this. I had a busy day scheduled and, as my assistant had just reminded me, was behind already. I had to admit, though,

Martha was no sucker, so the woman probably was genuinely in distress. Whether what she wanted to talk to me about was truly important or not was another story. *If this Brandy person is going to try to sell me a timeshare in Hawaii, Martha will never hear the end of it from me.* I went to the nurse's station, picked up a phone, and dialed for an outside line. Then I punched in the seven-digit number Martha had given me. There was no area code, so I assumed it was a local number. No sooner had I dialed than someone answered. I heard a young woman's anxious voice. "Hello?"

"Can I speak to Brandy Monroe?"

"This is she. Who's this?"

"Dr. Erica Rosen."

"Oh, thank you," Brandy gushed. "I'm so glad you called. You have no idea. I was afraid you wouldn't call."

I heard the woman burst into tears.

"Please, Brandy, tell me what this is about. I have a full schedule, and I'm already behind. If you—"

"Sorry, Dr. Rosen. Sorry. I feel you're the only one I can talk to. The only one who will understand."

"Understand what?"

"My kids, I love them all. I would never do anything to—"

"Did you hurt one of your children?" I asked, raising my voice. I wondered if this was an Andrea Yates type of situation. She's the woman who went bonkers and drowned her five kids close to twenty years ago. I remembered my mom telling me about her.

"No. Never. Not me. But—" her voice trembled, and she broke down crying again.

"Who? Who hurt your children? Where are they? Why are you calling me?"

"I brought one of my kids to your clinic last year. They're all . . . they're all special. Not many people see them as worthwhile. Even doctors. But I could tell you were different."

I still had no clue who this person was. I'm the one who sees most of the special needs kids, if what she meant by "special" was handicapped in some way. All the clinic staff knew I had a place in my heart reserved for them, having had a brother with cerebral palsy and deafness. He'd died a few years before, leaving me with an emptiness. I suppose a shrink would diagnose me with some sort of disorder in which I cared for disabled children because I was constantly trying to fill the void left by my brother's death.

"I'm sorry, but I'm not sure I remember you," I said. "Can you tell me more about your visit last year and what the problem is now?"

"I know, I'm not being very clear," Brandy said, sniffling. "I run a day school for older kids with autism here in San Francisco. It's called Bright Lights. Age sixteen to twenty-one. It's a small program, with eight students. All boys, none with severe behavior problems. Last year we went on a field trip to the aquarium at Pier 39. These kids are often the object of ridicule and cruelty by others. One of my boys, Arthur, was making funny noises like he often does, and a kid nearby stabbed him in the hand with a switchblade and ran off. It was horrible. I took Arthur to see you in the clinic and had my assistant take the others back to our program. You were so nice and patient with Arthur. I've never forgotten. You might remember me. I'm, um, very fat."

It was coming back to me now. She was a rather obese woman with long blond hair. I could tell she was very caring. Affixed to her collar was a blue puzzle piece pin, a symbol of autism awareness. Arthur was a Black teen, about seventeen years old and clearly autistic. He was nonverbal and, like she said, made a lot of funny noises. He reminded me of some of the boys I'd taken care of when I volunteered as an aide in a home for autistic children while I was in high school. Gentle and sweet, Arthur let me examine him and stitch up his wound without resistance.

I also remembered seeing what looked like cigarette burns on his arms. I asked about them at the time, and Brandy told me his mother had burned him with cigarettes when he was younger, before he became a ward of the state and was moved to a group home. When I commented that some looked fresh, she said Arthur had a habit of picking at them and making them bleed. I remembered Arthur but didn't remember Brandy much.

"Has something happened to Arthur? Has someone hurt him?" I had to get to the bottom of this. Soon. Even though I had patients waiting, I needed to find out what was going on as someone may have been seriously hurt.

"Not Arthur, no. Steven." Brandy started crying hysterically.

"Brandy, please, you've got to tell me what's going on, or I can't help you. Or Steven." My patience was wearing thin. The noise at the nurse's station was distracting me, it was difficult to hear, and I was growing more anxious every second, knowing I was falling further and further behind.

I heard sniffling on the other end before Brandy spoke again. "If I call the police, they'll think I'm a crackpot. He'll find out, and I'm sure he'll hurt the others if I don't stop him. I've met you, I've seen you on TV, and I know I can trust you. You could make sure no one gets hurt and put an end to this. You've got to come see me so I can explain."

"Explain what?" I heard only crying. "Okay, tell me where you are. I'll visit you and take care of Steven." I planned to hang up as soon as I got an address and phone 911 to send help.

"Steven's dead. But you can help the others before it's too late."

My heart sank. One of her boys, as she called them, was dead, and the others were in danger.

"What happened to him? Who did it?" A moment earlier, I'd been unfocused, trying to get off the phone as quickly as possible, but her words snapped me to full attention.

"It was Don. I didn't know he'd do anything like that. Maybe I should have figured it out, but I didn't. I had no idea. You've got to believe me."

"What? What did Don do? Is he there? Does he have a gun?"

"I can't talk about it over the phone. You've got to come here."

"You have to tell me more, or I won't come."

"Okay, okay. Don's not here right now. Last week, he told me Steven suddenly got sick in the night and had to go to a special hospital in Los Angeles for treatment. I thought Steven was still there. But now I know Don lied. Steven's really dead. Don trained them. Now I'm sure he trained all of them. Steven was the first one he used. I knew that when I saw his picture on TV earlier today."

"Trained them? Trained them to do what?"

"Trained them to be suicide bombers."

Chapter 3

I sat in stunned silence while my brain recuperated from what I'd just heard. *Did Brandy really say that? Suicide bombers?*

"Hello?" Brandy interrupted my mental paralysis.

"Did I hear you correctly?" I asked.

Brandy started crying again, but managed to blurt out an answer to my question. "Yes."

I pushed the conversation further. "Is this related to the Oracle Park incident?"

After a few moments of silence, I heard a door slam and a man's voice. "Who are you talking to, Sweetie?" he asked. That's the last I heard before the call was disconnected.

I've got to do something, was my first thought, followed by, *why is this happening to me?* I snapped out of self-pity mode and sprang into action. I hurried down the hall toward Martha, who was ushering my patient Aiden and one of his dads into Room Eight. I bent over to be at eye level with Aiden, a cute freckle-faced boy, and commented on his cool new high fade haircut. Then I straightened up and spoke to his dad. I explained I'd been called away on an emergency, and unfortunately, Martha would have to fit Aiden's visit in with another clinic doctor. I sensed Dad's disappointment, but he said he understood. Martha looked at me with her *Are you kidding?* expression, with which I was very familiar.

"Look," I whispered. "That woman, Brandy Monroe, the one you made me call. Turns out there may be something urgent she needs to tell me, but our conversation got cut off before she told me much. She could be a nut job, or this could be terribly important. I need to check it out, so please squeeze my patients in with the other docs. Fortunately, I only have routine check-ups scheduled today, so it should be easy for them to handle. I'll probably be gone at least two hours, depending on traffic. Sorry."

Martha's expression turned to one of resignation. "Whatever. I hope it's worth it. Don't worry, Dr. Rosen. I'll take care of everything. Let me know when you're on your way back."

Martha was well aware of my tendency to be impulsive when it came to children needing help. On several occasions, I'd left suddenly to tend to a child too sick to come to the clinic, the parents afraid to call an ambulance fearing deportation of a family member.

I entered Bright Lights into Google maps on my phone. Located in the Bayview District of San Francisco, I thought twice about going there. I'd never been to that area, known for its poverty and high crime rate. Did I truly need to go? It was the middle of the day, and the sun was out. If it were ever safe to be there, this would be the time. Given the possible emergent situation at hand, I didn't take the time to carefully weigh the pros and cons. I hurried home and went directly to the garage, where I kept my mom's car. A ten-year-old silver Honda Accord, it was a dependable workhorse. I was in the driver's seat twenty minutes after I'd left the clinic. Checking my phone, I noted the travel time to Bright Lights was estimated to be over thirty minutes due to heavy traffic. Shit. I was going to be AWOL from the clinic longer than I had hoped. Fortunately, there wouldn't be any real consequence for me, a perk of being the clinic director.

It took me almost twenty minutes just to reach the I-280 exit. I was still fourteen minutes away from my destination. After a series of turns, I was in a relatively undeveloped area of San Francisco, with warehouses, empty lots, and poorly maintained apartment buildings on both sides of the road filled with potholes. Groups of teenage boys smoking, vaping, and probably selling drugs stood on street corners. Ten minutes from my destination, thoughts of danger caused me to slow down. What was I getting into? The neighborhood might be the least of my problems. Why had the call been disconnected? Was it Don's voice I'd heard? Had Brandy hung up, or had Don disconnected the call? Was he violent? Was he still there?

I berated myself for not bringing Brandy's phone number so I could call her to make sure it was safe. I remembered exactly where I'd left the piece of paper with her number. I could have phoned Martha to read it to me but imagined several scenarios instead. What if I called Brandy and she told me she was in danger? What if she didn't answer the phone? Should I do the safe thing and turn around? My internal argument was won by the brave, one might say foolish, me. I stepped on the gas and continued toward Bright Lights. It didn't take long before my more cautious self started nagging, questioning my decision. I put my phone on speaker and dialed 911. It took longer than it should have before someone answered. I told the operator some autistic boys at a day program were possibly in danger, and he needed to send police to the school. No, I wasn't certain there was a crime taking place there, but I had good reason to believe that was the case. I was careful not to mention anything about suicide bombers. The operator told me to hold on, and he would notify police.

Knowing there had been a number of police shootings of autistic individuals in the past, I wanted to be at Bright Lights when law enforcement arrived. I wanted to be sure none of the kids were hurt by a police officer who didn't know how to interact with young autistic men. Appearing to be normal physically, they could seem threatening if they responded inappropriately to police orders or questioning.

I was on a curved street flanked by bare dirt, with one dilapidated warehouse-like building after the other. I hadn't seen another vehicle for a full five minutes, other than a few old cars parked on the side of the road. Heading around the final curve, I jammed on the brakes to avoid rear-ending a police cruiser parked in the middle of the street in front of the driveway leading to a squat gray building with a colorful sign over the red entry door. I'd reached Bright Lights.

I was wondering how the police had gotten there so quickly, as I disconnected my 911 call. Two uniformed officers, one male, the other female, exited the vehicle and approached me with their hands on their weapons. *Shit. What have I stepped into?*

The female officer walked to the passenger door, while the male officer, a tall white man in his mid-thirties with a pudgy face, came up to my door. "Please roll your window down, ma'am."

I complied and noted the nametag reading "Porter" pinned to his uniform.

"How'd you get here so fast?" I asked.

"Please get out of the car, ma'am, and keep your hands where I can see 'em." His voice was deep, his expression unfriendly.

I opened my door and slowly, deliberately swung my legs around and rose to a standing position, my elbows bent and my palms facing outward in front of my chest. "What's going on? I'm the one who called this in."

The female officer, a short-haired heavyset Black woman I estimated to be fiftyish, silently walked over and frisked me. I caught a glimpse of her nametag, which read "Wells." She nodded to her partner. "It's okay, Forest. She's clean."

"Okay, ma'am, you can put your hands down," Porter said. "Please show me some identification."

I reached into the car slowly and retrieved my purse. The officers watched as I fished around and pulled out my wallet, then removed my driver's license and handed it to Wells, who was nearer to me. She looked at it, then gave it to her partner. "Check it out," she said. Porter walked to the police car and started speaking into the dash-mounted radio.

"Now tell me, why are you here?" Wells asked. She seemed more agreeable than Porter, yet guarded.

"I came to see Brandy Monroe, the teacher in charge of the Bright Lights day program. I explained it all to the 911 operator. Weren't you told?"

"What's your business with Brandy Monroe?"

So far, the police had completely ignored my questions and appeared to be treating me as a suspect. Still, I had to admit to myself I was glad they had gotten there so quickly. "Brandy called me earlier and asked me to meet her here."

"Why?"

Porter walked back to where we were standing and returned my license. "No record," he said to Wells.

"She was worried about the safety of some of her students. She's expecting me."

The officers looked at each other a few seconds before Wells said calmly, yet firmly, "You can't go in there. We may have a dangerous situation."

"Are you responding to my 911 call, or are you here for another reason?" I asked, for the first time considering the possibility the police had been sent there independent of my emergency call.

"We don't know about your 911 call," Wells said. "Like I said, you can't go in there. But tell me what you know."

"Brandy said she has important information about some criminal activity and wants me to help her de-escalate a potentially violent situation."

"Does this have anything to do with recent events in the news?" Wells asked cagily.

She neglected to specify what events she was referring to exactly. I wondered if the officers were there on account of the suicide bombing. If so, what had brought them? I doubted Brandy had called them. "Yes, I believe it does," I answered, not specifically mentioning the explosion. I could be as evasive as they.

"Is this about the suicide bombing?" Porter asked. Both he and his partner were looking at me warily. They were done playing games. Now I knew that they had arrived at the same place as me, for the same reason. I thought it best if I leveled with them and told them why I was there. On the other hand, I didn't want to say anything to alarm them, not wanting this encounter to spiral out of control.

"It is, but let me explain. I'm a pediatrician and am the director of the county pediatrics clinic." I thought that last bit of information would lead them to appreciate that I was not a criminal type. "Brandy Monroe called me earlier today. I don't know her but had met her when she'd brought a student of hers to the clinic. She thought I'd be the best person to help, with my understanding of her special needs kids. All her students here are autistic."

"What do you know about what's been going on here?" Wells asked.

"Not much, actually. Brandy told me very little, only that someone named Don had trained her students to—I know this sounds strange, but this is what she told me—he had trained them to be suicide bombers. I believe she was trying to tell me that one of her students was the Oracle Park bomber. Our conversation was cut off after I heard her speak to a man who walked in on her."

I thought the two officers would start laughing, tell me Brandy was a known conspiracy theorist nutcase, and they were there to investigate a neighbor's complaint about noise or garbage or thefts in the neighborhood and send me on my way. Instead, Porter looked at his partner. "Okay, April. What do you suggest we do now?"

I focused on Wells, who was considering their next step. "We need to proceed with extreme caution here."

Chapter 4

"You think Brandy was on to something?" I asked. "You think she's in danger?"

"I think we all could be in danger," Wells said. "My partner and I are here following up on a lead, one of literally hundreds we've received about the bombing."

"Brandy called the police, too?" I asked.

"Not Brandy."

"Should you be telling her all this?" Porter asked. "Let's just go in." He was rubbing his gun holster, seeming eager to use his weapon.

Wells turned to her partner and spoke. "I want her to understand what's at stake here, why she can't go in. I don't want her trying to second guess what we're doing and give us trouble. She'll see it on the news soon enough, anyway." She turned back to me and continued. "A man called in earlier. He's a bus driver for the school district. Said he recognized the drawing of the bomber he saw on TV this morning. He used to drive him to this Bright Lights program every day until a few years ago when the boy moved to a different group home. Sweet kid, never caused any trouble, he said. Autistic and nonverbal. Name's Steven Swanson. Is he the one you saw in the clinic?"

I gasped. "No, but Steven is the name Brandy gave me—the name of the student she said she recognized from the picture on the news this morning—the one she said was the suicide bomber."

It was becoming clear now. Don, an incredibly evil man, had trained Steven to be a suicide bomber. It made sense. It was a remarkably ingenious plan. Steven would have had no understanding of what he was doing. It followed that no behavioral scientist would have detected any nervousness in him, since Steven had no knowledge of what lay in store for him. It would be easy to train someone like him to wear a heavy, bulky vest under his shirt and walk normally. He was probably expecting a reward, like a Coke or a burger, the next time he saw his trainer, Don.

"We'd better go in and check things out," Wells said to Porter. "Like I said, we'd better approach with extreme caution. This Don fellow may be inside. I'm calling for backup." She went to the police cruiser, then returned shortly and said, "Backup's on the way. Turns out the 911 response unit will be here soon." As she spoke, Wells pulled her gun from its holster, and Porter followed suit. Turning to me, Wells said, "Stay here, Doc. I'll come back for you if it's safe."

The officers walked up the driveway cautiously, guns held in both hands, pointed at the door. The driveway was approximately fifty feet long. When they were halfway to the door, I began to follow quietly. Stupid, I know, but I didn't trust the cops, especially Porter, to exhibit restraint if confronted by one or more of the boys. I needed to try to prevent the situation from spiraling out of control, into a disaster.

When they got to the door, I stopped. Porter reached out and slowly turned the handle. From what I could see, it moved freely. He looked at Wells, who was standing on the other side of the doorway. She nodded.

In a burst of energy, Porter flung the door wide open. He and Wells stormed in, Porter on the left, Wells on the right, guns pointing down at forty-five degrees in front of them. Almost in unison, they yelled, "Police! Freeze! Police! Freeze!"

Hearing nothing more, I ran to the threshold and looked inside. In front of me was a large L-shaped room, some of which was out of view. Several tables, most covered with papers, pencils, crayons, and books, stood adjacent to the white walls decorated with pictures. Porter was standing toward the far end of the room, facing ninety degrees to the left, pointing his gun at someone out of my view. He yelled, "Hands up! Hands up, or I'll shoot!"

Why fear didn't overcome me at that moment, I'll never know. I ran in to see what was happening. The first thing I noticed was a heavyset young woman with long blond hair splayed out, lying on the floor to Porter's right, face-up. A sizeable pool of coagulated blood had collected on the tan linoleum next to where her right ear would have been had her skull been intact. Looking around, I saw blood spatter on nearby walls and furniture. I looked back at the woman. She looked vaguely familiar, and I surmised it was Brandy. She'd been shot or clubbed to death. As I got closer, I looked to my left, in the direction Porter was pointing his gun.

Bloody footprints led from the blood pooled around the woman's head to a handsome fair-haired boy I estimated to be sixteen to eighteen years of age, sitting with his hands on the tabletop, facing Porter. He appeared calm despite the gun pointed at his head as he picked out one of the puzzle pieces in front of him and carefully placed it in the partially completed jigsaw puzzle on the table. He seemed unperturbed by the drops of blood sprayed over the table and puzzle.

"Don't shoot!" I yelled at the top of my lungs.

"Get back, Doc," Porter yelled, not letting his eyes stray from the suspect in front of him. "We told you to stay put."

"Officer, please listen. He doesn't understand you. Look at him. He doesn't even seem to notice you. He's autistic. Let me try something."

"Like what?"

"I think I can talk to him. Let me get closer. Give me five minutes with him, and you'll see he's not dangerous."

"Let her try," Wells said. "Lower your gun, Forest."

"He better not try to run," Forest said, bringing down his gun, "or I'm gonna get him."

I stood between Porter and the young man and opened my purse.

"I better check that," Wells said. "Protocol, you know." She walked over to me and took my purse. After looking through it, she handed it back. "Go on with what you were doing," she said.

I dug around in my purse for a few seconds and found a stray mint-flavored Tic Tac. I tossed it on the table, on top of the puzzle the boy was focused on. The blue morsel caught his attention, and he grabbed it, then put it in his mouth. As he did this, I raised my arms above my head and yelled, "Do this."

The young man looked up at me. Without changing his expression, he raised his arms.

"See," I said, looking at the officer. "You just have to know how to talk to him. I'm sure he didn't do this," I said, looking at the mayhem evident on the floor. "He's innocent. Don't hurt him."

Porter mumbled, "Fuckin' idiot" under his breath. Then in a gruff voice, said, "Well, I'm gonna cuff him anyway. Maybe you should help, so no one gets hurt."

Chapter 5

Porter handcuffed the young man over my objection. As he did so, I spoke gently to the boy so he would stay calm. I was glad Porter secured his arms in front, a much more comfortable position than in back. Wearing a long-sleeve pullover shirt, jeans, and tennis shoes, the youth looked like a typical high school kid. The two officers searched him carefully as he stood looking into the distance, making humming noises, occasionally rising on his toes. They found no visible blood on him other than on the soles of his shoes, his hands, and the back of his shirt. This was likely transferred from the blood on the floor and spattered over the puzzle and the back of the chair he'd been sitting in. Wells surmised he had been out of the room when Brandy's murder took place and returned after the killer had left. Unless, of course, he was the murderer and had changed his clothes and washed his arms, face, and hair, a scenario I explained was highly unlikely.

When the officers finished inspecting him, Wells made a phone call out of my hearing range, then asked me to look after the youth while she and Porter spoke to two officers who had just arrived at the scene in response to my 911 call. I lightly held the young man's arm and directed him to a nearby folding chair. After seeing a small kitchen behind where he'd been sitting, I filled a glass with water and gave it to him. Despite the cuffs, he had no difficulty drinking the entire glass as the officers disappeared down a hallway.

Ten minutes later, I found cookies in a kitchen cabinet and fed them to the boy as the room began to fill with cops. Porter and Wells re-emerged from the hallway and spoke to their colleagues in hushed voices.

"How about removing his handcuffs?" I asked Porter as he walked by. "You can see he's not dangerous."

"I know no such thing. The cuffs stay on. I'm gonna have to move the two of you." He looked around, then escorted us to one of the tables I'd seen earlier when I entered the building, the one closest to the front door. He pulled the table away from the wall and moved two nearby folding chairs behind it. I noted it was the only table with a bare surface—not even a pencil or piece of paper to occupy our time.

"Sit there and don't move until I give you permission," he ordered. "I'll be watching."

I squeezed behind the table and sat in one of the chairs. The young man followed my lead, looking uncomfortable with the table constricting him. When Porter looked away, I pushed the table out a few inches. I wondered where the other students were. So far, I hadn't seen any sign of them.

Soon the building was swarming as crime scene investigators, FBI agents, and a medical examiner arrived. With each new entrant, the noise level rose. The youth started rocking back and forth in his chair, putting his fingers in his ears, even though his wrists were still held together by the cuffs. I was sure the racket upset him, so I softly repeated "It's okay" over and over, hoping to calm him. I wasn't sure it helped or if he heard me, but he didn't seem to mind.

Twenty minutes later, the voice of a woman outside, yelling, rose above the other sounds. "What do you mean I can't go in? I'm here to see my daughter. She works here. I need to see her." This was followed by a low voice I couldn't understand. Then the woman screamed, "Let me see her! Goddamn you. Let me see if it's my daughter."

I recognized the voice of Wells. "I'm terribly sorry, ma'am. Your picture matches the woman inside. I think it would be best if you didn't see her just yet."

Hysterical crying ensued as Wells tried to comfort the deceased woman's mother. When she finally started to calm down, Brandy's mother repeated over and over between sobs, "I knew he was no good. I just knew it." Then she added, "Brandy was such a good person. The best daughter ever. She didn't deserve this."

I bent forward as far as I could and saw the grieving woman outside. She appeared to be in her mid-fifties, dressed in black pants and a white blouse. Her blond hair was medium length and looked disheveled.

"Why did you decide to visit your daughter today?" Wells asked.

"Brandy called me this morning. She seemed so upset. Said she needed to break up with that boyfriend of hers."

"What's his name?"

"Don. Don Brock. I'm sure he did this."

"Can you give us a description of him?"

"Wish I could, but I never met the son-of-a-bitch. Brandy said he was shy and didn't want to meet us, my husband or me."

"Why do you think he did this?"

"Things she told me, like he had a temper. She said he was handsome, athletic, intelligent. Very ambitious. To be honest, not the type who would choose to be with Brandy. Don't get me wrong. She's a beautiful girl. Was a beautiful girl." Brandy's mom had to pause as she began crying again. "He wouldn't meet us, even though they'd been dating for over a year. No ring yet, either. When she called this morning, she sounded like she was afraid of him. I thought something bad was going to happen. I live in Merced. Instead of going to work, I jumped in my car and drove straight here, even though it's almost a three-hour drive. I tried to call her an hour ago. When she didn't answer, well, I think I knew then." Brandy's mom started crying again, as Wells comforted her and asked for her contact information. Still sniffling, she walked away to call her husband, then returned to say she'd drive to the train station to meet him, assuring Wells she'd be okay.

"One more thing, ma'am," Wells said. "Did your daughter have a cell phone?"

"Yes. A Samsung, I believe. Always had it on her."

"You sure? We couldn't find it anywhere."

"Then the bastard took it. She never went anywhere without it." I heard her walk away, crying.

When it became clear I wouldn't be leaving any time soon, not wanting to leave the young man without an advocate, I called Martha and told her I couldn't return to the clinic that day. She took the news in stride and assured me she'd handle fitting my patients in and rescheduling them as necessary. As Porter walked by, I asked if I could look through the files in the office to learn more about the young man I was with, but he coldly informed me I was not authorized to touch anything, and I needed to stay seated next to the boy.

I tried to entertain the youth with cartoon videos on my phone, but he ignored them until I showed him a Mickey Mouse movie. That caught his attention, so I let him hold my phone. I watched as officers and technicians took pictures, dusted for fingerprints, and carried boxes outside to waiting vehicles, I assumed. My attention was diverted for a few seconds when an officer stumbled over a box and dropped a large crate, creating a loud noise. When I turned my attention back to the boy, my cell phone was on his chair, but he was no longer sitting beside me.

I panicked for a few seconds until I saw him seated at the table where he'd been when we first arrived. With no officers nearby to notice him, he was busy completing the jigsaw puzzle. Porter was out of sight, so I quietly left my seat, walked over to the young man, and pulled up a chair next to him. I tried to help with the puzzle, but he swatted my hand away.

Two hours after we'd arrived, Wells informed me I was free to leave, and she and Porter were going to take the young man back to the station. He had completed over ninety percent of the thousand-piece puzzle, a jungle scene, despite his wrists being held together.

As we left the building, it was still a beehive of activity. I asked Wells and Porter if I could follow them in my car so I could help with the young man at the station. Wells said she'd appreciate my help, while Porter seemed none too thrilled. I watched as Porter pushed the youth into the back seat of the police cruiser, then followed them for a half hour until we arrived at the 3rd Street station. I parked in the visitor's lot and went to the reception and waiting area just past the entrance to the building. *What am I getting myself into?*

Chapter 6

Before I had a chance to take a seat in the waiting area, Wells came and escorted me through a secure door. The smallness of the reception area belied the sizable police complex behind it. As we entered a spacious room with numerous desks, Wells informed me the interview rooms were occupied, so we needed to wait. She sat at a desk across the aisle from where Porter was already sitting, the boy seated in the aisle between them. I took an empty chair a few feet away, in earshot of the officers. I warned them that questioning the young man was unlikely to be fruitful, especially for anyone who didn't know how to talk to him. So far, he hadn't uttered a word. I thought he might be completely nonverbal, although he appeared to understand the few simple commands I'd given him. I hadn't tried to coax words out of him, given the noisy, hectic environs we'd been in.

I checked my cell phone for messages as the officers chitchatted.

"Did you hear McNeal is getting a divorce?" Porter asked Wells.

"I hadn't heard that, but I'm not surprised. He seemed to be getting awfully chummy with the new redheaded rookie. It's too bad. I like his wife. By the way, Forest, I'm gonna need someone to cover for me when I take my son in for his wisdom teeth to be pulled. Think you could work with Nelson that day? It's not for a while now, not until October thirteenth."

"Wednesday."

"Yeah, I guess it could be Wednesday. Does it matter?"

"Huh?"

"You said 'Wednesday.' Like October thirteenth is Wednesday. I'm not sure about the day of the week. I just know it's the thirteenth." I heard a hint of irritation in her voice.

"Well, why did you say 'Wednesday' then?"

"What are you talking about? I didn't say 'Wednesday.' You said 'Wednesday.'"

"Now you're getting on my nerves," Porter said. "Why would I say 'Wednesday' when I don't have any fucking idea what day of the week it is?"

I'd been half-listening to this conversation as I scrolled through my emails, mostly ads for clothing, cruises, jobs I could do at home, and Facebook notifications.

I got up and stood in front of the young man who was staring at a piece of lint he'd picked from his sleeve and released into the air. "August twenty-second, two thousand thirty," I said loudly.

The response was instantaneous yet delivered in a soft voice. "Thursday."

Wells and Porter stopped their bickering and stared at the youth in silence. Then they looked at me.

"He has calendar skills," I explained. "I'll bet if you check, August twenty-second, two thousand thirty is a Thursday."

"Damn, if it isn't," Wells said, looking at her smartphone. "How'd he figure that out?"

"A lot of people would like to know the answer to that," I said.

"I get it," Wells said. "He's the one who said 'Wednesday.' And I thought he couldn't talk." She looked at the boy and asked calmly, "Why were you trying to fool us?"

The boy sat in silence, focused on another fleck of lint floating in the air.

"Listen, you little shit, you'd better tell us what happened back there at the house," Porter yelled, his face red with rage.

The young man looked down and started rocking back and forth, humming loudly.

"Don't talk to him like that. You're upsetting him," I interrupted, putting my hand gently on the boy's shoulder. He flinched as soon as I touched him, so I removed my hand. I squatted and looked up into his eyes, which were focused elsewhere. I began to speak in the gentle, soothing voice I'd used many times before with young children and developmentally delayed older children. "Everything's okay. Would you like something to eat?"

The young man returned a blank stare. I had seen a cookie on Wells's desk. I turned to her and asked, pointing to the cookie, "Can I give him your cookie?"

"Sure," she said, handing it to me.

"Would you like a chocolate chip cookie?" I asked, holding the treat in front of me.

"Yes." The voice was soft, difficult to hear. I handed him the cookie, which he grabbed quickly. He devoured it in three bites.

"What's your name?" I asked.

"Zaron."

"What's your last name?"

"Johnson."

"Can you tell me what happened at Bright Lights today?"

My question was met with a blank stare.

"This is a waste of time," Porter said.

"Hold on a second," I interrupted, holding out an arm and hyperextending my hand, motioning Porter to stop and shut up. I looked at Zaron. "Who was on the floor at Bright Lights?"

"Brandy."

I looked at Porter. "You need to be gentle with him. I can't tell how much he understands or how much he can talk, but I would bet he's got some information stored in his head," I said. "It could be just a little, but he may know something helpful. You have to know how to get it out, though, or it's useless."

"What's Brandy's last name?" I asked, turning back to Zaron.

My question was met with silence again.

"I'd say he doesn't know her last name. Why would he?"

"He's bullshitting you," Porter said. "I have a niece with Down's syndrome. She's a retard, but at least she's not sneaky. She'll tell me anything I want to know. She loves to sit on my lap, no matter what I say to her."

"I can just imagine what you say to her," I said under my breath.

"Huh?" Porter said.

"People with Down's syndrome are much different than those with autism. They're sociable and usually have pretty good verbal skills. But they lack the cognitive abilities of many with autism, who can be surprisingly capable in some areas."

"Look," Porter said. "Matt's signaling the interview room's available. Officer Wells and I are going to take him there. If he doesn't cooperate, I'm going to book him." He raised his voice and turned to the youth. "You hear that, Zaron, if that's even your name?"

"I want the doctor to come with us," Wells said. "She knows how to talk to him. Is that okay with you?" she asked, turning to me.

"Of course. I'm happy to help."

"We have to Mirandize him," Porter said.

"He won't understand a word of that," I said.

Wells thought for a moment. "I don't think any of us thinks he's the murderer. Isn't that right, Porter?"

Porter was silent for a moment before he begrudgingly answered, "I guess not. He's too stupid."

"I don't want to waste a lot of time getting an attorney in here to figure out what to do. Technically, we don't have to read him his rights because he's free to go. All he has to do is ask."

"That's not going to happen," I said.

"I know. But I'm also pretty sure he's not going to give us a blow-by-blow description of how he killed his teacher," April said, "so, let's just see what we can learn from him. You better take the cuffs off, Porter."

After Porter removed the cuffs, Zaron flapped his arms in the air, jumped a few times, and smiled. As we entered the interview room, me following in the rear, an officer handed Wells some papers. The room was windowless with gray walls, just big enough for four chairs and the rectangular oak table in the center. Wells led Zaron to one of the seats and motioned for me to sit next to him. She sat opposite Zaron, her partner adjacent. Zaron leaned over and sniffed my hand, which was resting on the table. Porter glared at him.

"A lot of autistic people like to smell things," I explained.

"Thank you for offering to help," Wells said to me. "Please give me a second to look over these papers." With a concerned expression, she examined the three-page document in her hand, then passed it to Forest. "Looks like they've gotten a lot of information already, Dr. Rosen."

"Please, call me Erica."

"Okay, Erica," Wells began. "I think we'll be working together for a while if you're willing, so please call me April. I hope you can get this kid to help us. The deceased woman has been positively identified as Brandy Monroe."

"I was pretty sure that was the case."

"She was the director of the school, Bright Lights. Just thirty-four years old. It looks like she died of a gunshot wound to the head. A bullet was found in the rear wall. Of course, the medical examiner will have the final say. We found files for eight clients registered at the school. They include information on Zaron Johnson, the name our young man here gave us, and Steven Swanson, who was the suicide bomber, according to the bus driver." April took a deep breath. She must have realized the enormity of having finally identified the suicide bomber.

"So, one of these morons killed the teacher," Porter said, interrupting the moment.

"I doubt it," I said. "It's unlikely any of the students even know what a gun is used for."

"Oh, yeah, sure. And what about the bomber? He was one of them. He knew plenty about murdering innocent people. Like that psycho with autism, Adam Lanza."

"You're talking about the guy who killed all those children in Newtown. I don't know exactly what his psychiatric diagnosis was, but his autism, if he had it at all, was the least of his problems. He was high functioning and went to a regular school. Not like the students in the Bright Lights program, who I'm surmising are—or were—like Zaron, here. Much less capable. Can't negotiate the confusing world by themselves. I doubt the bomber had any idea about what he was doing," I said. "He was an unwitting pawn, trained by somebody else. Find that person, and you have the one responsible for the bombing."

April looked at me. "Didn't you say Brandy told you someone was training these guys?"

"That's right. Someone named Don."

"Last name?"

"Sorry, she never gave it to me."

"So, we've got to find this guy, Don. Probably the boyfriend, Don Brock. Then, theoretically, we've got our guy."

"Let me see what I can learn from Zaron," I said. "I doubt he'll know Don's last name since he didn't know Brandy's. Maybe I can get a description, something that might help."

"Please try."

"How about something for him to drink, like a soft drink?" I asked.

"Sure. We have a machine in the back," April said.

I turned to Zaron. "Would you like a Coke?" I asked.

"Yes." Again, the voice was soft, hard to hear.

"Be right back," April said, leaving me alone with Zaron and the Neanderthal, Porter.

"You really think you can get him to say something useful?" Porter asked, sounding skeptical.

"I'll try. I don't know him, though. Every person with autism has his own idiosyncrasies, just like the rest of us. But I have some experience with behavior modification. They probably used that technique at his program."

"The only behavior modification I know about is putting criminals behind bars. That definitely modifies their behavior."

"That's one approach. I like to use rewards. Basically, reward good behavior. Once it's understood good behavior is rewarded, you're likely to see more of it."

"What are you going to reward him for? Just sitting there without biting and kicking?"

"If he were normally belligerent, then yes, that's what I'd reward. Behavior refers to anything someone might do, not just acting up or being aggressive. In this case, I plan to reward the behavior we're after now. Speaking."

April returned, carrying a can of Coke. "Should I give this to him?" she asked, looking at me.

"I'll take it," I said, reaching for the can. I opened the tab and saw Zaron's full attention focused on what I was holding. I turned to Wells and Porter. "When I get what I want from him, I'll give him a little sip. If he doesn't give me what I want, no sip. Some behaviorists use punishment to extinguish bad behavior, but I don't. I surely don't want to punish him for not answering a question he doesn't even know the answer to."

"Makes sense," April said.

"Hell, I'd put him on the rack if I thought it'd help," Porter volunteered.

I shot a glance to Porter, intending to convey a message: *You're a jerk.* He didn't seem to notice, appearing to be more interested in his own opinions than in what others had to say. "Years ago," I said to April, "when I was an aide for autistic kids in a large group home, I learned about using behavior modification for teaching the residents. The technique was popularized in the '80s by a UCLA professor. In his earlier work, he punished some of his severely autistic patients by shocking them with a cattle prod."

"Ouch," April said. "That doesn't seem right."

"He thought his method was justified when, for instance, he used it to stop one man from hitting himself in the face after he blinded himself. The aversive therapy was criticized by many, and the professor later eliminated the use of painful punishments. Many programs for teaching autistic children today are based on his work but use only positive reinforcement. They use rewards to teach language and other skills in small steps, or exercises, called discrete trials."

"Does it work?" April asked.

"In my limited exposure, I've seen behavior modification work, up to a point." I turned to Zaron. "How old are you, Zaron?" I asked.

"Nineteen."

He looked a bit younger, but I had no reason not to believe him. I gave him a sip of Coke, allowing him to place his hand over mine. After he'd swallowed, I took the can back.

"What puzzle were you doing today at Bright Lights?"

"In the Jungle."

I gave Zaron another sip, remembering the jungle puzzle he almost completed at his school.

"Who is Don?"

Blank stare. I realized my mistake. "Sorry," I said to Porter and Wells. "That was a bad question. Too open-ended. He needs something with a more discrete answer." I turned back to Zaron. "What color is Don's hair?"

"Brown."

I didn't know if his answer was correct, but I figured it was. It had been my experience that severely autistic people like Zaron didn't see the point of lying. Sometimes I imagined they thought we were all somewhat unpredictable robot-like creatures. We had no mind of our own, but knew everything they knew, so nothing would be accomplished by trying to hide the truth. I rewarded Zaron again with a swig of Coke.

"Did you see Don today?"

"Yes."

"Did you see Steven today?" It made me queasy to ask the question. I knew Steven had died in the bombing, but I needed to be sure Zaron didn't say "yes" indiscriminately.

"No."

"When did you see Steven?"

Zaron's expression didn't change as he said, "Wednesday, August twenty-fifth."

I knew that date, as did the officers. That was the date of the bombing.

Chapter 7

It was clear to all of us that Zaron had information stored in his head—how much, we didn't know. If he knew anything else that could be useful, it would be difficult to access. It was as if his brain were encrypted, and we needed to hack it, figure out how to get him to give us the information. It wasn't that he was belligerent or defiant, it was that he operated by a different set of conventions, namely his own. Like he came from a planet so different from ours that gesturing, the most primitive form of communication, was lost on him.

I noticed him squirming a bit.

"Zaron, do you need to go to the bathroom?"

Blank stare. I'd try something else.

"Zaron, do you need to go potty?"

"Yes."

April and I looked at Porter. He sat motionless, but when we failed to turn our attention away from him, he finally volunteered. "Okay, I guess I'd better take him. C'mon, Zaron. I'll take you to the bathroom."

Zaron sat motionless. I sighed and stood up. I held out my hand and said, "Let's go potty." He grabbed my hand as I turned toward Porter, who pointed to the restrooms. There were two gender-neutral bathrooms, one of which was unoccupied. I waited outside while Zaron took care of business. When he emerged a short time later, I checked inside the bathroom. There was some water on the floor near the sink, but everything else looked in order. I was relieved, remembering that some of the autistic children I worked with left the bathroom a disaster. Fortunately, Zaron appeared to be potty trained and didn't see the need to smear feces on the wall or pee on the floor.

I brought Zaron back to the interview room where we returned to our seats.

"We've got another problem," April said. "I just heard from an officer who is still at the school. Zaron, here, as well as all the other Bright Lights clients, live in a group home located directly behind the program. The director, and as far as I can tell, the only one working in the home, was someone named Donald Brock."

"Donald Brock?" I said. "He must be Brandy's boyfriend."

"Right. He's most likely the one responsible. And, surprise, surprise, he's nowhere to be found. Neither are any of the remaining six clients."

"Which means," Porter said, "Brock's got 'em."

"So not only do we have six missing autistic children, who happen to be potential suicide bombers, but Zaron has no place to go tonight," April said. "We can't send him back to an empty house. We need to call Child Protective Services to find him a place to stay."

"That could be a disaster," I said. "What are the chances they can find someone to handle a kid like Zaron on such short notice? He could become so shaken up, he won't talk at all." I thought for a moment. Lim might be upset, but I could deal with him later. "How about I take him home with me? We have a sofa bed in the living room where he can sleep. I'll gain his trust some more, and try to figure out how to question him. Maybe he can tell us more."

"We can't release him to someone who isn't in the system," April said.

"Hold on a minute," I said. "He's nineteen. He's not a minor. He can decide for himself where to go." I turned to Zaron. "Zaron, would you like to come to my house to sleep and eat cookies?"

"Yes."

"Then it's settled."

"He's probably conserved and can't legally make that kind of decision himself," April said.

"Have you seen the conservatorship papers?" I asked.

"No, I haven't, but those papers are likely at the group home."

"Unless you have those papers, you can't be sure, right?"

"You do have a point, Erica."

"So, I can take him?"

"Okay, for tonight."

"Can someone pick up some of his clothes and bring them by my condo?"

"Officers are searching the group home right now. I'm guessing they won't be done for quite some time. We can't take anything until they've finished going through it all," April said. "I hope to have a report on what's been found there before noon tomorrow. After that we should be able to drop off some of his things if he's still staying with you. If we're lucky, we'll have caught this Don fellow by then. If not, we may have a lot of questions we'd like Zaron to answer. Also, we'll have to find a more permanent place for him to stay."

"It may take you awhile to find a suitable residence for him." I wrote my cell number on the back of one of my cards and handed it to April. "Call me when you get some of his clothes, or if you find him a place."

"Appreciate it."

I grabbed the Coke can, still over half full, and escorted my new houseguest to the parking lot.

*

I opened the passenger door on my mother's car, and Zaron got in. He buckled the seat belt without me saying a word. The belt has a tricky clasp most people had a hard time with, but he was able to quickly figure out how to operate it. Before starting the engine, I placed the Coke can in the beverage holder closest to me. On the way, I spoke to Zaron.

"My name is Erica. What's my name?"

Silence.

I repeated this several times, until finally, when I asked, "What's my name?" I got a response.

"Erica."

I gave him the can of Coke and let him take a swig as a reward. Once done, I grabbed the can and put it back in the cupholder. He didn't resist.

I hadn't forgotten how to use behavior modification to teach skills. The drills I'd done years ago to teach the autistic kids under my care were coming back. Patience and repetition were the keys. Along with rewards, of course. Everything had to be taught. Not just words—nonverbal communication, too. These things didn't come naturally. I remembered spending almost three months trying to teach one ten-year-old boy how to point. By the time I'd finished volunteering there, he was starting to get it. I wondered how he was doing.

I pulled into my designated spot in the parking garage, and we got out. I locked the car and led Zaron down the two flights of stairs to the lobby of my condo. Zaron was flapping his arms and rocking back and forth, a big smile on his face. A heart-melting smile, to be exact, as he looked me in the eye. Autistic people often avoid eye contact, but for the first time, Zaron was looking directly at me. He felt comfortable in my presence. I was becoming attached to this young man who I found charming in his own way. I was more determined than ever to protect him. Just like I'd done whatever I could to protect my brother while he was alive.

I called Lim as we walked and tried to break it to him gently, but there was no good way to tell him. A young autistic man with no place to stay would be living with us, possibly for a few days. I tried to put a positive spin on it.

"He doesn't talk much," I said.

"We don't have room."

"Considering how you lived in China, I'd think you would say we have plenty of room."

"That was different. Now I'm used to your decadent western ways."

"You can always stay with your parents while he's here."

"That would be too Chinese."

"So, you're okay with it?"

"If you think it's necessary. I don't want to see him out on the street. But only for a really, really, short time."

"Thank you, Amazing Husband. See you real soon."

Next, I called Martha at home and told her I needed to help someone out. I'd be away from the clinic for at least one more day. She kidded me for being too soft but promised to take care of rescheduling my patients and squeezing in those who needed to be seen.

As if I didn't feel badly enough springing my strange guest on Lim, I felt worse when I walked into our unit and saw he had set the table for three and was busy making rice and stir-fried vegetables. Intentional or not, Lim was making me feel terribly guilty by being so accommodating.

"Dinner's almost ready," he said. "I'd already started to make dinner when you called. Luckily, I made enough to have leftovers, so there should be plenty."

I walked over to kiss him. "Sure smells good," I said. Gesturing with my arms, I made introductions. "Lim, this is Zaron, Zaron this is Lim."

"Hello, Zaron. Nice to meet you," Lim said, holding out his right hand.

Without saying a word, Zaron brushed by him and started looking around, opening all the cabinets, checking out the bedroom, bathroom, and study. He picked up a few things to examine closely, then gently placed them back in their original positions. Fortunately, Lim was looking away when Zaron picked up the elephant his father had carved for him in China, when Lim was a child. I'm sure Lim would have rushed over to grab it from Zaron had he seen it. I watched, ready to jump in if needed, as Zaron studied the carving, sniffed it, put it back, and moved on to the next item of interest. He seemed particularly drawn to a decorative metal apple painted red on the coffee table, a wedding gift from a coworker. After studying it for a while, he tried to bite it, then placed it back where it had been.

Zaron jumped and waved his arms a lot, but unlike the bull in the china shop he superficially resembled, he failed to damage a single thing. I assumed that was how he behaved when he was excited. Lim served up dinner, and the three of us sat around the table. Zaron was all smiles.

Lim and I picked up our chopsticks and began to eat. As I started to explain the events of the day to Lim, I noticed Zaron wasn't eating but was closely studying our handling of the chopsticks. I watched as he silently picked his up and tried to mimic our motions. He awkwardly began eating his rice, his chopsticks often slipping past each other, the food falling back on his plate. Slowly he was able to get through the pile of rice before him. He never once asked for help or requested a fork. His vegetables, other than the carrots which he had carefully picked out and eaten, went untouched. Many people with autism are picky eaters. I'd have to figure out what he liked. Probably junk food, if my past experience was worth anything.

After dinner, Zaron sprang into action, clearing the table and putting the dirty plates in the dishwasher. He did all this without me saying a word. He put the leftover food in refrigerator dishes, which he had apparently located during his earlier cabinet exploration. Lastly, he wiped the table with a sponge. Although he went through the motions, he didn't actually get the table clean, missing some areas and not rubbing the dirtier spots where it was needed. I concluded he didn't understand the purpose of cleaning the table and likely never would. I checked the dishwasher to see if it was full enough to run and saw Zaron had piled cups and bowls on top of each other on the upper rack. He obviously didn't grasp the way the dishwasher worked either. I rearranged the dishes as needed, which took very little time.

Once the kitchen was cleaned up, I tried to determine Zaron's ability to speak. I showed him objects around the condo, each time asking, "What's this?"

"Plate."

"Book."

"Chair."

He knew most of the things I showed him, including a cell phone and sunglasses. He failed to identify lipstick or a power cord. I noticed that if I didn't understand what he said, he never repeated it. Missing it the first time meant missing it forever.

Verbs were harder to test, but through my actions, I got him to identify clap, jump, run, and walk when I asked him what I was doing. I was trying to think of something else to test when Lim walked in the room and put the iPad he'd just used for a Facetime conference on the kitchen table. Zaron grabbed it and found the Netflix icon. Within seconds, he was sitting on the couch, watching a Disney movie, and smiling as he gently rocked back and forth.

"It's nice to see him acting a little normal," Lim commented, "although he's ten years too old to be watching that."

"Look at the time," I said, glancing at my watch. "I completely lost track. It's after nine-thirty. How about we let him watch his video for a half hour, then see about getting him to sleep?"

"Did you get any of his clothes? Does he have something to sleep in?"

"Doesn't look like they'll be bringing any of his things by tonight. Could he borrow a pair of your pajamas?"

"Not a problem. I have two sets, neither of which I've worn since we've lived here."

"As it should be. At least not until you're old and fat."

Smiling, Lim went back to the study to do some work while I read a few articles from the journal *Pediatrics* and skimmed *The San Francisco Chronicle* at the kitchen table.

After close to thirty minutes, Lim appeared from the study. "Move him to a chair at the table, and I'll set up the bed."

"I think you should tell him to move to the table."

"I don't know how to talk to him."

Zaron was ignoring us, even though he could hear us talking about him. Lim pulled out one of the chairs around the table and looked at Zaron. "Sit here," he said.

Zaron didn't move, but remained engaged with the video.

"He doesn't know you're talking to him. You need to get his attention. Call him by his name."

"Okay. Zaron!" Zaron looked up. "Come sit here."

Carrying the iPad, Zaron moved from the couch to the chair by the table, where he continued to watch the singing mermaid.

"See? Not so hard."

"I see he's a lot easier to manage than you are," Lim said, smiling as he pulled out the sofa bed.

"I'll get the sheets and a blanket," I volunteered. I found what I needed in the hall linen closet and began to make up the bed, Lim helping. Zaron came over and pretty much pushed Lim out of the way, then took over for him.

Lim didn't seem to mind. "Maybe we should keep this guy," he said.

I gave Zaron a fresh towel, a pair of Lim's pajamas, and a new toothbrush. "Go in the bathroom and get ready for bed," I instructed him. I had no idea what he would do. Would he need help changing?

Brushing his teeth? I didn't think it would be appropriate for me to give him a shower. He wasn't a baby, after all. I doubted Lim would eagerly volunteer to help.

Zaron disappeared into the bathroom and closed the door. I heard the sink faucet turn on and off, then the shower. Then the sink again. The toilet flushed twice. Twenty minutes later, Zaron emerged. Dressed in Lim's pajamas, his arms and hair were dripping wet. He was carrying his dirty clothes, socks on top. One navy sock, one brown argyle. I figured that was no accident. He probably wore different sock combinations on different days, as a boy did in the place where I previously volunteered.

"What color socks do you wear tomorrow?" I asked.

"White, black," he answered. I'd look for those colors in Lim's sock drawer in the morning.

As I grabbed a towel and dried Zaron's hair, I realized I hadn't seen his arms before. The shirt he'd been wearing was long-sleeved, but the pajamas were short-sleeved. Now I noticed he had the same type of scars on his arms as the patient Brandy had brought to me a year ago—circular, classic for cigarette burns.

Chapter 8

Happily, Lim and I were able to sleep through the night without being disturbed by Zaron. For once, I woke up before Lim, although to be honest, I suspect he languished awake in bed so he wouldn't have to confront Zaron alone. I dressed quickly and went to the living room. The sofa bed had been folded away, and Zaron was sitting at the kitchen table, quietly watching a Disney video on Lim's iPad. I made coffee and brought a cup to Lim, who by then was getting dressed in our bedroom. When I returned to the kitchen and tossed the coffee filter in the garbage, I noticed two empty Pepperidge Farm bags in the trash. Zaron had helped himself to our complete stash of cookies before I got up.

In the bedroom, I grabbed a T-shirt from Lim's dresser, along with one black sock and one white sock. Zaron would have to wear the same pair of pants and the same underwear—I could only ask so much from Lim. Upon seeing the clothes, Zaron made a distressed noise and ran into the bedroom. Lim looked on helplessly while Zaron rifled through the dresser until he found what he wanted—a yellow T-shirt. Without thinking, I had given Zaron a blue shirt.

I looked at Lim and shrugged. "I guess Wednesday is yellow." Turning to Zaron, I said, "Go in the bathroom and get dressed." A few minutes later, our guest emerged from the bathroom completely dressed, although his shoes were untied. He stood still as I tied them.

Zaron had cold cereal for breakfast with Lim and me, choosing Cheerios from our limited selection, apparently not full from the cookies he'd eaten. After breakfast, he smiled as he cleared the dishes, put the milk and cereal away, loaded the dishwasher, and superficially cleaned the table with a sponge. I adjusted the dishes in the dishwasher and was about to start it when April called and asked if she could come over. She had some additional information and hoped to get more from Zaron.

"Now's a good time," I said. I told Lim a police officer would be coming by soon. He decided to leave for the office before she arrived so he could work without interruption. I assured him I'd be fine staying with Zaron and told him to give his parents my best when he checked on them as he always did when he left for work. Fifteen minutes later, I buzzed April in.

Carrying a banker's box, she sighed with relief when, after I'd ushered her to the kitchen table, she plopped the carton down.

"Whew, that was heavy," she said, shaking her arms. "Normally, we'd do this at the station, but I thought it would be better to meet in a place more comfortable for Zaron."

"I'm glad you came here without Porter. I don't like dealing with him."

"He won't be involved with the case anymore. To be honest, I shouldn't be working on this either, since the FBI has the case now. For the time being, given the unusual circumstances, the department's giving me some relief from patrol duty to act as a liaison between you and Zaron and the FBI. I've offered extra help off the clock as long as I'm needed."

"I appreciate that. I'm sure working with you will make things a whole lot easier for Zaron. Thanks for understanding."

"Glad I can help. By the way, nice place you've got here." April looked out the window, toward the bay. The sky was clear, so she could appreciate the unobstructed view of the Bay Bridge. "Not very far from the explosion, I see. Nice views, though." April turned and shifted her attention back to me. "How'd he do last night?"

Zaron walked over to the box, opened it, and sniffed the contents."

"We had a good evening, didn't we, Zaron?"

No response or acknowledgment.

"I didn't think he'd answer me, actually. Impossible question for him," I said. "He was absolutely no problem, really. Even helped with kitchen cleanup."

"Amazing. Say, you're probably wondering what I've got in the box."

"Sure am. Before we get started, though, I want to show you something." I grabbed one of Zaron's arms and held it up. "Look at this."

April walked closer to inspect the arm. "Looks like someone's been abusing this poor kid. I'm told there were similar marks on the bomber's arms. They remained pretty intact." She lifted Zaron's shirt in the front and the back. "Interesting. Nothing there."

"The other client I saw from Bright Lights had the same pattern of burns. Brandy told me it happened before he came there."

"You think Brandy did this?"

"No. I can't be sure, of course. But I could tell she really cared about her kids. I don't see her doing this. It's more likely she was trying to protect the guilty party. I'm guessing it was her diabolical boyfriend, Don Brock."

"I'd sure like to get to the bottom of that. For now, we can start going through some of the evidence I've got here."

April put on a pair of disposable gloves, retrieved a three-ring binder from the box, and opened it. "Here's a list of all eight Bright Lights clients, including Zaron Johnson and Steven Swanson. What was the name of the other kid, the one you saw in the clinic?"

"Arthur. I don't remember his last name."

"Here he is," April said, looking down the list in front of her. "Arthur Purcell. The paperwork shows all the boys are wards of the state."

"That's convenient. No parents to check up on them."

"Just what I was thinking. Now, look at this." April opened the notebook to a different page and laid it flat on the table. "I believe there were pictures of all the Bright Lights students above their names on these pages, but the pictures have been ripped out."

April showed me four pages, each with the names of two boys. Above each name, the surface of the paper was ragged, as if something had been glued there and torn off.

"We couldn't find photos of the boys anywhere. But I do have a picture I'd like Zaron to look at. When they searched Brandy's apartment yesterday, there were no photos displayed anywhere. It looked like things had been removed, including pictures, from the look of the dust patterns. What I have here was found in a locked diary she kept under the mattress. The only picture in the whole place."

April removed a box from the carton, opened it, and took out a photo sealed in a Ziplock bag. She put it on the table, facing Zaron. I recognized Brandy. She was smiling, standing next to a man with one arm around her shoulder. He was smiling, but it looked like a fake smile to me.

"Tell me who that guy is, Zaron," April said.

Silence.

"Here, let me try," I said. I turned to Zaron. As I put my finger on the man in the photo, I asked, "What is his name?"

"Don."

April and I looked at each other. The police now had a picture of the prime suspect, Donald Brock. That was momentous, the revelation followed by a moment of silence.

April interrupted the feel-good moment, saying, "The group home behind Bright Lights where all the students lived looked like it had been hurriedly evacuated. Half the clothes in the laundry room were folded. The refrigerator had plenty of food, and the dishwasher was almost full. Most, if not all of the clothes, remained. The whereabouts of the director of the home, Donald Brock, and the other six clients is unknown. We suspect Brock has them hidden away someplace. The FBI is looking into his background right now.

"What's the home like?" I asked.

"Not bad, I'm told. It's pretty large. Two beds in each bedroom, so we assume they each shared a room. Four shared a bathroom. Better than a lot of group homes I've seen. A large master bedroom had a queen bed, probably where Don lived. There were longish blond hairs in the bed, not as long as Brandy's, so he may have been keeping company with another woman.

"They found a small, detached unit, just a bedroom, bathroom, and kitchenette, behind the house. There was an empty tampon box in the bathroom, so unless we get evidence to the contrary, we're pretty sure a woman was living there. There is no record of a female employee in the group home, though. Looks like most of the belongings were removed from Don's room and the separate unit, but we have plenty of latent prints to check out."

"I wonder if the blond hairs in Don's bed are from the occupant of the detached unit."

"Just what we were wondering. Some blond hairs about the same length as those found in Don's bed were found in the bathroom of the disconnected unit, so we'll have our lab see if they match. Interestingly, there is an adjacent building that looks like an old, abandoned warehouse. In it, we found metal detectors set up like they might be at a sports arena."

"The boys must have been trained there."

"That's what we all figured." April removed another binder from the box. "This is the daily log of activities and events from the school. The last entry Brandy made is from the morning of her murder. It states Zaron scraped his leg on a rusty garden tool. A man in the neighborhood drove him to a local doctor for a tetanus shot. Looking through previous notes, it seems this sort of thing has happened before. The doctor and the man who drove Zaron there are being questioned this morning. And there's another thing."

"Oh?"

"Brandy's assistant is missing. Had you met her?"

"No, never."

April stood and fished a large Ziploc bag from the box. In it was a green paper bag with the logo of a local sporting goods store imprinted on both sides. She removed the contents, including a receipt for the purchase. Paid for in cash was an olive green Bassdash fishing vest, still with the tags attached. From the large number of compartments and pockets, it was obvious what this might be used for other than fishing.

"This was found outside the house. I think it was dropped when Don made a hurried escape. I'd appreciate it if you could help me find out if Zaron knows how to put this on. I'll put it here on the table. Please don't touch it. I have gloves for the two of you."

"No problem," I said as April handed me two pairs of vinyl gloves, then unfolded the vest and laid it face down in front of Zaron. I put on one pair of gloves and handed the other to Zaron. He struggled slightly but got them on. They were a tight fit.

"What is it?" I asked Zaron, touching the vest.

"Vest."

"Put the vest on," I said.

We watched intently as Zaron turned the vest over, unzipped the front, stood, slipped his arms through the armholes, adjusted the Velcro straps at the top, zipped the vest up, put his hands in his pants pockets, and stood as if waiting for instructions.

Tears came to my eyes as I realized that what I had suspected had happened. Seeing this play out in front of me made it so much more real and horrific. This sweet, innocent young man had been trained to put on an instrument of pain, death, and destruction, then put his hands in his pockets. With his hands sequestered, he wouldn't flail his arms as he sometimes did. The training probably included cigarette burns to his arms whenever he moved oddly, something that came so naturally to him. Once successfully trained to keep his hands in his pants pockets, he would fit in with any crowd.

I decided to push my luck. "What did Don put in the vest pockets?" I asked.

"Clay."

"Clay, my ass," I mumbled.

"Plastic explosives are clay-like," April said, "so Don probably used real clay during training to mimic the feel of the explosives, so they'd be used to it."

"Take the vest off," I instructed Zaron, who unzipped the vest and returned it to the table. April folded it and put it back in the paper bag along with the receipt, then returned everything to the Ziploc bag. Zaron remained standing. "How did these vests get through the metal detector with all the wires needed to detonate the explosives?" I asked.

"These types of bombs don't require much metal. Only a few thin wires which metal detectors don't pick up. He probably needed a lithium battery to detonate the explosion, though. That's a different story. We figure Don got the battery through security inside a device, maybe a fake cell phone, then placed it in the bomb and took off."

"What are you going to do now?" I asked.

"Terribly sorry, but I can't give you any more details about the ongoing investigation."

"What about Zaron? He could be in danger from this Don Brock psycho."

"The FBI doesn't think that's likely. They believe he's taken the other boys and fled the area. He must realize coming back would be dangerous. We really appreciate all you've done, Erica. I hope you'll be available should we need your help in the future. I'm happy to say I can take Zaron off your hands now. We've found a group home that can accommodate him."

"You're going to take him?" For some reason, I was surprised. I didn't expect to keep him forever, but I was getting attached to him and felt disappointed they were going to take him away. I wondered what sort of place he'd be moving to. I'd heard my share of group home horror stories.

"How long do you think it will take to find Don and the missing boys?"

"Sorry, there's no way to know. As soon as I get back, I'll be using this photo to put out an all-points bulletin throughout the state. The FBI will set up a national search. With a little luck, we'll catch him and the boys soon."

"You owe this guy," I said, taking Zaron's hand and patting it. I was pleased he didn't pull away. "Without him, you'd have no photo identification of Brock."

"That was helpful, but we do have other means. Brock probably has a driver's license, passport, or some other picture on file someplace."

"At least Zaron helped you get a head start."

"And I appreciate it. Now, I'm going to have to take him with me."

"Now? Can't you wait?"

"Sorry, but according to protocol, we need to place him now."

April gently wrapped her hand around Zaron's upper arm and pulled him toward the door, but he didn't budge.

"Zaron, you need to go with April," I said.

Zaron became more agitated than I'd seen him. Instead of walking with April, he squealed loudly and started pulling his hair frantically.

"At least let me take him," I said. "I'm parked in the garage here."

"Okay, you and Zaron can follow me in your car. I'll wait for you—I'm parked right outside the building. But you're going to have to leave him with me. This only prolongs things."

"I understand." *Here I go again. I'm such a sucker for the helpless.* I was trying to think of ways to convince April that Zaron should stay with me a bit longer. I escorted Zaron back to the garage, carrying the shirt and socks he'd worn the day before in a paper bag.

*

With Zaron seated beside me in my mom's car, I followed April to the police department, where I pulled into the visitor's lot. April met Zaron and me inside the waiting area and escorted us past the receptionists, through the door leading to the large room we'd been in the day before. She took a seat at one of the desks and motioned for Zaron and me to sit in adjacent chairs.

"Someone should be here soon to pick him up. If you could walk him to the car when the time comes, it would be a big help," April said. As she spoke, I was already dreading the moment I'd have to leave Zaron with a stranger.

No sooner had we sat down than an officer I hadn't seen before rushed over to April. "Something important's come up," she said, nodding her head sideways, undiplomatically signaling April to walk away so they could have a private conversation. April took several steps, but it wasn't enough. Straining, I was able to hear their muffled conversation.

"There was another threat from the bomber," the unfamiliar officer said.

"Damn," April responded.

"I found out about it thirty minutes ago. The FBI kept it secret from us. There's a Los Angeles Angels home game in two days. If they don't pay five million dollars, there's going to be another bombing."

"Oh, boy. Since the pictures of the boys were taken from Bright Lights, we don't know what the other potential suicide bombers look like." April paused as she appeared to be thinking of a strategy. "Maybe with Dr. Rosen's help, we could get Zaron here to monitor the crowd coming in, tell us if he recognizes anyone. He could pick out Donald Brock, although Brock might use someone else to bring in the next bomber. I think our best strategy—"

"Don't worry about coming up with a plan. MLB decided to pay. Just made the transfer to a bank in the Cayman Islands."

"Shit. Played right into that asshole's hands."

"Can you blame them? Really? They have a lot on the line."

The conversation couldn't have taken much more than ten seconds. When it was over, I turned to Zaron. His seat was empty.

Chapter 9

I told myself not to panic and headed toward the restrooms. Both empty. Then I panicked. I felt queasy as my pulse quickened. It was coming back to me now how some of the kids I used to care for could disappear when my attention was distracted for a moment. Zaron had already demonstrated that ability when he'd left my side at Bright Lights and moved to the puzzle table without my noticing. I should have paid more attention.

April was still involved in a conversation with the other officer when I returned from the restroom check. "Zaron's gone," I blurted out. "He was sitting next to me one second, then a few seconds later, he was gone. I checked the bathrooms. He's not there." The two officers stared at me blankly before April sprang into action, looking in every cubicle, and around every desk in the room. Convinced Zaron had left, she radioed dispatch, instructing them to send out a BOLO for a nineteen-year-old man approximately six feet tall, with sandy hair and blue eyes, wearing a yellow shirt, blue jeans, gray tennis shoes, one white sock, and one black sock. He wasn't armed or dangerous and should be approached in a nonthreatening manner.

"He can't have gotten far," April reassured me.

"Maybe not, but I'll bet he can make himself very hard to find if he wants to. This wouldn't have happened if he'd been allowed to stay with me." I was annoyed with myself as soon as I said it. It must have sounded like I was blaming April, but I knew it wasn't her fault.

"It wasn't my decision."

"I know, I'm sorry. I don't blame you for anything. But maybe now you can talk some sense into whoever did make that decision. Let's hope Zaron's okay."

"I'll look for him with Porter," April said.

"I don't think Zaron likes Porter. He'd probably hide from him."

"Okay, I agree Porter hasn't endeared himself to Zaron. I'll look for him myself. Wait here 'til I get back. Then we'll see about where he stays."

I must have waited close to twenty minutes. During that time, I noticed two officers standing nearby, discussing something in hushed tones. I opened my wallet and splashed pennies, dimes, nickels, and quarters onto the floor, directing the majority of them towards the officers. Collecting the loose change, I spent most of my time near the officers, working as quietly as possible while listening intently to their conversation.

I had, in fact, hit a jackpot of information with my coins—I learned Donald Brock was thirty-eight years old and had been born in a small town in Appalachia. He had no criminal history, no academic history, and no employment history until two years earlier when he got a license to open a group home. His first income tax filing was for revenue he received while operating the group home, the money coming from the clients' Social Security payments and the Regional Center, a California agency set up to help the developmentally disabled. I knew those payments were never generous. Someone was checking on the application Brock had filed for the group home.

With so little information available on the suspect, one of the officers raised the possibility that the perpetrator had taken over the identity of a dead person named Donald Brock. His colleague assured him that was impossible, as all relevant information is computerized and interconnected. The Social Security number of a person known to be dead would never pass muster with the IRS.

I was back in my seat when April returned. Looking visibly upset, she said, "Can't find him. Believe me, I looked all over the area. Asked everyone I saw. One person thought she'd seen him eating food from a garbage can. It sounded like something he might do, so I parked and looked all around. Called his name, but no luck."

"It's not safe for him to be out there alone. I imagine he has all the street smarts of a young child. He could be hit by a car or kidnapped by anyone with a candy bar. I'll call my husband, Lim," I said. "He can run around on foot with a bag of chocolate chip cookies. I think Zaron likes him. Maybe he'll come out for Lim and cookies."

"Going up and down every street nearby is a lot of running," April cautioned me. "I don't know how far he'll get before he tires out, but I suppose it's worth a try."

"My husband can run quite a distance. He's fast, too," I assured April. I didn't think she believed me, but saw no need to describe Lim's past accomplishments in that area.

I phoned Lim and asked him to get a bag of chocolate chip cookies and meet me at the police station, prepared to run around the neighborhood. Fifteen minutes later, I received a text letting me know Lim was waiting outside. April and I met him in front of the building where he was stretching his legs, dressed in running shorts and a tank top.

I introduced Lim to April and explained what we needed him to do. "Wish me luck," he said, giving me a kiss and heading north while glancing at Google Maps on his cell phone. April followed close behind in a cruiser.

I returned to the building and waited on one of the few chairs in the public area. I hadn't seen my mom in four days, so I used the time to call one of her caregivers. I was assured she was stable, with no recent deterioration.

My thoughts returned to the bomber. He'd managed to get five million dollars from MLB. Would he stop now? Or would he continue to extort more money? How much did he want? Something else took hold in my thoughts.

A few years ago, I had a patient whose mother came from Appalachia. The mother was proud to have gotten her son a birth certificate at the time he was born. While most of us take such things for granted, she'd come from a poor family and had been born at home. Her single mother hadn't bothered to get her a birth certificate, a common omission at that time and place. When she was eighteen and wanted a Social Security card, she had to jump through hoops. Getting a Delayed Certificate of Birth required presenting the issuing agency with various supporting documents that weren't easy to procure. She vowed to herself no kid of hers would have to go through a similar ordeal.

Now I wondered if the same could happen with death certificates. In a rural area where people might not have money for burial expenses, someone who died might be laid to rest on the family's land. No death certificate would be issued because the county coroner wouldn't be notified. If someone adopted the identity of that person, it would never be discovered by cross-checking on government computers.

I was looking downward, those deliberations occupying my mind, when twenty minutes later, my thoughts were interrupted by the sound of someone chomping on food in front of me. I looked up to see Zaron scarfing down a chocolate chip cookie. Behind him stood April and Lim, both smiling broadly.

"Zaron," I shouted in relief. I regretted my enthusiastic reaction when Zaron put both his hands over his ears, upset by the noise. "Sorry, Zaron," I said quietly. "I was just so glad to see you."

"We did it," April said. "Or, to be honest, he did it," she said, pointing to Lim. "That man of yours sure can run."

"I forgot to mention he was a member of the Chinese Olympic track team," I said.

"Well, that explains it."

"How'd you find him?" I asked, looking at Lim.

"I went behind some stores about a half-mile from here and called his name," Lim said. "I think he smelled the cookies. He dashed out from behind a dumpster and tried to grab the bag. I'd like to think he was also happy to see me."

"Well, I'm glad he's back. Now what?" I asked, turning to April. "If he gets sent to a new home, he'll probably run away. You've already seen how helpful he can be. He may know something else that could facilitate catching Brock, and find the missing boys. See if you can get authorization for me to take him back to my place. I'll make sure he's safe, and available—"

April held up her hand as if to say "halt" and nodded in agreement. "Already done," she said. "We don't want to lose him. I'll bring his clothes by your place after I get them delivered from his old house. All the clothes are labeled with names, so it won't be hard to figure out which ones are his."

*

Lim ran home from the station, entering our condo shortly after I arrived there with Zaron. I filled him in about what I had learned at the police station. The bomber had just become five million dollars richer by way of a payoff to his Cayman Islands account. There was nothing on record for Donald Brock before the previous two years. The fact that he'd been born in Appalachia led me to suspect the real Don Brock had died as a child years ago, and had been buried on his family's property without being recorded in the state's vital records.

"Where's Appalachia?" Lim asked. "I've never heard of that state."

"It's not a state. It's a region, covering parts of several states, including Kentucky, Pennsylvania, West Virginia, and Tennessee, where the Appalachian Mountains are. There are areas of extreme poverty there."

"If this guy is just pretending to be someone named Don Brock of Appalachia, we need to know that."

"If only I could find out for sure," I lamented. "I don't think I could expect April to look into this. After all, it's only a hunch."

"May I suggest one of two ways to accomplish that?"

"Like what?"

"One way would be to go to Appalachia and look for his grave in all the family plots you can find."

"That would probably take no more than ten or fifteen years working full-time," I said.

"Or you could use the internet. Even in most backward places of the US, people have access to it."

"How's that going to help? How in the world can I find out about this guy on the internet?"

"There's lots of sites you could try. I'd start with genealogy sites."

"I wouldn't know where to begin."

"Now that I think of it, maybe I could help," Lim said with a sly smile.

"I was hoping you'd come up with one of your brilliant ideas."

"I could use some of the proprietary software I've been developing. In addition to collecting data on specific IP addresses, it can target IP addresses in particular locations."

"Meaning?"

"I can send emails to people in Appalachia. In particular, I can target people with the last name of Brock, so I don't spam too many people."

"That would be fantastic. How many days would it take you?"

"Tell you what. If you entertain Zaron, I'll spend the next hour or so working on it. Then, if your hunch is correct, it's just a question of time until someone responds with the information you want, namely that Donald Brock, who would be thirty-eight years old today, died years ago."

"Then all we need to do is figure out who the guy impersonating him is. Thanks, Amazing Husband." I gave him a kiss. "I'll take Zaron for a walk."

When I returned an hour later, it was almost time for dinner. I had discovered that while Zaron enjoyed walking outside, he had no clue how to cross streets safely, seeming to lack any understanding of traffic safety. He tended to walk ahead of me, requiring me to yell "stop" each time he approached a street corner. Fortunately, he was compliant and waited patiently for me each time. Now that we were home, Zaron was smiling and bouncing the new red ball I'd bought him at a nearby toy store. I placed the bag I was carrying with a few other items I'd purchased on the coffee table. Lim was reading the newspaper.

"Well?" I asked.

"Done. It's a pretty big area, and there are a lot of Brocks there. I sent out over two thousand emails. Now we wait and see if someone responds. It would be nice to have several responses, to corroborate each other."

"What if the bomber finds out? What if he tracks us down from the email you sent?"

"What's your expression? 'Not to worry?' Well, don't worry. I doubt he'll get one of these emails. If he does, and he has the ability to trace it, he'll be led to Liam Altermatt in Switzerland."

"A fictitious person you invented?"

"Of course."

"Clever. What did you write in your email?"

"I said I was dying of heart failure and took great pleasure in tracing my genealogy. I had recently become aware of relatives in the eastern part of the US. A third cousin once removed told me there might be a distant male cousin named Donald Brock living in that area who was around the same age as my thirty-eight-year-old son, Elias. If true, I wanted to let Elias know about it before I died. I also mentioned I was poor, so they wouldn't expect any money. I didn't want people making things up to get paid."

"Good thinking. Thanks. I hope you hear something soon. Now on to another important topic. What would you like for dinner?"

"I've got that covered. Mom's making a special dinner for us. My parents want to meet Zaron."

Chapter 10

I had mixed feelings about getting together with Lim's parents. I always felt like an outsider, being the only one who didn't speak their language. On the other hand, Lim's mother, Fung, was a really good cook. His dad, Enlai, always made sure my water glass and teacup were full.

"Do you think I could invite Daisy?" I asked. "I'd like her to meet Zaron, too." Daisy had been invited to our big family dinners several times in the past, twice bringing her own parents who grew up in Taiwan and were able to speak to my in-laws. Daisy herself understood a few words of Mandarin but never learned to speak it. She had grown close to Ting and her children, especially Mingyu. We all joked that she was Mingyu's second mother, having smuggled him out of the secret Chinese gene-editing facility under a fake pregnancy belly.

"Sure. Mom always makes plenty of food."

I called Daisy and learned she was up against a deadline on her work project and couldn't come for dinner but would take a break and stop by afterward. I told her about Zaron for the first time, and she looked forward to meeting him.

I took a jigsaw puzzle I'd bought earlier at the toy store when we went to my in-laws. As soon as we entered their condo, I smelled the food Fung was preparing. A delectable combination of garlic, ginger, onions, sesame, and I-don't-know-what. My mother-in-law was busy tending to multiple woks on the stove, mixing things in bowls, and shouting orders to her husband. As Enlai darted around, bringing her things and setting the table, I noticed something different about him. It took me a minute to figure out what it was. In contrast to the balding pate with salt and pepper hair he'd had when I first met him, he was sporting a full head of straight, thick black hair. He had obviously invested in a wig. I hadn't appreciated that even a middle-aged man just out of a labor camp might be vain. The way he was rushing around, it appeared the new wig gave him extra energy.

Ting and her children were already there. At first, the kids kept their distance from Zaron, observing him as he made strange noises while looking around the condominium, inspecting the contents of every cabinet. Then they followed my lead and held up objects for him to identify, objects they themselves had only recently learned to name in English. Zaron seemed to enjoy it and was able to identify quite a few. Lim's parents watched as they continued to get dinner ready but didn't know if he was naming things correctly until their grandchildren cheered and said "Yes," a word they understood.

We finally sat down to eat the banquet Fung had prepared. I think she was particularly pleased Zaron scarfed down most of what she served—a beef dish, a chicken dish, long beans, and rice. I was surprised he liked the long beans but left the delicious stir-fried bok choy untouched. His skill with chopsticks had already improved. For dessert, Fung had made scrumptious sesame fritters. Zaron unabashedly stuffed them in his mouth, one after the other, until they were gone.

After dinner, he jumped up and started clearing the plates as my in-laws looked on in amazement. They were talking to Lim and Ting in Chinese, smiling and laughing as he put the dishes in the dishwasher.

Daisy rang from downstairs, and Enlai buzzed her in. He opened the condominium door for her a short time later and waved her in, just as I finished correcting the mistakes Zaron had made loading the dishwasher. Seeing Zaron, Daisy walked over to him and smiled. "Hi Zaron, I'm Daisy," she said. Her voice was loud, and Zaron looked away, covering his ears.

"It's okay, Daisy," I said, noticing her distraught expression. "It's best not to be too loud around him. He doesn't take to new people easily." I looked at Zaron and pointed to Daisy. "Look at Daisy and say, 'Hi, Daisy.'"

Zaron looked at Daisy for an instant, then looked away again and said, "Hi, Daisy."

We both laughed. "That's as good as you're going to get right now," I said.

Zaron walked away and opened the jigsaw puzzle I'd brought with me. He dumped all 200 pieces on the kitchen table and got to work. The rest of us stood around and watched as he completed it, smiling while putting the pieces in place a lot faster than any of the rest of us could have. Daisy held Mingyu so he could watch. Once the last piece was in, Zaron immediately took the puzzle apart and tossed the pieces back in the box. I heard an audible gasp from the others as he did this. He wasn't one to sit back and admire his accomplishments.

"Why'd he do that?" Daisy asked, looking flustered. "Nobody takes a puzzle apart as soon as they finish it. Everyone I know leaves it out for weeks, or glues it together so they can hang it on the wall."

"You have to remember, Zaron doesn't think or react to situations like the rest of us. But he's clearly got a lot going on up there," I said, tapping my second finger on my temple.

"That was quite a show," Daisy said. "Unfortunately, I have to get back. I hope I get a chance to spend more time with Zaron."

"You will if I still have him after you're done with your project."

Lim, Zaron, and I stayed a short while after Daisy left, then departed ourselves. Upon returning to our unit, I spent the evening with Zaron as Lim worked in the study. I unwrapped a package of flashcards I'd bought earlier. The cards were simple, with pictures of items on one side. I wanted to find out how many words Zaron knew and started going through the pile. Car, broom, lamp, shoe, bear, tree. He knew them all. I'm aware it doesn't sound like much, but I was stoked knowing this young man, who initially appeared to be completely nonverbal, knew much more than was apparent on the surface. Nothing prepared me for what happened next. He started telling me what was on each card before I showed him the picture. All the cards were in a pile, face down.

"Boat," he said, so quiet I could barely hear him.

I picked up the top card and looked at the picture. It was a boat. No sooner had I done that than, in a voice barely audible, he said "clock." I picked up the next card. A clock. It was eerie, as if he had some sort of ESP. Then I laughed at myself for being so dense. The words for each item were printed on the back of the cards. Zaron had been reading the card backs upside down before I turned them over. Now I knew he could read. With more testing, I learned that although he could read almost anything, often with an odd pronunciation after sounding out an unfamiliar word, his comprehension was limited. Although his writing was unreadable, I discovered he was able to type on my laptop and could use it to spell common words and answer simple questions.

I reflected on Zaron's indifference towards impressing others with his ability to read, spell, or put puzzles together. He wasn't concerned with what others thought of him. He was like the autistic kids I'd looked after before. None of them bragged like normal kids. They didn't care.

I wondered if Zaron knew anything important, something to help us find Don and the boys. I decided to test his memory. The better it was, the more likely he might provide us with a detail we could use. "Zaron, what is the address of Bright Lights?"

"760 Amador Road."

"That's right!" So far, so good. "Zaron, what kind of cereal do I have in that cabinet?" I pointed to the closed cupboard where we kept our cold cereal.

"Cheerios, Wheat Chex, Raisin Bran, Froot Loops."

We had Cheerios, Wheat Chex, and Raisin Bran, but neither Lim nor I would ever buy Froot Loops. I looked in the cabinet to be sure and saw only the three cereals we normally had. I wondered if he misremembered or had mistaken something for Froot Loops. "Show me the Froot Loops, Zaron," I said.

Zaron walked to the cabinet, opened the door, and reached behind the cereal boxes I was familiar with. He turned to me, carrying in his hand a single-serving-sized sealed cup of Froot Loops, the kind often doled out in restaurants. Only then did I remember Ting asking me to remove the Froot Loops from her condominium several months earlier after Wang Shu had brought them home from a party. Instead of throwing the junk food in the garbage, I had placed it behind the other cereals and forgotten about it. I concluded Zaron's memory was pretty good, and his observational skills were at least normal, probably better than most.

Next, I asked, "Zaron, what did I have for dinner April 17, 2015?" That was a date I pulled out of thin air. I didn't remember what I'd eaten that evening, and there was no way he'd know. He sat down without answering. Then I asked, "Zaron, what did *you* have for dinner April 17, 2015?"

"Chicken, rice, peas, water, bread, butter, vanilla ice cream."

I had no way to prove his answer was correct, but I was sure it was, as he'd never fabricated information in the past. From then on, I was convinced Zaron's memory was impressive. If only there were a way to get him to tell us what he knew.

"Time for bed," I said as I threw the Froot Loops in the trash.

Zaron opened the sofa bed without being told. While he was getting a pillow from the storage cabinet, someone slipped a sheet of paper under our door. Zaron stopped what he was doing, bolted toward the door, picked up the paper, and threw it in the kitchen garbage. It alerted me that due to his compulsion to clean up, I'd have to keep an eye on him to be sure he didn't throw out something important.

I fished the paper out of the trash and recognized the peculiar logo of our condominium board—a cable car riding on the Golden Gate Bridge. I read the message, signed by our board chair, stating management would be replacing the carpeting in the hallways over the next few weeks, and they would do their best to minimize the inconvenience. We got such notices frequently. There was always something to fix or update, a way of justifying our high monthly fees, I suspected.

Zaron brushed his teeth, showered, put on the pajamas he'd worn the night before, and got into bed as if he'd done it a hundred times. He now had a routine. If there's one thing I remembered, autistic people love routines. Comfortable. Predictable.

I read for a while, then went to bed myself as my husband remained ensconced in the study.

As usual, the next morning Lim woke before me and brought me coffee at seven thirty. I sensed he wanted to tell me something.

"Good news," he said.

Still sleepy, I took a sip of coffee. "Give me a hint."

"Remember those emails I sent out yesterday?"

Now completely alert, I asked, "You got a response?"

"Yap."

I laughed. "It's 'yep,'" I corrected him before taking another sip of coffee.

"Right. Yep. Not just one, either. I got five."

My eyes widened reflexively as I finished the sip and sprung out of bed. "That's wonderful. What did they say? Is Donald Brock alive or dead?"

"All five confirm. Dead."

"How long?"

"More than thirty years. Just as you suspected, Don Brock was buried on the family farm. The property is in a small town called Grundy, located in Buchanan county. That's in Virginia."

"Who'd you hear from?"

"An older brother, an uncle, and three cousins. The kid got whooping cough, the local doctor couldn't save him, and he died. With no money for a funeral or burial plot, the parents buried him on their land. I got the exact address from the brother and uncle. The parents are dead now, but it's doubtful a death certificate was ever obtained.'

"If they had registered his death," I said, "Social Security would have a record of it, and he wouldn't have been able to open the group home—not using the Social Security number of a dead man."

I was satisfied that the guy we were after had taken over the identity of a child named Donald Brock who died years ago, but whose death was never recorded. I didn't know how the murderer had found out about the dead boy, but that didn't matter.

"You'll need to tell April about this," Lim said.

"I know. Maybe they know about this already, but I doubt it."

"Meanwhile, we can celebrate our fine detective work."

I gave Zaron a five-hundred-piece puzzle of colorful fish swimming in the ocean. Once he was engaged, Lim and I retired to the bedroom and locked the door, something we hadn't done since we moved in. We made love or, to be more accurate, had wild sex.

When we were finished, I wondered what my next step should be. *How do we find out who this guy really is? Where are the other boys? Are they being fed and taken care of? Can we stop this psychopath from killing more people and extorting more money?*

Chapter 11

I watched, almost in a trance, as Zaron finished his puzzle, having what seemed like a preternatural ability to manipulate the pieces, rotating some close matches, trying to insert them quickly, then placing the ones that didn't fit to the side before picking the next one. Often succeeding on the first try, it didn't take long to place the next piece. He frequently rocked back and forth gently, smiled, and made a humming sound in celebration after each success.

I wondered how life must be, not understanding the world. No concerns about finances, the health of loved ones, responsibilities, planning for the future, politics. On the other hand, having no ability to control one's life, or express wants and needs had to be frustrating if not downright scary. Being at the mercy of non-caring or abusive people would be the most terrifying of all. I worried that if Zaron developed appendicitis, no one, even someone thoughtful and caring, would know. As I watched him, I found myself hoping it would take a long time to find a suitable place for him to live.

My thoughts were interrupted when Lim emerged from the bedroom, dressed and ready for work. After an affectionate goodbye kiss, he was out the door.

I was about to test Zaron's reading ability some more when I received a call from April. She was about to leave the station to bring me some of Zaron's clothes and promised to update me on the investigation. I wondered how much she would divulge. I liked her and felt we were becoming friends. However, she was still a police officer and obligated to keep most official business private.

I looked forward to telling her in person what Lim and I had found out about the man calling himself Donald Brock. I'd wait for the right moment to explain what Lim had done and hope I could convince her Lim and I would be valuable unofficial additions to the investigative team. I was motivated to remain involved, worried that without my input law enforcement would consider the safety of the missing boys secondary.

I didn't have to wait long for April to arrive. Shortly after I buzzed her in, she was at my door, carrying two bags. I welcomed her and showed her the box containing the puzzle Zaron had finished and put away earlier. I felt proud and wanted others to appreciate his ability.

After letting Zaron know how impressed she was with his puzzle skills, comments Zaron completely ignored, April put one of the bags on the table while still holding the other one.

"I have your clothes," she said to Zaron.

He glanced up, grabbed the bag from the table, and emptied its contents on the sofa. Making humming noises, he picked up each item and felt it between his fingers before putting it aside. He'd handled three shirts, two pairs of pants, and some underwear in this way before he picked up a light blue shirt. Instead of feeling it ceremoniously as he had done with the other items, he simply put it back in the bag and said, almost inaudibly, "Steven."

I walked over and took the shirt from the bag. The name tag read "Steven." My heart sank. The shirt had belonged to the dead boy.

"That was found in his room," April commented. "I see now it looks a little small for Zaron. Sorry, it must have gotten mixed in with his stuff by accident."

"Steven was Zaron's roommate?" I asked.

"Afraid so."

I was relieved Zaron never asked where Steven was or how he was doing.

"Maybe you could take Steven's shirt back with you," I said to April.

"Sure, no problem," she said as she placed the bag she was still holding on the table. "There's a few other things I'd like to show you." She pulled out a beautiful, framed, pencil drawing of a building I recognized, Bright Lights. I hadn't seen the picture before, but the style reminded me of other pictures I'd seen hanging on the walls of the school. "This was found in the group home, along with many others done by the same artist," April said. "I want to know if Zaron knows who drew this."

"Why would he know that?" I asked.

"Please, just ask him. I don't think he'd answer me."

I turned to Zaron and held the picture up. "Zaron," I said, tapping the picture. "Who drew this?"

"Derrick."

I looked closely at the lower right-hand corner of the picture but saw no signature. I turned to April. "What's going on? Who's Derrick?"

"He's one of the missing boys. We noticed a lot of these pictures in the group home as well as the school. Looking through the information we got from the office, an inspector read that one of the boys, Derrick, has phenomenal artistic abilities. Brandy wrote she was encouraging him to draw buildings he saw in the area and on field trips. Apparently, he did this all from memory. Zaron just confirmed these were done by him—none of them are signed, so we weren't sure."

"Interesting," I said. "Artistic ability—that's one of the savant skills autistic people sometimes have."

"I see. That must explain Zaron's ability with dates. Do they all have some of those skills?" April asked.

"No, but approximately ten percent of them do. What do you know about the others enrolled at Bright Lights?"

"Not too much. We learned Arthur, the Black fellow you met earlier, always wears a necklace with an "A" on it. Has a fit if you take it off."

"I remember seeing the necklace, now. It was made of a yellow metal and covered in rhinestones."

"I'll make a note of that," April said, pulling a small notepad from a pocket and jotting something down. "It could be an important detail to help us identify him since we don't have pictures."

"What else did you find out about the boys?" I asked.

April flipped a few pages in her notepad before answering. "Martin. He likes to memorize baseball scores. Apparently, he's memorized all the major league scores from at least the past ten years. Another savant skill, I suppose."

"Yes," I said.

"Another one named Zachary has calendar skills like Zaron here. Patrick loves to make paper origami cranes, so the school kept special paper on hand for him. Kyle won't eat anything that's green. Apparently, trying to slip in small pieces of healthy green vegetables doesn't work. He does like carrots and cauliflower, though. That's all I know."

"What about Steven, the boy who died? Let's not forget about him."

April glanced at her notepad again. "All I have here is he always carried a small pink ball he liked to hold up to his ear and tap with his fingers."

"I'm sure there's a lot more to know about all of them than what you have written down. They all have their own personalities like the rest of us, their special quirks, and their likes and dislikes. I sure hope they find them soon. Any luck locating the murderer?" I asked.

"I'm not at liberty to say, but we're still looking. You can interpret that any way you want."

"I don't think Donald Brock is his real name."

"We checked that all out because it's unusual to have so little information on someone. I shouldn't be telling you all this, but I don't see the harm. Our people confirmed Don Brock is a real person. He's alive and used his real birth date and Social Security number while running the group home, filing taxes, and paying into Social Security."

"I think he took over the identity of the real Donald Brock who died some years back."

"You've been reading too many mystery books. There was a time when a person could take on the identity of a deceased person. But those days are long gone."

"I know about all the cross-checking the Social Security Administration does with death records. But that only prevents someone from stealing the identity of a dead person if the Social Security number matches up with a recorded death."

"Well, of course. As I said, that's all been checked."

"I don't doubt it, but something may have been overlooked. Knowing there had been no information about Donald Brock until he showed up here and became the director of a group home, Lim and I thought maybe he had taken over the identity of a dead person."

"Like I said, we'd know if he'd done that."

I sensed April becoming annoyed. I needed her to stay on my side, so I spoke as tactfully as I could. "You'd know if he'd taken over the identity of a dead person only if the death had been registered. Remember my husband, Lim? You met him when we were trying to find Zaron after he ran away from the station."

"How could I forget?" April seemed to be making an effort to hide her impatience so I wouldn't feel insulted. I surmised we both understood the value of maintaining our cooperative relationship. Even so, April gave me a look as if to ask, "Where are you going with this?"

"Lim is the lead computer engineer for his startup company, Cyber Protection. The company is developing software to gather data in different ways to protect businesses from cyberattacks and allow them to hide their true IP addresses from possible attackers. Since we thought Don Brock might have died but hadn't been issued a death certificate, Lim put his company's software to use. He sent an email from a fictitious European relative to all the Brocks in Appalachia, where a Donald Brock was born thirty-eight years ago."

"How did you learn his age and place of birth? I know I didn't tell you."

"I overheard two officers talk about it while you were looking for Zaron."

"You're a dangerous one, aren't you?" April said, smiling. "I'll bet no one gets anything past you. I'm glad we're on the same side. Tell me, did anyone respond to the email?"

"They did." I told April what Lim learned from relatives of the real Don Brock.

"Interesting," April said when I finished. "I'm still not completely convinced, but I'll run it by my boss. Maybe he could ask the local department there in Virginia to check it out for confirmation."

My cell phone rang as it often did at inopportune times, like a jealous child seeking attention. Without checking, I declined the call, not wanting to interrupt my conversation with April. "I'm guessing the guy posing as Donald Brock is originally from that area and knew about his death," I said, wondering if April had even noticed I'd received and dispensed with a call.

"Could be. One step at a time, though. Are you still okay with keeping Zaron? I'm supposed to be checking on his welfare right now, as my chief says we may be held responsible if anything happens to him."

My phone pinged, letting me know I had a voice mail message. I ignored the notification as I responded to April. "As you can see, he's doing great here. Seems to be very happy, so I'd just as soon keep him until something better is worked out. I'm worried the murderer might try to get him back, though. He's got six trained suicide bombers, and he might want a seventh."

"I don't think Zaron's in danger, if that's what you're worried about. Again, I'll run it by my chief. Meanwhile, let me know if you notice anything suspicious."

After April left, I checked my phone and listened to the recent phone mail message. It was from my friend, Shanika, a geneticist. She'd been on maternity leave ever since I'd returned from China.

My mom, who suffered from the neurodegenerative disorder Huntington's disease, was living in a wonderful care facility not far from me. I visited her several times a week, often bringing her chocolate, her favorite food. She was still conversant, but less so each time I saw her. Strange movements beyond her control, including tremors and random writhing motions of her arms and legs, were taking over her body. I felt her slipping away, each visit more ominous than the last—especially since I knew I had a fifty percent chance of inheriting the disease from her. I had the dark cloud of uncertainty hanging over me, as I'd been waiting for Shanika to return to work so she could test me. Lim had suggested I get tested by someone else, but I wanted to wait until my friend could do it.

Shanika told me in her message she would be returning to work on Monday and wanted me to schedule a visit for Huntington's disease testing her first day back. Soon I would learn the secret that had been locked in my DNA since before I was born.

Chapter 12

I wasted no time in calling to make the appointment with Shanika. I needed to find out once and for all if I would suffer the same fate as my mother. Even though my mind was occupied with other matters, not knowing was taking its toll.

If the result came back negative, it would be a relief better than any other. I feared how I would react if the test were positive, my fate sealed. I felt I could handle it, but one never really knows until it happens. Nevertheless, I needed to find out.

After making the appointment, I began doing laundry. Zaron sprang to action, grabbing the detergent from me before I dispensed it. He measured the laundry soap, added it to the washing machine, and with little guidance from me, started the load.

I reflected on the fact that aside from the possibility of later suffering from a debilitating neurologic condition, my life was finally settling into something that could be considered normal. I enjoyed my clinic work, seeing old and new patients, and mentoring the younger physicians. While many patients came in with routine problems, challenging cases had a way of presenting themselves on a regular basis, keeping the job interesting.

April called to tell me her chief wanted the address where the child Donald Brock was said to be buried. I asked her to wait while I searched for it on Lim's computer. Once located, I read the address to her while wondering how long it would take the police to confirm the existence of the grave.

I decided to explore Zaron's ability to follow written instructions. Taking a blank piece of paper, I wrote, "Turn on the light in the bathroom." Zaron grabbed the paper from me, then put it on the table. He walked into the bathroom, turned on the light, and returned. As I reflected on Zaron's untapped abilities, I heard a knock on the door.

As always, I checked through the peephole. Fung. I prepared myself for the usual awkwardness between us when Lim or Ting wasn't around to translate. I opened the door and attempted to tell her Lim wasn't home, when she abruptly interrupted me.

"Zaron," she said. I noticed she was carrying a plate filled with sesame fritters, which smelled freshly made.

Zaron ran to her and grabbed the plate. As he stuffed one fritter after the other in his mouth, Fung looked pleased. When he'd finished eating them all, Zaron sniffed Fung's shoulder. She laughed, then reciprocated and sniffed his shoulder.

"Fung," she said, pointing to herself as she looked at Zaron. "Fung." Zaron looked past her, but she moved into his line of sight. She pointed to Zaron and said, "Zaron." As Zaron tried to look away from her, she moved around, staying in his line of sight while pointing back to herself, saying, "Fung."

She repeated this several times until Zaron said, "Fung" when she pointed to herself.

Fung smiled, waved to me, and left. Surprisingly, my mother-in-law demonstrated a natural ability to relate to Zaron. I sensed the beginning of a friendship of sorts. Fung and Zaron were well-matched in some ways. Neither was comfortable speaking English. Fung enjoyed cooking treats, and Zaron enjoyed eating them. Watching them interact was curiously captivating.

I checked my calendar and saw it was time to collect blood from Ting's kids for testing. I'd get their samples after dinner, when Ting would be available to comfort them. As Zaron watched a movie on my iPad, I searched the internet and made a few phone calls before finding a lab offering a test for myostatin deficiency, or double muscling. I'd send a tube of Kang's blood there and, while I was at it, I'd have Mingyu tested, too.

Meanwhile, I needed to decide what to do about Zaron. I wanted to keep him with me until the Don Brock impersonator was captured. On the other hand, I couldn't shirk my clinic responsibilities forever to ensure his safety. I wouldn't be comfortable watching him placed in a random group home even after the murderer was captured. I know, there are thousands of intellectually disabled children and adults in group homes nationwide, and many of those facilities are fine. But lots aren't, and they need to be carefully screened, something I didn't have time to do. Now that I was familiar with him, I wanted Zaron to have more opportunities than would be offered in most available living arrangements. I didn't know exactly what I wanted for Zaron, but I would know it when I saw it.

I considered hiring a caretaker to watch Zaron when I was at work. Perhaps I could find another day program for him since Bright Lights was no longer operating. I considered asking the Regional Center to recommend the best schools for him but thought twice about it. Since he was a ward of the state, I feared if I brought attention to the situation, the bureaucracy would wake up and force Zaron into a group home. I'd have no say in the matter. Something to discuss with Lim when he came home that evening.

April called. A mere four hours after I'd given her the address, the local police in Virginia confirmed that Donald Brock, born thirty-eight years ago, had indeed been buried on the family property in Grundy at the age of seven.

"Now what?" I asked.

"We have this guy's fingerprints and the photo from Brandy's apartment. The prints have been entered into a national database, but so far, no hits. If any crimes are committed, and the fingerprints match, we'll find out right away. We have a BOLO out on him, so police up and down the state are looking for him. If he's changed his appearance significantly, he may be hard to find, but really, if you ask me, it's just a question of time. He's bound to slip up. Meanwhile, it's time to think about moving Zaron to a more permanent residence."

That's not what I wanted to hear. "Let me keep him longer," I said. "Find this dirtbag you're after, and the missing boys. Then we'll talk about finding a permanent home for Zaron."

"Okay, I won't contact the Regional Center if you don't want me to, but eventually they're going to wonder where he is and insist on placing him in one of their homes. He won't be able to slip through the cracks forever, but as far as I'm concerned, you can keep him for now."

"Thanks," I said, happy one problem was solved, at least temporarily. I glanced at Zaron, still watching the video on my iPad. He smiled as he gently rocked back and forth while making the sounds he made when he seemed happy. I would miss him terribly if he moved out.

Lim worked hard for his company. Just as one problem was solved, two more popped up. He was good at what he did, and the product he was developing was over ninety percent complete. Lately, he'd been concerned mostly with debugging the software. Each glitch found was frustrating. With all the pressure he was under, I felt guilty burdening Lim with my problems. But that didn't stop me. As soon as he came home, I unloaded my concerns about Zaron.

"I have an idea," he said. "My parents love watching their grandchildren during the day. When Ting has the kids, they get lonely. Other than going to Chinatown, where they get together with other Chinese immigrants, they don't have much to interest them. They like Zaron, although they haven't seen him much. I think they would enjoy watching over him. They were always such hard workers, and proud of it. Ever since they've been here, they've wanted to be useful. They're so full of life, it's hard to believe we thought they were dead for so many years."

"They're so busy as it is, taking care of Ting's kids. I'd hate to ask them to do more."

"You have to understand—they want to do more. I think caring for Zaron will make them very happy, and you could see him as often as you want. Zaron could help them with things like the heavy housework and carrying groceries home, although they would never admit to wanting any assistance. Also, with him around evenings and weekends, they won't be so lonely. Win, win as you say. They have an extra bedroom they don't need."

I must have been smiling because Lim commented, "I haven't seen you smile like that since you found him."

"If I understand what you're saying, Zaron could stay with your parents?"

"Yes, until we have a better solution."

"Just today, your mom came by with some of her sesame fritters. I had the feeling she connected with Zaron on some level. I think he likes her."

"I'm sure he likes her fritters, if nothing else."

"Let's give it a try. But you'll have to explain to them Zaron needs supervision. He doesn't have common sense. When confronted with something unfamiliar, there's no telling what he'll do. If there's a fire, he might not leave the building."

"I'll explain everything."

"Let's try writing down things your parents might want him to do on notecards. Like set the table, or do the laundry. On the backs, you can write the Chinese translation. They can hand him cards telling him what to do. They read one side, he reads the other. We can see what happens after a day. If he does okay, and your parents are comfortable with the arrangement, I could go back to work."

"Good idea. I think it's going to be great for everyone."

Dinner arrived, thanks to DoorDash, and we sat down to eat. Lim talked about his meeting with an angel investor earlier that day, while my mind wandered. Something Lim had said earlier made me uneasy. "Thought they were dead." Why did that make me uncomfortable? I was silent as I thought long and hard.

"I know that look," Lim said. "You're thinking. Wondering if my parents are up to the task."

"That's not it," I said. "Something you said, about thinking your parents were dead." A thought took form in my head. More of a hunch. "Of course! The murderer has no fingerprints in the system because they're probably searching a database with fingerprints of living people only. I'll bet he's got a criminal history, all right. But if I'm right, he faked his own death, then took Don Brock's name."

Chapter 13

After dinner, Lim and I had fun making note cards together—English instructions on one side, Chinese on the other. Zaron didn't resist when we collected his clothes and took him downstairs to my in-laws' condo. As soon as we were inside, Zaron made himself at home. He picked up the iPad on the kitchen counter but seemed confused until Lim changed the language from Mandarin to English. I loaded a Word Search app, which he played while gently rocking back and forth, making his happy sound. We'd think about buying him his own iPad if this worked out.

Once he seemed settled, I went next door to see Ting and get blood samples from her kids. They were unusually cooperative for kids their age. Perhaps they figured they had it easy now, having been stuck with needles so much more often when they lived in China. It was still light out, and I walked to the lab with Lim to drop off the specimens, including the extra tubes I drew from Kang and Mingyu to test for myostatin deficiency. It was a good time to talk and brainstorm about what to do next.

"Do you think I should tell April what I'm thinking? We certainly can't be sure this guy faked his death, but I think it's likely."

"If he did, there are only a few possible ways he could have done it. He could have found a dead body or killed someone and made it look like it was him. Or he faked his death in a way there would be no body. Like a drowning or terrible fire."

"It appears this guy showed up around two years ago. So, if he faked his death, it was probably around then, or earlier."

"That helps, but it's not enough."

"We could narrow it down by assuming he was born and raised in the vicinity of the real Donald Brock. It's unlikely anyone who wasn't from that area would know about the unregistered death. He was probably born within five years or so of the boy since in his picture he looks about the same age Donald would be if he had survived."

"Maybe there's some sort of national database we can check. Someone born in Virginia, around thirty-eight years old who died in the last few years?"

"It's worth a try."

After returning to our building, we first checked with Lim's parents. All was going well. In the short time Zaron had been there, Fung had taught him to repeat a few words in Chinese. As far as I could tell, his pronunciation was pretty good, although I doubted he knew what the words meant.

Lim and I returned to our unit and began an internet search. Finding the information we wanted wouldn't be easy. I learned of a national database of recorded deaths available to researchers. However, using it required waiting for approval, which could take months. We didn't have that much time.

"The cops or FBI can probably get the information in a few days if they assign enough people to it," Lim said.

"You're right. I'll ask April about it in the morning."

*

Morning came, and I felt myself missing Zaron. I assumed he was doing well at my in-laws', as we'd heard no complaints from them. I called April to tell her about my new hypothesis. She told me that while it was possible the murderer had faked his death a few years earlier, the idea was far-fetched. The FBI was busy following the myriad tips still pouring in. They were stretched pretty thin as it were. Sifting through the records of people who had died two or more years ago, at an age between thirty and forty-five, wasn't going to be a priority. I called Martha and brought her up to date on why I had missed work. Not surprisingly, she had lots of questions. I knew I could trust her but held back a lot of information for her own protection. She seemed happy when I told her I'd be returning to the clinic in the afternoon after I checked on my mother.

When I got to the care facility, Mom was lying in bed as usual. I sat and held her hand. She seemed happy to see me, but I wasn't sure. The young woman dispensing medicines told me she required increased sedation due to agitation.

I asked Mom some simple questions about her day, but she didn't answer. I held up a pen I found in my purse and asked her what it was. Again, she didn't answer. Sadly, my mother was less verbal than Zaron.

A caretaker came by and suggested I call my mother's doctor because my mom was having difficulty eating, and the staff was worried she might aspirate food when she swallowed. I called her doctor, who asked if I wanted to have a feeding tube inserted into her stomach so she could get the nutrition she needed without eating and risking aspiration.

I declined, not wanting to deprive my mother of the ability to eat, the one activity that might still give her pleasure. The doctor indicated his agreement with my decision. I left wondering if this was the beginning of the end for Mom. It sure looked like it.

When I got to the clinic, I had no time to mull over my mother's condition. My afternoon schedule was filled with patients Martha had scheduled earlier that day. The first three had minor injuries from scooters. I gave each parent my scooter lecture, insisting their children wear helmets if they continued to allow them to participate in such risky behavior.

I had to reign in my emotions when I saw my fourth patient, who came in with her mother. Five years old, she had been in complete remission from childhood leukemia for four months, following aggressive treatment. Now she had a textbook measles rash and a fever of one hundred three. Due to her recent leukemia treatment, she had lost all immunity from her previous measles vaccine but wasn't yet ready to be revaccinated. When I saw her, she was quite ill, with difficulty breathing. Some kid had exposed her to the virus, most likely because his or her parents were anti-vaxxers—suckers for junk science, rumors, discredited studies, and probably Russian trolls. I had my patient taken by ambulance to the pediatric ICU immediately. The most likely diagnosis was measles pneumonia, a serious complication. As the ambulance pulled away, I hoped the girl would survive.

The remainder of the day was fairly uneventful, with mostly stomachaches and ear infections. All in all, it felt good to be back to work. I stayed late, catching up on administrative tasks that seemed to have multiplied while I was gone. I checked on lab results for Ting's kids. Most of the routine tests had been completed and were in the normal range. I didn't expect to receive the results of the myostatin tests for days. They would come by way of a secure email directly from the East Coast lab performing the test.

I left in time to attend a get-together of the staff at a colleague's house, something we did one Friday evening a month. It was a time to unwind, talk about interesting cases, and gripe about problems in the clinic. With so much on my mind, I didn't want to go, but as clinic director, I felt obliged to attend. It was at these gatherings, where people were relaxed and a little inebriated, that conversations flowed more freely than at work, and I often came up with solutions to workflow issues. As usual, I drank only club soda so I could stay sharp.

I left a little after seven, looking forward to a quiet dinner with Lim. It was a warm San Francisco evening, and we don't get too many of those. Walking home, I made a small detour to pick up a bottle of wine. Upon exiting the liquor store, I texted Lim I'd be home in fifteen minutes.

The scent of basil and garlic wafted in the air as I entered our condo. Lim greeted me with a quick kiss, then rushed back to attend to the stir-fry medley of chicken, vegetables, and spices on the stove.

"I'm trying something new," he said, running around the kitchen frenetically.

"Smells good. How about a glass of wine before dinner?"

"Great idea. Give me a minute."

I removed two wine glasses from the cupboard, opened the cabernet bottle, a twist top, and poured two generous portions. I placed one glass next to Lim, who took a quick sip while remaining focused on his culinary mission. Shortly after that, he said he'd keep the wok on low heat while we enjoyed the wine together.

"How about the balcony?" he asked.

"Great idea." The sun was starting to set as we sat on the rarely used balcony chairs. "This is the life," I said. "Not a worry in the world. Well, hardly a worry, especially with a little wine on board."

"Agree. We should do this more often. Isn't this view of the San Francisco Bay from the balcony one of the major reasons we bought this place?"

"So much has happened, I hardly remember. But sounds reasonable."

"Now that you're nice and relaxed, something I haven't seen for quite a while, how about we talk a little about that thing you don't like to talk about?"

"Somehow, I knew you'd be bringing it up."

"Since you're going to be tested soon, I want to remind you of our previous discussions. I hope you don't have Huntington's like your mom. But if you do, I want you to know, we'll deal with it. I'll always be here for you. There will probably be better treatments for it in the near future, anyway."

"Do you know how often I've heard that sort of thing? Better treatments in the future? Sometimes I even say it to my patients' parents. But only to give them hope when there really is a new treatment brewing. I don't like to give false hope. Sure, some company out there may develop a new treatment, but it's not likely anything will come down the pike to help me. It could be a good fifty or hundred years. I've seen many a patient come and go, waiting for that one important discovery, just around the corner, to help them."

"I understand how you feel. But it doesn't change the fact that I want Mingyu, Kang, and Wang Shu to have cousins. I want us to have a family."

"I know. Let's wait 'til I get the test results before we make any more plans. I would never pass this bad gene on if I have it."

"We've discussed that. If you have it, we'll do in vitro and test the embryos. As you know, it's been done before. Only embryos without the abnormality would be implanted."

"What if both my genes are abnormal? My dad died fairly young. It's possible he had Huntington's, too."

"You know that's very unlikely. There's no reason to think he had the gene. His two older siblings are alive and well, and there's no reason to think either of them has the bad gene."

"I just want to prepare you for all possibilities. I don't want you to be hurt."

"Don't worry about me. If you have two copies of the bad gene, we'll adopt. Okay?"

"Okay."

Lim smiled. "My parents will be so happy. Ting, too. And her kids."

"I wish my mom could experience the joy of being a grandmother."

"I know, baby. I know." Lim put his arm around me and held me tight. "But that's no reason not to go on with our lives."

I knew Lim was right. I agreed with him completely, but it was comforting to hear him say it. "Let's eat," I said. "I'm drunk, and I'm hungry. The last thing you want is a mean drunk on your hands."

We went inside, and I started to put plates on the table. "Too bad we don't have our manservant here to take care of us," I commented.

"Yeah, I miss Zaron. He took a little getting used to, but he did grow on me, as you say."

"I think he'll be good for your parents. How long till we eat?"

"Two minutes."

"Just enough time to check my email." I went to my laptop and logged into my personal Gmail account. Mixed in with the usual ads for things I didn't want was a message from the Golden Gate Regional Center. The subject was Zaron Johnson. My heart pounded. Did April tell them I had Zaron? She told me he could stay with me for the time being. If it wasn't April, then who? Just when I was starting to unwind from all the tension, now this. I clicked on the message.

> *Dear Dr. Rosen,*
>
> *It has come to our attention that you are illegally housing Zaron Johnson, a client of the Regional Center. This is in violation of his rights as a ward of the state. We order you to bring him to the Golden Gate Regional Center office in San Francisco Monday so he can be placed in an appropriate residence. Failure to do so will result in criminal charges.*

The letter was signed by the Golden Gate Regional Center director. I felt my face turn red as I sat frozen for a moment, rereading the message. This would be devastating to Zaron and likely eliminate him as a future source of information for the ongoing investigation. Without thinking, I rang April's cell phone. I was furious with her. I trusted her, and now I felt betrayed. She was off duty, but she answered.

My words started flowing faster than I could process them. "What were you thinking? Why did you tell the Regional Center about Zaron?

He's safe here, and he's happy. You know he's probably got a lot of information you could use to catch the bombing mastermind. Now, thanks to you, I've got this letter from the paper-pushers at the Regional Center, who want me to turn him over. I'm supposed to bring him there on Monday—"

"Whoa, Dr. Rosen. Whoa." April was speaking over me. I stopped speaking mid-sentence and let her talk. "I didn't tell the Regional Center anything about where Zaron is. And I'm sure no one else in our department did."

"Then how do they know where he is?"

"They don't. As a matter of fact, I spoke to someone from there earlier today. They called about him. It took them all this time to figure out they didn't know where he was. That's bureaucracy for you. All I told them was our department had placed him somewhere safe, and I'd look into finding out where."

"Could they have found out he's with me between the time you spoke to them and the time the email was sent?"

"What time was it sent?"

I checked my computer. "Five-thirty this evening."

"I must have spoken to them around four-thirty. Considering the speed at which they work, I'd say that would be nearly impossible."

"So now what? What should I do?"

"First of all, I don't want you to take him to the Regional Center. I smell some sort of a trap."

"They said I could be arrested."

"That won't happen. We wouldn't arrest someone just because somebody at the Regional Center asked us to. Everyone needs to go through proper channels. Don't go there or contact them in any way until I give you the okay. I'm going to talk to one of our cybersecurity experts to look into the possibility the email is a fake."

"Fake? How could someone fake an email?"

"I'm not an expert, but I know fake emails can be sent. That's why I'll check with our experts tomorrow." I detected a bit of irritation in her voice.

"Okay, sorry I was so mad. Please call me when you find something out."

"Will do."

"Dinner's getting cold," Lim said as soon as I'd finished the conversation with April. "I thought you were just going to check your email."

"Sorry." I could tell his feelings were hurt. He'd tried to make a perfect evening, only to hear me yakking on the phone as the dinner got cold. "Well, it's not cold, just not steaming," I said as I took a bite. "It's delicious."

Lim smiled.

"I was speaking to April because I got a strange email from the Regional Center ordering me to bring Zaron there for placement in a residence. I needed to talk to her about it right away."

"That doesn't sound good," Lim said.

"She thinks it might be fake. She's going to check with her computer experts tomorrow." I glanced at Lim between bites, noticing he looked upset. "I couldn't tell her not to bother. But of course, I'd like you to look into it, Amazing Husband. I know you're much better than anyone in her department could possibly be." I'd said the magic words, and Lim looked happy again. "And better looking, too."

Before the dinner plates were cleared from the table, Lim was on my computer. It didn't take long before he turned to me. "You've been spoofed."

"What does that mean?"

"This email isn't from the Regional Center, but someone tried to make it look that way."

"Who's it from?"

"Excellent question. That's going to take some digging, but I'd say it's the Brock impersonator unless proven otherwise."

"How did he know Zaron was with me? How'd he find my email?"

"Don't know, but if I had to guess, he knew you were the one speaking to Brandy just before he killed her. All he had to do was look at her phone. He probably dug around, learned where you work, and that you deal with developmentally disabled kids. He likely also accessed information on group homes in the area and knows Zaron hasn't been placed in one yet. He put three plus three together and concluded you're taking care of him."

"It's two plus two," I corrected him.

Lim smiled. "I'll compromise. He put two plus three together. Meanwhile, you better not take Zaron near the Regional Center."

"You think he's in danger of being kidnapped?"

"Either that, or worse. I'll let my parents know not to let him out of the building until further notice."

Chapter 14

The next morning Lim promised to look into the origin of the mysterious email. I was relieved to know I wasn't going to be prosecuted by a government agency, but that relief was overshadowed by my fear of the message's sender. I spoke briefly with April who was still off-duty but wanted to come by to pick up my laptop so their cyber specialists could study it. With me not keen on giving up my much-needed internet access and leaving the investigation up to the police department or FBI, the two of us came to a compromise. I forwarded a copy of the email to her, and she agreed to have patrol officers give extra attention to my building.

Being Saturday, the clinic was closed, but I had signed up to do a day shift in the pediatric ICU. I left for work assured Zaron would stay safely inside our building and Lim would chase down the source of the phony Regional Center email. My mind was kept busy all morning working up two admissions and tending to abnormal lab results coming in on other patients in the unit. Lim called me at noon to let me know that using the software he was developing, he'd traced the email to a computer located in a neighborhood grocery store less than two miles from our condominium. Someone there had spoofed the Regional Center email address using commercially available, easy-to-use software. I was surprised the murderer was so close by and took no comfort knowing that if he wanted to kidnap Zaron, he wouldn't have far to go.

I called April. As I suspected, her team hadn't made a dent in the task of finding the IP address, much less the actual location, of the computer that had sent the email. I gave her Lim's number so her people could speak directly to him and get the street address of the grocery store the spoofed message was sent from. Hopefully, they could apprehend the scumbag who was responsible for the bombing before he moved on. I reminded her there were also six innocent young men, still missing from the group home, who needed to be rescued.

I awaited news of a police raid on the grocery store all afternoon, worried the perpetrator might escape, and innocents harmed or killed. I tried to stay focused on my patients as they deserved the best care I could give them. Nonetheless, I allowed myself to check my phone every fifteen minutes for news of finding the man responsible for the Oracle Park bombing.

Finally, an update from a local news station popped up on my screen at 3:30 p.m. Police had raided a small grocery store in the Tenderloin. As was often the case, people from the neighborhood showed up in large numbers to observe. There was some reference to the bombing at Oracle Park, but local activists weren't buying it. The couple who owned the store were handcuffed and ordered to lie on the floor, while neighborhood kids made off with candy bars before the area was secured, knowing the cops wouldn't chase them down. Police searched the store, and a computer found in the back office was confiscated. The owners and a store employee were taken to the police station for questioning. The store would remain closed indefinitely. A police spokesperson said no injuries were reported and promised updates as they learned more.

I called April. "I heard the computer was found," I said before she could say hello.

"Yes, even though I'm off today, I came to work to see what's going on. We have the computer, but to be honest, I don't think the people taken into custody are involved. Not knowingly, anyway. The computer was in an unlocked office in the back of the store. According to the owners, they always left it open so people in the neighborhood—kids, homeless people, whatever—could access the internet. The computer wasn't even password protected. Nothing would have prevented a stranger from walking in and using it, as long as the store was open. A lot of people knew about the computer and used it."

"Where are the store owners now?"

"They're being questioned. From what I've been told, they aren't very sophisticated. I doubt they'd have the wherewithal to open an account in the Caymans. The store was searched, as were the residences of the owners and the employees. I'm sorry, but there was no evidence or sign of the missing young men. Everything happened so fast, I'm convinced that if someone working in the store had the boys, they wouldn't have had time to hide them, and the boys would have been found. We think our murderer learned about the unprotected computer, wandered into the store, used the computer to send the email, and left. And before you ask, no. The store had no videos of customers. Seems they only had fake cameras mounted."

"Damn," I said. "We're dealing with someone who's pretty sharp."

"Agreed."

"What about the email threats to the MLB? Has the source of those been identified?"

"Our people have traced them to an IP addresses in Bucharest. That's probably not the real origin, though."

"Maybe the origin doesn't really matter—not if he uses computers of innocent people with low computer security. It would help in determining his general location, though. Unless he has someone else send the emails. If you want, I'm sure Lim could help. I don't want to insult your staff, but he has more resources available. He has a very powerful program for locating spoofed emails."

"I already took the liberty of asking our team to contact him, pointing out he located the computer that sent you the fake email. They won't hear of it."

"I was afraid of that. Now what?"

"There will be more questioning, the neighbors will be interviewed, and the investigation will be completed. I'm not optimistic this is going to lead to anything. We still have officers nationwide looking for the Don Brock impersonator and six missing young men we don't have pictures of. So far, nothing. I believe our suspect is still in the area, given the location of the computer he just used and the fact that he wanted you to bring Zaron to the Regional Center office."

"You think he's watching it? Waiting for me to bring Zaron so he can grab him?"

"That's one possibility. He might want one more trained suicide bomber. The FBI, on the other hand, thinks he's gone to an awful lot of trouble to find Zaron. Now they think the murderer is worried that Zaron will tell you something to help us find him. I agree with them. Frankly, I'm worried that if this Brock character can't kidnap Zaron easily, he'll kill him. That would be easier to do without attracting immediate attention to himself."

"How?" I asked.

"The most obvious would be to shoot him from a distance. There's lots of other ways, too. You need to watch more TV."

My stomach felt tense as I thought about Zaron being the target of a murderer. "I wonder what Zaron might know that could be so important."

"See if you can find out. It's clear our bomber is very motivated to find him." April paused. "There's something else I should tell you. You can tell Lim, but no one else. Not until it's made public."

"You have my word."

April lowered her voice. "I'm not supposed to be sharing this. I'm only telling you, so you'll be sure to keep Zaron inside where it's safe. Later today, it will be announced there has been another threat and demand for money. Ten million dollars to prevent a bombing at the Oakland A's game in two days."

"I see his price has gone up."

"He probably figures since they already paid five million, why not try for ten?"

"What are they going to do? I hope they pay the money."

"I agree with you. It's too risky not to. But I'm afraid Homeland Security has become involved and is urging the A's to announce the threat, yet carry on with the game. They're very focused on catching this guy, so the extortions don't go on forever. I've been told some folks at Homeland Security are having conversations with receptive newsgroups, suggesting they issue a series of announcements emphasizing that going to the game as planned is the patriotic thing to do. If people don't go, the terrorist wins."

"But who wins if people go and they get blown up?"

"I hear you, believe me. I don't like this plan, but I don't have a brilliant alternative idea to stop this guy, and, let's face it, I'm just a patrol officer. Nobody listens to me. In the announcements to come, Homeland Security will claim they're confident the FBI will spot the bomber in time with the additional information they have. They now know how the previous bomb was hooked up and will be able to disarm it in seconds. They've been practicing with a mock-up."

"I hope they can stop it, but I'm worried they won't."

"That's why I want you to try your hardest to come up with some good questions for Zaron. That may be our best chance for preventing another disaster," April said before hanging up.

It was near the end of my shift. I needed to finish up my notes in the electronic medical record after checking on a few labs. Once done, I got ready to go home, have a glass of wine with Lim, and unwind. Then I'd rack my brain to dream up more questions to ask Zaron.

As I was walking out of the building, I received a call from Ting.

"I sorry bother you," she said. "Kang, he playing soccer at school near our building. I need pick him up at six, but my father fall and maybe have broken arm. I need go with him to emergency room because not always have translators. Lim in Mountain View at meeting and no can get back in time. My mom can watch Zaron, Mingyu, and Wang Shu, but I wonder—"

"You want me to get Kang?"

"Sorry, yes. Bring him to my mother. He finish six o'clock."

"I'd love to. I'm leaving work now, and I can get there in plenty of time. Don't worry about a thing. Go ahead and take care of your dad."

After what seemed like close to a hundred thank yous, Ting hung up. The hospital where I had just finished my shift was much farther from my neighborhood than the clinic where I usually worked. I wanted to get a walk in before it got dark, so I decided to have an Uber drop me off in front of the clinic building and then head to the soccer field on foot. I'd walked by the school many times. It now dawned on me I'd never watched Kang play soccer before. Picking him up, and hopefully seeing him play for a bit, would be a welcome relief from my usual routine of late, which consisted of work and worrying about Zaron.

Fifteen minutes to six, I exited my Uber ride in front of the clinic building. As I walked in the direction of the soccer field, I noticed out of the corner of my eye a petite blond woman in sunglasses emerge from a nearby stairwell and follow in my direction. I had an eerie feeling of déjà vu. Something similar had happened when I left work the day before. I wasn't heading home then, but to the Friday night get-together at a colleague's house. Was it the same woman?

Chapter 15

I stopped abruptly and pretended to answer my phone several times. Each time I stopped, the footsteps behind me slowed down. Maybe I was being ridiculously paranoid, but I didn't want to take any chances. I ducked into a bookstore I was familiar with and exited the back door. I was sure I wasn't being followed by the murderer, who was a man. Could this person be working with him? Why would he want someone to follow me? Was this woman the blond living in the detached unit at the group home? Was this an attempt to locate Zaron? If so, why? I didn't have answers to my questions, but I had a solution. I turned ninety degrees, walked a block, then entered another store I often shopped in. I exited on a different street and headed to my destination.

Confident I had lost my tail, if that's in fact what it was, I arrived at the soccer field five minutes before the game ended. Parents were on the field videoing their precious darlings as the children ran around, seemingly at random, occasionally kicking the ball. It was a happy time, and I enjoyed the moment.

Out of nowhere, I noticed a powerful kick, different from the others. The ball arched up and over the heads of three of the children, then landed about a third of the way down the field. I turned to see who had kicked the ball, thinking a parent hadn't been able to resist showing the kids how things should really be done. When I found the source of the kick, I saw it wasn't a parent. It was Kang.

I heard the other parents comment, "That kid's amazing." "How does he do it?" "He never seems to get tired."

The coach, the father of one of the girls on the team, announced practice was over. I called out to Kang and told the coach I was there to pick him up because his mom had to take his grandpa to the doctor.

One of the fathers came over to me. "Are you a neighbor of his?"

"Actually, I'm his aunt."

The man looked surprised. Since Kang and I didn't exactly look alike, I was used to that reaction.

"His mother is my husband's sister," I explained.

"I see," he said. "Well, your nephew is something else. If I didn't know better, I'd say he's taking performance-enhancing drugs. Or maybe he's had some of that genetic engineering I read about that they're doing over in China." He laughed. "When he grows up, I'll bet he's gonna be a great athlete."

I knew the man was being friendly, but his words had a chilling effect on me. He'd probably heard the news months ago about the genetically engineered children brought over from China, but never suspected Kang was one of them. I wondered what was in store for Kang and his siblings as they grew older. Looking at my nephew standing next to his peers, it was obvious—he was much more muscular than they were. I didn't have the test results for a myostatin mutation yet, but I was pretty sure he was going to test positive.

While I walked back to our condominium building with Kang, I told him his mom had taken his grandfather to the hospital because he hurt himself, but would be fine. I struggled to understand Kang as he talked about the soccer game and said he made the most goals. He thought the other kids didn't like soccer as much as he did because they didn't seem to be trying very hard. None of them kicked the ball nearly as far as him. I told Kang he was probably a lot more talented than the other children. I also complimented him on how well he was speaking English.

We arrived at my in-laws' unit, where Fung was waiting. She was able to say "Hello" and "Thank you" to me, at least that's what I thought she said. Her accent was so heavy, I couldn't be sure.

I sat across from Zaron, who was doing a puzzle at the kitchen table. He looked up and smiled when he saw me. Yes, I was hooked. I'd do whatever I could to protect this sweet, innocent young man. I wanted him to stay in my life. But at the time, I needed to get more useful information from him.

"How tall is Don?"

No answer.

"Does Don take any medicine?"

No answer.

"Does Don have a nickname?"

No answer.

"Does Don have a hobby?"

No answer.

"What does Don watch on TV?"

No answer.

"Does Don have a friend?"

No answer.

I was getting nowhere. Zaron either didn't know the answers to these questions or didn't understand the questions as I asked them.

"TV, Don."

No answer.

"Another name, Don."

No answer.

"How can we stop the next bombing?" I asked in frustration, knowing Zaron wouldn't understand the question.

No answer. I was running out of ideas.

I returned to my condominium and tried to occupy my time until Lim came home. While I was waiting, Ting phoned to let me know her dad was fine—an x-ray showed only a hairline ulnar fracture requiring a sling for a few weeks. No sooner had the call ended, than April called to update me.

The computer taken from the neighborhood grocery store had been dusted for prints. A thumbprint matching several prints taken from the group home was found. The couple who owned the store were religious Seventh Day Adventists, as were the employees. They had spent their lives helping others. Despite having little money, they were always quick to assist a neighbor in need. Not the profile of someone willing to kill innocent people for financial gain. There was not one iota of evidence any of them had been involved in the bombing or had six autistic youths stashed someplace. All the suspects arrested earlier had been released. At the end of our conversation, April mentioned that the latest bomb threat had recently been announced on the radio and TV.

I turned on the news and didn't have to wait long until I heard it. "There is a bomb threat for another baseball game, this time for the A's game at home on Monday. Law enforcement believes the threat is low, but they will have increased security. Information learned from the last incident will be very helpful in preventing another attack. Anyone who wants to turn in tickets will get a full refund. However, in a show of support, local groups are urging people to attend the game. They claim that staying away lets the terrorists win. So far, we are told, very few requests have come in for refunds. Moreover, ticket sales have increased, and sales are predicted to outpace any in recent history. This game may even be a sell-out."

When Lim came home after eight, he had already heard about the new bomb threat. I filled him in on the hunt for the murderer. He was disappointed but not surprised the computer didn't lead us directly to him. Over dinner, we tried to brainstorm helpful questions I could ask Zaron. We didn't come up with anything I hadn't already asked.

Chapter 16

Sunday was uneventful. Uneventful, yet stressful. I visited my mom and did some cleaning in my condo. Lim worked most of the day at his company and Zaron stayed with Lim's parents. They knew to keep him inside, where they could occupy his time with chores, puzzles, and videos. We all had dinner at my in-laws that evening. Once again, Fung made a delicious meal. Zaron seemed to like his new environment, smiling and making his happy sounds. I tried again to get more information about the man he knew as Don but was unsuccessful in learning anything new.

Lim and I returned to our condo and relaxed, listening to Beatle's music while answering emails and paying bills. My sleep that night was peaceful, even knowing I'd be getting my blood drawn the next day to test for Huntington's disease.

Monday morning, Lim brought me coffee in bed as usual. We walked together to meet Shanika in her lab, located in a nondescript building housing several medical practices. We entered the Golden Gate Genetics suite and checked in with the receptionist. Before we had time to take a seat in the small waiting room, Shanika appeared through a side door, wearing a white lab coat.

She ushered us down a short hallway into an office on our right. I could see only a portion of what appeared to be a large laboratory farther down the hall. Once we were seated, I noticed a floor-to-ceiling bookcase behind Shanika's desk, filled with books and journals. A large computer monitor stood on her desk near several short stacks of paper. I introduced Lim and asked Shanika if she had any pictures of her new baby.

"Not at the moment," she said. "I have some at home, but I forgot to bring them. This being my first day back at work, my morning was a bit hectic. I even forgot to bring my cell phone. But enough about me. Let's talk about you."

Shanika explained the significance of testing for Huntington's disease and had me confirm I was ready to learn if I would get the same disease as my mother. Our meeting lasted less than ten minutes, after which I signed a legal document giving my consent. Shanika directed me to the station where a phlebotomist drew my blood as Lim sat next to me. Then Lim and I left to have breakfast together at a nearby café.

My omelet was perfect, but the coffee wasn't as good as Lim's. Too weak. Nevertheless, I enjoyed the relaxed pace of our leisurely breakfast. I'd cleared most of my morning calendar ahead of time, so we wouldn't feel rushed.

Meanwhile, I was glad my test was finally being processed. I'd be hearing back in a week or so. I felt like I was in for a thumbs up or thumbs down branch in my life, like a gladiator in ancient Rome. I was ready.

I got to work around 11:00 a.m. as planned. Kids with fevers, sore throats, and diarrhea were waiting. Thankfully, I didn't have to give bad news to any parents, only reassure them their sons and daughters would recover and be fine. I worked through lunch and started to eat a sandwich Martha brought me from a food truck around 2:00 p.m. as I caught up on my medical records entries.

My sandwich was half-eaten when a three-year-old collapsed in the waiting room, and his mother began screaming. I rushed to the scene where I got a brief history from the mom between wails. I learned the boy had been suffering from diarrhea for three days. He showed all the signs of dehydration—sunken eyes, dry mucous membranes, skin tenting. I arranged for him to be transported immediately to the emergency room for hydration. No sooner had I seen him safely on his way than Martha informed me my next scheduled patient was in Room Three.

Waiting for me in the exam room was a darling one-year-old girl brought in by her mother and father for loss of appetite. I soon discovered she had an abdominal mass. Although it might be something benign, I didn't have a good feeling about it. A one-year-old shouldn't have an abdominal mass. I worried about a malignant tumor, such as neuroblastoma, hepatoblastoma, rhabdomyosarcoma, or Burkitt's lymphoma, to name a few. I explained to the parents that I was concerned about their daughter, and she would need to undergo some tests, starting with a CT scan. Hysteria doesn't begin to describe the reaction of both the parents. A part of me wanted to tell them I was sure their daughter would be okay, but that would have been a lie. At times like this, it isn't easy to be honest.

My next patient wasn't much easier—a young boy with cystic fibrosis brought in for a routine vaccine. I could see that his parents, both of whom were in attendance, had grown weary of the stress and the regimen of daily treatments. I suggested they get respite care so they could have a break, something they denied needing. I advised them to think about it. They asked about a lung transplant, and although I thought it was premature to be thinking about it, I encouraged them to discuss the procedure with the pediatric pulmonologist they took their son to regularly.

I was still in the exam room, finishing up my note, when I heard screams. I couldn't tell for sure where they were coming from, but it sounded like they were originating near the reception desk down the hall. I peeked out of the exam room and saw a group of doctors, assistants, and receptionists gathered around a cell phone. Two were screaming hysterically. The remainder looked on in silence. I approached one of the physician assistants standing on the periphery.

"What's going on?" I asked.

"They're watching the news, live."

"Watching what?"

"Another bombing. The Oakland A's."

I was filled with dread.

"Well, you can't say they weren't warned," someone commented.

I'd been so distracted, I hadn't thought about what April told me two days ago, or the announcements from Homeland Security. I felt sick to my stomach. While to my knowledge, no one close to me was at the game, I knew it had been well-attended. I'd have to wait to hear about the number of dead and wounded.

This was likely another bombing carried out by an unwitting autistic suicide bomber. I thought about April's descriptions of the other boys, and wondered which of them had been killed. I also thought about all the other innocent people who had gone to the game to have a good time in the company of friends and family. I wondered how this could happen. Why did the FBI stupidly recommend not paying the money, instead deciding to watch the crowd for suspects? It didn't work the first time. Sure, they knew more now. They had a picture of the man responsible, the ringleader, but there was no guarantee he would attend the game, and as far as I knew, they had no pictures of the six young autistic men trained to wear explosives into a crowd. For some reason, I had thought the FBI would cave in at the end and tell MLB to pay the ten million.

Irate, I phoned April, but only got her voicemail. After leaving a message requesting a call-back, I went to see my next patient. Martha directed me to Room Five, where I examined a girl with pink eye, an easy problem I could dispatch in my sleep, thankfully. After the girl and her mother left, Martha informed me that news of the bombing was spotty.

"Are you going to be okay?" she asked. "You look pretty shaken up. You only have one more patient, and I can reschedule him if you want."

"Thanks, but I'll be fine." As Martha walked away, I hoped nobody noticed as I wiped tears from my eyes. My last patient, a young boy, was uncomplicated. That was a relief for me, and considering my mental state, probably a good thing for him.

I left the clinic building as soon as I finished my last chart. Once outside, I looked around for the blond woman I thought might have been following me two days earlier but didn't see her. Lost in thought, I didn't give the mysterious woman another thought until I reached the front door of my building, turned, and saw a petite brunette wearing sunglasses walking and looking my way. Around the same size as the blond woman, she suddenly stopped and turned as if she were watching something in the street. The road in front of her was empty. Hungry and anxious to get inside, I convinced myself I was being ridiculously paranoid. I punched in my passcode and entered.

After checking to be sure Zaron was safe in my in-laws' unit, I went to my condo, grabbed leftovers from the refrigerator, and turned on the TV to find out more about the bombing. I saw footage, complete with sound, of a young man being carefully grabbed around both forearms and handcuffed as he remained standing. His shirt was quickly cut away with scissors, revealing a vest packed with bars of what was later identified as C4. An officer deftly reached in and cut wires protruding from the explosives. Many people were screaming as a wide berth formed around the area, most in the crowd doing their best to get as far away as possible while others stared, frozen, as if unsure what to do. Within seconds, the youth being held became flushed and agitated, then slumped forward. His legs appeared limp, the surrounding officers seeming to support him. As they slowly dragged the young man away, a loud explosion could be heard coming from farther inside the stadium.

A different camera showed the crowd swarming into the stadium a few seconds earlier, then a loud bang followed by screaming, smoke, and a clearing filled with people and bodies on the ground. In the words of one bystander who had witnessed the Oracle Arena bombing, it was "like seeing my nightmares following the previous disaster come back to life." The second video was from a distance and less graphic than it would have been if closer. The scene nevertheless portrayed horror beyond what anyone should experience. So far, nine had been pronounced dead, and more were seriously injured. It would be days before the final numbers were in.

At seven-thirty, my phone rang—a call from April. I was furious with her. Why hadn't she called me sooner? Although she didn't work for Oakland where the bombing was, I imagined she'd been pretty busy. I was mad anyway. I had so many thoughts swirling around. Why hadn't they paid the money? Why hadn't they watched the crowd more carefully?

I knew my anger was misplaced. It wasn't April's decision whether to pay the ten million bucks or not. Of course they had been watching the crowd. By "they," I mean the FBI, local cops, stadium security, mall cops, whatever. They thought they knew what to look for, and they missed it. On second thought, they didn't miss it. They just hadn't anticipated a second bomber. Once they stopped the first bomber, they'd let their guard down, and probably everyone in security had rushed to the site. Very clever, I had to admit to myself. I let my phone ring several times before I answered April's call.

"What happened?" I asked.

"I'm sure you've been watching the news, so you know almost as much as me."

"Is there any doubt this is the same guy?"

"None. The boy who died in police custody had cigarette burns all over his arms. Just like Zaron."

"Who died in police custody?"

"The first one. The one they spotted and grabbed before the bomb went off. Sorry, you probably haven't heard about that yet."

"He died?"

"You probably saw him go limp after they had him in custody. It's been played on TV over and over."

"I figured the commotion was too much for him, and he fainted."

"He didn't faint. He died. The police did nothing wrong. It couldn't be prevented. You didn't hear it from me, but he was foaming at the mouth at the end. We figure it was poison. No one knows how it was administered. Hopefully, the autopsy and toxicology will tell us."

I felt sick. Two more innocents had died, the boy in custody and the second one whose bomb exploded. I had been hoping the boy whose bomb hadn't detonated would be another source of information about the killer.

"I hate to bring this up so soon," April said, "but we have pictures of both of the young men. We assume they are part of the same group, but we need verification. We'd like Zaron to identify them. That's the only way we can be one hundred percent sure."

I hated to involve Zaron, but I knew how important this was, and he was the only one who could do it.

"Okay, I'm sure he'll cooperate."

"Any chance you could bring him by the station?" I heard hesitancy in April's voice as if she knew what my response would be but felt she had to ask me anyway.

"Sorry, but there's no chance of us going there. I can't risk letting Zaron leave this place."

"Okay. I'll come over."

"Wait!" I said. "You could be followed. Then he'll know where Zaron is."

"I'll make sure I'm not followed."

"Not good enough."

"You have a better idea?'

I thought for a moment.

"Can you email me the pictures? I'll have Zaron look at them on my laptop."

"That would be against regulations. It's not that I think you would make anything up, but the identification should be done in the presence of an officer."

"How about Facetime or Skype?"

"I'll see if I can get my chief to approve it. Let me call you back."

The callback came in less than fifteen minutes. It was a go. I called Ting, explained the situation, and asked her to help. Carrying my laptop, I met Ting as she was talking to her mother in the hallway in front of her parents' unit. Ting was holding Mingyu, and I followed them inside. Zaron was sitting at the kitchen table, working on a puzzle. I put my laptop next to the puzzle and established a Skype connection with April. Knowing I needed the room to be completely quiet, Ting took her parents next door to her apartment, leaving me alone with Zaron. April brought up the picture of the first boy, the one who had died in custody. So young and innocent looking. If I didn't know better, I would have thought he was asleep.

"Who is that?" I asked Zaron.

"Patrick. Bird."

I remembered Patrick was the one who liked to fold origami cranes.

"What is Patrick's last name?" April asked.

Zaron looked behind the computer as if searching for the source of the voice. I repeated the question. "What's Patrick's last name?"

Nothing.

Next, April showed a second picture, this one an image of the head of the boy who was blown up by the bomb. The photo was cut off just below the chin, so there was no way to tell the head was detached from the rest of the body. Again, a young, sweet face, this one with a deep gash on the side. Zaron paused a moment, rocked back and forth a moment, excited, then said in his usual quiet voice, "Brother."

I almost lost it. "Is this your brother?" I asked, my voice shaking.

"Brother."

Now I saw the resemblance. His brother had a beard and long hair, tied in a ponytail. Once I subtracted the long hair and beard, I saw that the face and coloring were the same as Zaron's.

"What's his name?"

"Zachary."

Not surprisingly, he was the other boy at Bright Horizons who had calendar skills. I was pretty sure Zaron would know the answer to my next question, and I knew what the answer would be, but I asked anyway, to be sure. "What's Zachary's last name?"

"Johnson." Same as Zaron's.

Even as I was being crushed by an overwhelming despair I was powerless to fight, I had a thought I couldn't shake. Knowing Zaron was nineteen years old, I asked, "How old is Zachary?"

"Nineteen."

Still, I had to be sure. "Zaron, what is Zachary's birthday?"

"March twelfth."

My voice cracked as I asked, "What is your birthday, Zaron?"

"March twelfth."

Chapter 17

I had to leave the room so Zaron wouldn't see me break down in tears. I returned a few minutes later to see April, still on camera, sitting in stunned silence. Like me, she realized that Zaron's twin brother had been murdered horrifically. Zaron still had no idea. How could we tell him? Would he understand? April broke the silence. Knowing full well Zaron was sitting in front of the computer and could hear everything she said, she asked me, "Are you going to tell him?"

"I don't know how. Maybe we should take him to see his brother's body. Maybe he would understand then."

"There's not much left—his head, legs, and one hand and arm."

I felt like throwing up. "I don't think Zaron should see that. I don't suppose there's a need to tell him. Not unless he asks about his brother, which is unlikely. Even then, I don't think he'd understand. What will happen to the remains?"

"They'll be kept in the morgue at the Medical Examiner's. No rush in deciding what to do with them. After some time, they'll be disposed of with the other unclaimed bodies."

"I'm very concerned about Zaron's safety now. I think maybe someone was following me."

"When was that? Man or woman?"

"A woman. Petite. I thought I was being paranoid, but with everything that's happened, now I'm not so sure. The first time she followed me for sure was when I walked from the clinic building Saturday, but I ditched her."

"Can you give me a description?"

"Other than being small, I can't say much. She had blond hair on Saturday. Then, I think I saw her again tonight, with brown hair. Big sunglasses both times. What do you think? Am I crazy?"

There was a short silence. "I think she may be someone who was working with our suspect."

"This is the first I've heard of someone working with him." I'm sure I sounded angry because I was.

"I'm sorry. Brandy's assistant—we were keeping it under wraps. We don't have a picture or any work history on her. No Social Security number, either. Brandy paid her under the table, probably because it's hard to find helpers to work for so little money. As you know, it's very expensive to live around here. We have no address on her. It's likely she's the female whose blond hair we found in the separate apartment at the group home. She may be working with our murderer, possibly romantically involved."

"You should have said something about her before."

"I didn't think it was necessary. We don't know who she is, what she looks like, where she is, or if she's involved with the bombings."

"There must be a way to find out something about her. Weren't there any fingerprints or DNA in the apartment?"

"There were, but we haven't been able to identify their source. We ran the prints through our usual databases, but there weren't any hits. Same with the DNA we extracted from hair roots. Whether the evidence was from our suspect's assistant, or someone else living there, we're no closer to finding her than we were on day one."

"Do you have her name?"

"We're keeping her name under wraps for now. Sorry."

"Doesn't she have a bank account or driver's license you could use to find her?" I knew someone in the SFPD must have already looked into these things, but in my frustration, I felt compelled to ask.

"All reasonable questions, but we've pretty much exhausted all leads. There are many people with the same name as her in the Bay Area. We've compared the prints we found in the group home apartment with fingerprints of all persons in the area with that name who could conceivably have lived there or worked there—none match. We haven't been sitting around. We've been busy."

"Sorry, I didn't mean to imply you haven't been trying. It's just that I'm a bit on edge. I wish there were a way to know if the woman following me is the murderer's sidekick, whatever her name is."

"If she follows you again, call this number right away." April typed a number in the Skype instant messenger, which I copied to a memo on my cell phone. "This is the number for dispatch. I'll make sure they get an alert to send a squad car right away if you call."

I felt uneasy and considered asking Lim to walk me home from work for a while, but that would be very inconvenient for him, especially since he was under so much pressure to get his company ready for sale. Zaron knew what Brandy's assistant looked like, but there was no way I'd be able to get a description of her from him. My subconscious brain must have been working hard because it suddenly pushed an idea into my thoughts.

"I need to have her name, at least her first name, so I can ask Zaron about her. Maybe he could help."

"I'm not sure how, but okay. I can't see the harm in telling you her first name, but don't tell anyone else."

"Promise."

"Her name's Isabelle. What the hell, Isabelle Watts. That's her full name. Ever hear of her?"

"No, but let's see what Zaron says." I turned to the young man as I tried to frame a question. "When did you see Isabelle?" I asked.

"Dinner."

Did he understand my question? I repeated it, but slightly differently. "Your teacher, Isabelle. When did you see her?"

"Dinner."

The answer confused me, but I had an idea for my next question. "Did you see Isabelle at dinnertime today?"

"Yes."

"Where did you see her?"

No answer.

I tried again, remembering the difficulty with pronouns common in autistic people. "Where did you see Isabelle?"

"Outside."

Lim's parents had been told not to let Zaron outside, and I was momentarily furious. "When did you go outside?"

Silence.

"Did you go outside today?"

"No."

"Where outside was Isabelle?"

"Sidewalk."

I walked over to the living room window and looked out. The sidewalk and traffic in front of the building were clearly visible. I called Zaron over.

"Zaron, point to where Isabelle was at dinnertime."

Nothing. I hadn't tested Zaron's ability to point.

"Zaron, point to the television."

The TV was in the living room a few yards away. He didn't point. I made a mental note to teach Zaron how to point. I looked out the window again and noticed a street sign and a garbage can.

"Zaron, was Isabelle in the street?"

"No."

"Was Isabelle in a car?"

"No."

"Was Isabelle on the sidewalk?"

"Yes."

His answers, when he gave them, were clear and consistent. I sat in front of my laptop again to continue my conversation with April. "Did you hear what he said?" I asked.

"Sure did. I think Zaron just confirmed that Isabelle knows where you live."

"Why would she be following me?"

"I'd have to say it looks like she followed you from work to your home so she could locate Zaron. Now she knows where he is."

"What do you think they're planning to do now?" I was pretty sure I knew what April would say, but I hoped she had a more optimistic take on the situation.

"Right now, they're doing their best to prevent him from telling us something. They're going to try to either kidnap Zaron or kill him, I'm afraid."

"What should I do?"

"I suggest you move him. Get him out of town, if possible. I could send a car around to pick him up, but we couldn't take him someplace he'd like to be. He'd be safe, but might have to spend the night in a jail cell."

"That would be awful. And then what? Where would he go in the morning that would be safe?"

"I'd have to ask my chief. In the meantime, although I don't think anyone's going to be brazen enough to shoot at Zaron through the window, I suggest closing all the curtains. Right now, they're probably only watching your unit because they think he's staying with you, but in time they'll see Zaron in your in-laws' condo. I'll have a car drive around there to check the area regularly. I can request 24/7 surveillance, but I doubt it will be approved."

"I'll let you know if I want him to be picked up tonight. Meanwhile, I'll close all the curtains here." We promised to let each other know of any significant developments and disconnected the call. Lim's parents watched in silence as I pulled all the drapes closed. I called Lim and asked him to meet me in his parent's unit when he came home. He said he'd be leaving work in ten minutes.

I went to Ting's unit and brought her and her children next door to her parents' condo. Ting knew about the earlier bombing, and I explained to her what I had learned from April. Speaking to her parents in Chinese, Ting told them everything she knew about the day's events, translating her words into English for me as she spoke. Her mom cried upon learning Zaron's twin brother had been killed. We all agreed it would be best not to mention Zachary's name in front of Zaron.

I asked Zaron, "Who teaches Zaron to wear the vest?"

"Don. Isabelle."

I should have asked him earlier if anyone besides Don gave those instructions. I had assumed it was Don and only Don, without asking. The information had been right in front of me, inside Zaron's head all this time. I had another thought.

"Who does Isabelle kiss?"

"Don."

Now I knew. They were romantically involved. Don wasn't alone in this, but had someone he could depend on. It made sense—he needed her help, considering how difficult it had to be, taking care of six—now four—autistic boys on the run.

When Lim arrived, we kissed briefly like a long-married couple and got busy planning. Just hours ago, Isabelle had learned where I lived, and by extrapolation, knew where Zaron lived. Had I not gone to the department meeting after work last Friday, she might have followed me home then, and Zaron might already be dead or kidnapped. One thing was for sure—Zaron had to be safely removed from the building as soon as possible. There was no doubt in my mind Isabelle had been watching the building, looking for him. She was probably out there at that moment.

Lim asked his parents a question in Chinese. Nodding their heads, they gave a long answer. As they spoke, Ting translated for me. Lim asked if they had friends in Chinatown who could put Zaron and them up for a few days. They mentioned several people they were sure would be happy to accommodate them. Lim asked them to arrange for Zaron, Ting, her children, and themselves to stay with one of them, preferably with whomever had the apartment farthest from the street.

The in-laws discussed their options back and forth. Finally, Fung made a phone call, then told Lim and Ting what had been decided. Lim explained to me they arranged to stay with a couple in Chinatown who lived in the back of a building above a restaurant, three floors up. The apartment was small, but they could make do.

It took us a half hour to work out the escape plan. We would disguise Zaron as a young Chinese man by darkening his skin with Ting's makeup base, hiding his eyes with dark glasses, and covering his head with Enlai's wig, giving him straight, black hair. Zaron would leave the condo with Ting, her children, and my in-laws. We would instruct Zaron to keep one hand in his pants pocket, and Ting, posing as his wife, would hold the other to prevent him from flapping it. Ting and her parents would speak loudly in Chinese. The entourage would appear to be a young Chinese family out for the evening with one set of grandparents. To add credibility, Ting would whisper to Zaron and have him repeat a few Chinese words her parents had taught him. Kang and Wang Shu, happy to participate, would look at Zaron and say "Daddy" several times.

We rushed around to get everything ready. Zaron's nose was large for a Chinese person but was fortunately not conspicuously so. With the black wig, sunglasses, and darkened complexion, he fit in with Lim's family. He looked like a Jimmy Buffet fan when we dressed him in Lim's Tommy Bahama shirt, worn over the blue T-shirt he had chosen to wear that day. He left the condo and walked toward the elevator with Ting holding one hand, Wang Shu and Kang in front, my in-laws in back. Fung carried Mingyu, who was holding a teething toy. Enlai, not wanting to expose his balding head, wore a hat. I watched from the window, my heart pounding. It seemed to take forever before they exited the building. I looked around for Isabelle, and noticed her in the shadow of a doorway across the street—the same petite, dark-haired woman I'd seen earlier. She was talking or pretending to talk on her cell phone. Finally, Zaron and the rest hit the sidewalk and started walking. They looked like they were having a pleasant conversation as they took their time strolling down the sidewalk. With one hand in his pocket, Zaron tried to shake Ting's grasp on his other hand now and then, but she hung on tenaciously. It all looked so normal. I held my breath as Isabelle looked at them for a few seconds. She raised her sunglasses to get a better look, then returned to her cell phone. I exhaled slowly, feeling assured that Isabelle didn't recognize Zaron in his disguise.

Looking out my window for several more minutes, I saw a patrol car circle around the block as Isabelle remained in place. I called the number for dispatch April had given me earlier, hoping the police would pick up Isabelle, and she would lead them to her boyfriend. The woman I spoke to at dispatch told me to expect a call back from an officer shortly. By bedtime, the return call still hadn't come. I was disappointed, but felt confident Zaron was safe for now. I went to sleep next to Lim that night, relaxed and optimistic everything would be okay, at least in the short-term. My feelings of well-being ended abruptly at three o'clock in the morning.

Chapter 18

I awoke to a blinding light in my eyes. Lim's quiet breathing was all I heard. I nudged him gently with my elbow as I tried to become oriented to the here and now, shaking the dream I'd been having of talking to my mother.

"What's going on?" I asked. "Who are you?"

The intruder lowered his flashlight. As my eyes adjusted, the dim light from my bedside digital alarm clock provided all the illumination I needed to see the form of a heavy-set man wearing a ski mask, pointing a pistol at me.

"Where is he?" he asked.

"Where is who?" I knew he was asking about Zaron, but I needed to buy time to collect my thoughts.

"Don't play games with me, Doctor. You know who I mean. You should have brought him to the Regional Center. It would have been much easier on you."

My heart raced, and my skin grew clammy. Saying I was scared wouldn't come close to describing my fear.

"He's not here."

"I can see that." The man kept the gun pointed at me. "I'm going to count to ten. If you don't tell me where Zaron is by the time I get to ten, I'm going to shoot him," he said, shifting his aim to Lim.

By this time Lim, still groggy from sleep, was half sitting up in bed. He hadn't said a word.

The man began to count, pausing two seconds between each number. "One. Two."

I could hardly breathe. I had to stop him from killing Lim, but I couldn't tell the man exactly where Zaron was even if I wanted to. I didn't know the address.

"Three. Four."

I was starting to regret my no-guns-in-the-home policy. I was desperate—I couldn't bear the thought of losing Lim. I thought my chest would explode as I started speaking quickly. "I don't know, but Lim can tell you. Lim, it's okay. I can't let him shoot you. Tell him. Please."

I heard a monstrous scream, like a battle cry. It took me a second to realize it was coming from Lim. To my astonishment, he'd reached under the mattress, pulled out something, and thrown it hard at the intruder, hitting him in the gun-wielding hand. The man yelled as his weapon dropped to the floor. With the speed of a panther, Lim sprang from the bed and retrieved the pistol. The intruder ran for the door, avoiding the large suitcase I saw later in the middle of the living room floor. Lim didn't see it in the dark and tripped, landing with a loud thump. At impact, the gun discharged.

I heard Lim leap to his feet in pursuit. My heart pounded as I worried about what might happen next. I turned on the overhead lights and saw what Lim had thrown at our visitor lying on the bedroom floor. Two-foot-long cylindrical light-colored wood segments connected by a heavy-duty five-inch chain. I'd forgotten about his nunchucks. I told him to get rid of them months ago, as outside of martial arts classes, they are illegal in California. Thankfully, he had ignored me. I didn't think he knew how to use them, but now I knew differently. I was examining the nunchucks when Lim returned a few minutes later. Seeing him, I felt an incredible release of tension, as if I'd just been untied from a medieval rack. He was a sight to behold—his black hair rumpled, chest covered in sweat, wearing only a pair of gray boxers.

"Dammit," he said. "He got away."

"That's okay. At least you're safe."

"I'd have gotten him if I hadn't tripped over that fucking suitcase. Shit."

"Suitcase? What happened out there?"

"Like I said, I tripped. By the time I got to the elevator, he was gone. I ran down the stairs just in time to see him peel out of his parking space out front. The car had no lights on, and it was too dark for me to get his license."

"I see you have a new vocabulary word. 'Peel.'"

"I'm full of surprises, aren't I?"

"I'll say. That was quite a Jackie Chan impersonation you did. I had no idea—"

"I know what you're thinking. You're thinking you should be mad at me because I didn't get rid of the nunchucks after you told me to. Yet, on the other hand, you're glad I kept them."

"You know me too well."

He grabbed me and held me tight. His embrace was so strong I struggled to breathe, yet found it comforting. Finally, his grip loosened. "Believe me," he said, "I'm just as glad as you that I kept them. You know he was going to kill us both, don't you?"

"Really? He said he wanted to know where Zaron was. I don't doubt he would have killed him, but why would he kill us?"

"If he didn't intend to kill us, he probably wouldn't have had the safety off."

"I suppose that's why the gun went off?"

"I guess you don't know much about guns, even less than me."

"Good assessment."

"There would be no reason to keep us alive once he got the information he wanted. He knows we'd have gone to the police or FBI. That wouldn't necessarily get him caught, but why take a chance? Killing us would guarantee we'd be of no help to law enforcement."

"What should we do now?" I asked as we walked into the living room. I turned on the light and saw an oversized suitcase, unzipped with the top open, in the middle of the floor. "What's that suitcase doing there? I've never seen it before."

"That's what I was telling you about. The suitcase I tripped over." He started to say more but was interrupted by a loud knock at the door, and a male voice shouting, "Police, open up."

Lim yelled, "Coming right now." He opened the door to find two police officers standing sideways on either side of the door, guns pointed ahead. Lim raised his hands and said, "Thank you for coming. Please come in." He pointed to the gun on the floor where he'd left it after falling and added, "The gun fell and went off accidentally after I tripped on the suitcase."

"Explains the calls we got reporting a gunshot," one of the officers said. He asked us to sit on the couch while his partner looked over the premises.

"You never saw that suitcase before?" Lim asked quietly as we sat on the couch.

"Never."

"Me either. Must have been left by our visitor."

Our conversation was cut short by the loud voice of the officer who was checking our unit. "Here's where the bullet hit," he said, pointing to a hole through a picture hanging on our living room wall.

"I never did like that picture," Lim said. "I haven't been corrupted enough to enjoy pop art."

With his gun still drawn, the officer tracked the trajectory into the bedroom. Upon returning to the living room, he announced, "The bullet is lodged in the bedroom wall near a window. It's a good thing no one was injured."

The officer disappeared for several minutes to investigate the rest of our unit. When he returned, he said, "All clear." Both officers holstered their weapons.

We explained what had happened, including the mysterious appearance of the suitcase in the middle of the floor, and told the officers we'd been working with one of their colleagues, April Wells. We hoped they'd find the gunman, the man behind the bombings, as well as his girlfriend. The officers bagged the pistol, which was still lying on the floor, and, despite the hour, called April. They told us April had corroborated what we had told them and said technicians would come by in the morning to remove the bullet and pick up the suitcase for evidence. They would arrange for a car to be stationed outside the building, and we could stay there if we wanted. After they left, I sat on the couch and cried for a good half hour as Lim held me.

Finally, I asked a question I'd been wondering about. "Why do you think he brought that suitcase?"

Lim got up to inspect it. He flipped the suitcase over and unzipped the false bottom. "You could probably stuff three bodies in there if they were cut up. I see he has sheets of plastic, a knife, and a hacksaw in here. Like on the show you told me about. What's it called? Dexter?"

I was speechless.

He added, "We need to stay someplace safe."

Chapter 19

At 7:00 a.m., Lim began arranging for a secure place where we could all stay. I had suggested a safe house owned by a security company I was familiar with, but he thought it would be better to stay at the large South Bay house of a wealthy investor in his company. Lim had been there before and assured me the house had up-to-date security features and was built like a fortress, surrounded by a high fence. A small staff monitored the grounds, including all the cameras around the property. The cybersecurity was the best. Conveniently, the owner would be away for at least two weeks.

Lim called Ting to tell her we'd be picking her up along with the rest of the family and Zaron later. Ting said she would call into work to ask for a few days of personal leave. As she was ahead of schedule on her project, it wouldn't be a problem.

I called Martha and told her I wouldn't be in for a few days. I didn't know how long I'd be out and apologized for again putting her in the position of cleaning up after me. Lim arranged for a small bus to meet us in front of a bookstore on the street behind our condominium. The bus was owned by a tech company, and at the time was making its morning run, transporting people living in San Francisco to their jobs in Silicon Valley. It would be available to pick us up at 11:00 a.m.

We packed our laptops and a small supply of clothes, toiletries, and miscellaneous items in two carry-on suitcases. Then we filled the luggage to the bursting point with similar items from Ting's and my in-laws' units. Allowing plenty of time, we exited the back of our building. Lim threw the suitcases over the fence bordering the rear of the property, and we climbed over—me first, after a much-needed boost from Lim.

We took a circuitous route, our suitcases in tow, to reach the back door of the bookstore before casually walking the length of the store inside to the front. There, we watched for our ride through the large display window. When the bus pulled up, and the driver opened the door, we grabbed our bags and rushed to get inside, deftly squeezing by a mother tending to her infant in a stroller, partially blocking the store entry.

Once we were seated, Lim called Ting. He directed our driver to a narrow street in Chinatown, where we found her leaning against a run-down stucco building near an alleyway. Ting was holding Mingyu in one arm as she looked at the phone held in her free hand. As soon as we stopped, she ran to the van with Mingyu, followed by my in-laws, Zaron, Kang, and Wang Shu, who emerged from the darkness of the alley. Once all were seated, Lim instructed the driver to make several detours. When we were convinced no one was tailing us, we headed down I-280 to our destination in Woodside.

We drove forty minutes on the freeway before exiting to a busy, tree-lined boulevard. After a few turns onto hilly, curved streets lined by large estates barely visible through the dense foliage, we pulled into a long driveway. A stocky man wearing a security guard uniform, standing next to a white brick booth, greeted us. After checking the adults' IDs, he handed Lim several keys and a card with the house Wi-Fi network name and password, then remotely opened the formidable iron gate several feet ahead of us. We proceeded through the gate as the doors swung open, towards a sprawling stucco, metal, and glass house.

We exited the van and stretched our legs as the driver unloaded our luggage, then departed. Lim turned the key in the lock of the massive black front door and pushed it open. We followed him into a dramatic two-story atrium, complete with trees and exotic plants. Furnished in ultramodern chic, the home had large windows overlooking the grounds, which included a small vineyard.

I walked past the large sunken living room and into the spacious kitchen, outfitted with stainless steel counters, sinks, and appliances. A granite table in front of a picture window had seating for ten. The pantry and refrigerator were stocked with food. I felt like I was in an Asian market: bok choy, long beans, lemongrass, bamboo shoots, noodles of all kinds, rice crackers, and an assortment of black and green teas. Instead of knives and forks, I found chopsticks. Lim had found for us the home of a wealthy Asian entrepreneur.

We turned down a hallway with eight bedrooms, four on each side. Every one of them was uniquely decorated and had a private bathroom attached. For Lim and me, I chose the room decorated in my favorite colors, teal and lavender. I put Zaron's suitcase in the adjacent room and told him he would be sleeping there. My in-laws, Ting, and her children selected their rooms on the other side of the hall. It was mid-afternoon by the time we had unpacked and felt settled.

I called April and told her about our safe new location. "I'm glad you found a secure place to stay with Zaron," she said. "The police are finished going over your place, but I suggest you stay away for at least a few days. The gun your intruder had was reported stolen several years ago and may have passed through several hands after that. No surprise there. The FBI thinks there's a good chance our Donald Brock impersonator and the boys have left the area, but they can't be sure, of course."

"Why do they think that?"

"He sent another email this morning. Now he's threatening to bomb an NFL game in Atlanta next week. Looks like he's moving from baseball to football. Probably figures the NFL has more money. He's asking for fifty million dollars this time."

"I'd say that nails down the motive. Money. Purely money."

"Right. But that doesn't help us."

"What are they going to do? If this guy isn't paid off, it won't be safe to go ahead with the game."

"Don't I know it. Of course, it's not my call. The FBI has set up a task force to deal with this, so they've taken over. We're completely out of the loop as far as the Atlanta situation is concerned."

"I wonder if this guy will keep demanding money until he gets what he thinks is enough."

"Either that, or until he's caught. By the way, someone from the FBI is going to contact your husband. They've heard about some of the things Lim can do with his software. The FBI cyber team hasn't made much headway, and they want to ask him to help trace the source of the emails. I think they're getting desperate because I know they hate to go outside of the organization. Their excuse is they have to do everything by the book. I don't know what book they're talking about, but my guess is, it needs rewriting."

An hour later, Lim was contacted by Special Agent Williams of the FBI Task Force. Despite being an expert in all things cyber, he wanted to meet in person. After promising he would make sure he wasn't followed, Lim gave him instructions to our temporary residence. Williams, a tall man with short, dark brown hair, arrived ninety minutes later. His manner of speaking reminded me of Detective Joe Friday from reruns I'd seen of the 1950's show, *Dragnet*. Even though he wore jeans and a T-shirt, he looked like an FBI agent to me.

Lim and Williams met behind closed doors for over an hour in the room Lim had adopted as his office. After the agent left, Lim sat at the kitchen table and told me the FBI had been running into dead ends. They hadn't been able to trace any of the bomber's emails past Bucharest. Clearly, the IP address had been spoofed. Williams doubted finding the real IP address or locations the ransom notes were sent from would be helpful if the perpetrator availed himself of random computers or used a laptop he moved around. Nevertheless, he wanted to trace the emails as far as possible.

The FBI had already determined the grocery store computer the fake Regional Center email was sent from hadn't been used for other emails written by the murderer. The bomber had probably tried to ensure that if the Regional Center email were traced, it wouldn't be linked to the extortion emails.

The FBI hadn't made much progress regarding the Cayman Islands account. They had the account number where the deposit had been made, but neither the Cayman Islands government nor the Cayman National Bank had been willing to provide information about the account or the account holder.

Williams hoped Lim could determine if the five million dollars already deposited there by MLB had since been transferred to another account. Notices to all US banks had been sent, directing them to notify the FBI of any transfers from Cayman National Bank in an amount of fifty thousand dollars or more. So far, nothing useful had turned up. Williams was hoping Lim would be faster at getting the needed information than either the CIA or FBI, here or abroad.

"I'm surprised they trust you with all the information they're giving you," I said.

"Because I look so inscrutable?"

"I was thinking more in terms of them not knowing anything about you."

"It so happens Williams's wife is also an agent in the San Francisco FBI office, and she remembers working with you last year to help get me from Alaska to San Francisco. She had a copy of my asylum application and the background check the USCIS people did."

"That explains it. I'm sure being an enemy of the Chinese government gave you a lot of credibility."

"It didn't hurt."

Chapter 20

After Lim returned to his study, I made a pot of chrysanthemum tea, a bowl of rice noodles, and a large helping of stir-fried vegetables. When done, I artfully arranged the provisions on a tray along with a teacup, plate, and chopsticks, and headed to Lim's office. Conveniently, the door was ajar, allowing me to nudge it open with my foot.

The room was large, with one side comprised of a floor to ceiling window overlooking a lush garden. The walls were white, decorated with several works of art I assumed were costly. A black and white Chinese rug covered most of the white marble floor. Lim looked up from his laptop as I placed the tray on the large white lacquer desk where he was working. I knew the sustenance I brought could keep him going for hours.

We spoke a few minutes, Lim assuring me the grandeur of the office wouldn't throw off his ability to concentrate. Not wanting to distract him further, I left to call Daisy and fill her in on recent events, starting with having my blood drawn to be tested for Huntington's disease and ending with hiding out in a secret location. She asked if there was anything she could do, but other than change my genetic makeup and render us all invisible, I had no suggestions. She wished me well, we disconnected the call, and I set off to explore the house.

I discovered a fully equipped exercise room opening to a garden outside, then descended stairs off the kitchen to the floor below. There I found a wine cellar with at least 300 bottles of wine, as well as a small movie theater with seating for ten. Maybe I'd watch a movie later. But then again, maybe not. Almost all the DVD's were in Chinese, something my in-laws would appreciate.

I went upstairs and called Martha to find out if there was anything I needed to handle in absentia. "Glad you called," she said. "A lab on the East Coast called. Said you should check your email for a lab result. Other than that, there's nothing needing your attention right now."

I thanked her, got off the phone, and retrieved the VPN token allowing me access to my hospital email account. I logged on and found two emails from the lab where I'd sent my nephews' samples for myostatin gene testing. Kang's results were in the first email I opened. The report was long, so I went right for the highlighted area near the top.

Summary: Positive for knockout myostatin mutation.

In lay terms, that meant Kang's myostatin gene was non-functional. Below the summary was a description of the exact location of the mutation as well as details of the deleted DNA base pairs. Next, I opened Mingyu's report which read exactly the same. I took no joy in knowing my suspicion was correct, and the mutation in Kang's myostatin gene was allowing his muscles to grow much larger than normal. Mingyu would no doubt develop similarly. I didn't know what else was affected by the genetic mutation causing myostatin deficiency. One thing was certain, though—I would have to tell Ting soon.

It occurred to me there was nothing I needed to do at that moment. No work. No cleaning. No shopping. I had that rare commodity known as free time. I was paralyzed with indecision at first. Should I read a book? Exercise, surf the web, or think? I chose to spend time with Zaron. He was so able, yet so unable. I explored his capacity to figure things out, including how to flush the strange toilets, operate some odd light switches I had discovered, and open a drawer I had managed to jam. What I found confirmed my previous observations—Zaron had an uncanny ability to figure things out as long as words weren't required.

After running out of things to test him with, I sat at the kitchen table with Zaron and let him watch a video on my iPad while I turned on the small wall-mounted TV nearby. All major channels were reporting the same thing. The NFL agreed to pay fifty million dollars in extortion money to the same party responsible for the two baseball game bombings. The safety of the fans was paramount, and the NFL wanted all their fans to enjoy the game without fear.

I wondered what would happen if teams kept paying the bomber, no questions asked. In that case, he wouldn't need the boys anymore. I felt a chill thinking about it. He obviously didn't care about them. I hoped that if any were still alive when he was through with his nefarious plan, he would desert them. Maybe leave them by the side of the road someplace where a kind passerby could rescue them. I feared it was more likely he would murder them.

My thoughts were interrupted by a call from April. "I wanted to tell you before you heard it on the news," she said. "We received the medical examiner's report this morning. Remember Patrick? The boy who died before the bomb went off at the A's game?"

"Of course. You know how he died?"

"Fentanyl overdose."

"How can that be? He was fine walking through the entrance. He certainly wasn't shooting up as he walked."

"What the medical examiner found was unlike anything he'd seen before. The boy had five small balloons—each around the size of a large pill—in his stomach. They were made from finger cots, those vinyl or latex condom-like things that fit over one finger—"

"I know what they are. They're used when just a finger needs to be covered, avoiding the need to use a whole glove."

"Right. So, this guy filled five of those with fentanyl. Then he poked a few holes in them, making each one like a slow-release capsule. He had the boy swallow them. When the fentanyl level in his blood got high enough, he collapsed."

By the time April was finished with her explanation, my eyes were brimming with tears. "That's so cold," I said.

"Don't I know it. We suspect he did the same thing with Zachary, Zaron's twin. Fentanyl was detected in his tissue. Of course, we didn't find the balloons because his whole torso was vaporized. I think our murderer was covering his tracks. Whichever boy was noticed first wouldn't be alive long enough to provide us with useful information but would distract law enforcement from intercepting the second bomber."

"This guy's smart," I said. "And a real psychopath. Not a good combination. Now what?"

"It's really in the FBI's hands now. I just hear bits and pieces of what's going on. As far as I can tell, they're at a standoff now. The NFL is planning to transfer fifty million dollars to this guy tomorrow. With all the publicity this story has gotten, tons of calls are coming in, with reports of spotting the perpetrator or the four missing boys."

"What are they saying about the boys?"

"Most of the leads aren't very promising, but we're following up on all of them. Almost any group of four teenage boys seems to raise suspicion. I heard there was one report of four teenage boys stealing food from a store. Another described four boys dressed in rags sleeping by some dumpsters in Chicago. Those are just some of the tips we've followed up on, but so far, none have panned out."

Nothing April said made me feel better. Her words only worried me more that the boys weren't safe and might be starving in a dirty shack someplace. "What about people claiming to see the bomber?" I asked.

"They're coming in from all over the country. Frankly, I think a high percentage are from people who are simply pissed off at someone. Almost like swatting."

"Swatting? What's that?"

"Someone calls in a made-up police emergency, such as a hostage situation at a house. The police respond, not knowing it's a hoax. At best, it's a very unpleasant situation for the innocent party when the SWAT team shows up. Sometimes, things don't go well, and the victim is hurt or even killed by mistake. Some people think it's a harmless prank, but it isn't. At best, it's a colossal waste of time."

"Other than chasing down these leads, what's the FBI doing?"

"Your husband knows more than me. I suppose they have people looking into our murderer's Cayman Islands bank account. Other than that, as I see it, there's nothing much more to do other than follow up on tips and wait for the bomber to ask for more money. If he ever does. Maybe fifty million is enough. It would be enough for me."

"They need to find those boys."

"Absolutely. I have no doubt our murderer will continue to blow them all up as long as he wants more money. He's so callous. I've never seen anything like this. Sure, I've seen desperate or greedy people do terrible, even violent things. I've come across premeditated murder of spouses for insurance money, to avoid divorce, or gain complete custody of kids. I even investigated a kidnapping for money. None of those cases involved anything near fifty million dollars, though. And none resulted in the indiscriminate murder of random people. Believe me, I'm worried about the boys. This guy has more evil in him than anyone I've ever dealt with before."

Chapter 21

I woke up in a funk the next morning, despite having spent the night with Lim in a beautifully decorated room, where we slept in a comfortable king-size bed between high thread count Egyptian cotton sheets.

Facing one wall stood a beautiful writing desk with inlaid wood, a crystal pen stand with a gold pen on top. The adjoining bathroom featured plush towels, two sinks, and a rain forest shower. I had nothing to do but worry, as I couldn't go to work or anywhere else. Lim was already up and, I assumed, busy in his newly-adopted office working on his startup company and hunting down the killer. He had left a large cup of coffee, now cold, by my bed. I took a few sips, got dressed, and meandered into the kitchen, coffee in hand.

I glanced into the adjacent family room. Ting was multi-tasking, talking to her parents in Chinese, playing Candyland with Wang Shu, and watching Mingyu as he cruised around, steadying himself on the furniture. Kang was excitedly going through a box filled with old Superman DVDs. I assumed they'd found the Candyland and DVDs in the nearby open cabinet.

I walked down the hall, peaked in Lim's office to thank him for the coffee, and asked if he wanted me to bring him anything. He declined my offer, so I returned to the kitchen and turned on the TV to watch the news. I sat next to Zaron who was seated at the kitchen table, gently rocking back and forth as he was entertained by a Mickey Mouse cartoon on my iPad. I decided it would be a good time to speak to Ting about Kang's and Mingyu's myostatin tests. Lim thought I should be the one to tell her about it, as I would be able to answer medical questions.

I started to walk toward the next room when a loud noise, the slamming of the front door, startled me. I froze. *How did he find us? Did he kill the guard at the sentry gate? Is he going to kill all of us?* My heart was pounding. I looked around for a knife to protect myself with, but didn't see one. Not that it mattered. I doubted I'd be able to bring myself to use it effectively.

Loud footsteps approached. Only one set, I thought. He was probably alone, and he wasn't even attempting to sneak up on us. In my mind, that meant he planned to shoot us on sight. Zaron remained absorbed in the video as I was about to come face to face with the killer again. I wondered if he bothered to wear a ski mask this time.

I took in a deep breath and held it as I slowly turned toward the sound of the intruder. Instead of a heavyset man pointing a gun at my head, there stood a diminutive young Asian woman dressed in black, with bright pink hair, a nose ring, and a tiger tattoo on her left arm. To say I was surprised would be an understatement. "Hi," she said in a friendly voice.

I stood in stunned silence for a moment. I imagined I had turned white, thinking I had just escaped death by execution and instead had met up with the girl with the dragon tattoo. Correction, tiger tattoo.

"I'm sorry. Did I scare you?" she asked. Despite her appearance, she had a soft, sweet voice. A key dangled from her right hand.

"You did surprise me. I wasn't expecting anyone."

"Didn't my parents tell you? Sorry. They can be so lame."

"You live here?"

"Yes, I'm Vanessa. I guess you could say I don't really live here anymore, or not much. Not since I started college two years ago."

I began to relax. She did have a key and had gotten past the gatekeepers. I didn't hear any gunfire, and she wasn't carrying a visible weapon. She had no resemblance to the woman who had followed me, the nose ring something I would have noticed. My mind was racing as I considered she could have removed the nose ring when she tailed me. Maybe I was being paranoid, but I had reason to be. I breathed deeply twice to calm myself, so I could think rationally about what to do next.

"Zaron," I said, interrupting his enjoyment of the video. "Who is that?"

Nothing.

"I don't know him," Vanessa said, appearing confused. "Honest."

"I believe you. Just making sure."

"Hi Zaron," Vanessa said. "I'm Vanessa."

"Hi Vanessa," Zaron said quietly, not looking up from his video.

Then and there, I realized I had just been surpassed by Zaron in the etiquette department. "Hi, Vanessa. I'm Erica," I said, extending my hand. "Sorry, you probably weren't expecting us."

"Just like you weren't expecting me. Don't worry, I'm used to it. My parents often have people stay here since they have so much extra room. Doesn't matter if they're in town or not. I like a lot of the people I meet here. You and Zaron seem cool. And you speak English, so at least I can talk to you."

"Let's go to the family room. I'll introduce you to the rest of the gang," I said. "The older couple doesn't speak English, but their daughter does, and her kids are learning."

We went to the next room, where Ting was holding Mingyu, Wang Shu was combing her doll's hair, and Kang was enraptured by an English-language Superman DVD with Chinese subtitles. I introduced everyone, and Ting translated to her parents.

"Glad to meet all of you," Vanessa said. "Let me know if you need help with anything. This house is so big, sometimes it's hard to find things, and you can get lost. We moved here when I was six, and I got all turned around trying to find my bedroom at first."

"I'm not surprised. I think I've only seen about half the house," I said.

"Some of the modern fixtures are hard to figure out," Vanessa said, smiling. "Very embarrassing for guests when they can't figure out how to flush the toilet."

Ting and I laughed, then her parents laughed after Ting translated.

"I'll introduce you to my husband, Lim, when he surfaces again. He's set up an office in one of your rooms. I don't want to interrupt him, but he'll come out for food eventually."

"I hope so. I've often worried someone might die in a back room and wouldn't be discovered for years." Vanessa's gaze moved to the older kids on the floor, then the infant in Ting's arms. "How old is the baby? What a cutie," she said adoringly.

"He a boy. Fourteen month."

"I'm two hundred forty-three months myself," Vanessa responded.

Quick with numbers.

Zaron and I helped Vanessa unload her car, a late model Prius. Together, we carried the suitcase, sleeping bag, and bags of miscellaneous items to her bedroom, located in a wing of the house I hadn't seen yet. Zaron started lunging back and forth and waving his arms wildly after we'd delivered everything to her room.

"You look excited, Zaron," Vanessa said.

Zaron ignored her comment and stayed in motion. "He's autistic," I said. "He doesn't talk much, but he's smart and sweet. Sometimes he waves his arms and rocks back and forth or jumps around when he's excited."

"Cool. I have a friend with an autistic brother. He's in graduate school in bioengineering at Cal. Very smart."

"Well, Zaron's not like that. There's a whole spectrum. There are people diagnosed with autism who, although odd, can get along in society, even get a good job. I think it's confusing to a lot of people to lump those like your friend's brother together with people like Zaron, who don't talk much, if at all, and can't make their way in this world by themselves. Your friend's brother is what would be called high functioning. Zaron is not. He's not at the lowest end, and is even normal or above normal in some areas, but is near the low end when it comes to verbal skills and social interactions. For that reason, he doesn't learn like the rest of us. Teaching him new things is difficult. His knowledge is pretty much limited to what he observes and what he figures out on his own. He'll always need someone to look after him and keep him safe."

"I see," Vanessa said. "Well, this is a great place for him. Sign me up for Team Zaron."

From then on, I liked Vanessa. We sat at the kitchen table drinking tea while she told me a little about herself. I found out she was studying economics at MIT and would be starting her third year soon. She planned to start a nonprofit organization when she graduated, probably something to do with renewable energy. For the last month, she'd been hiking and camping out with friends in Arizona and Utah, visiting National parks including the Grand Canyon, Bryce, Zion, and Arches. She had less than three days to relax, catch up on sleep, wash her clothes, and pack for the fall semester before returning to Massachusetts.

It didn't take long for me to feel I could trust Vanessa completely. I told her why we were staying in her house, as she clearly hadn't been told by her parents. She listened intently as I explained we were being hunted by the man behind the deadly baseball game bombings.

Her eyes widened. "Holy shit," she exclaimed. "I had no idea. We all heard about the bombings on our trip. No one could understand how anyone could do such a thing. I'd like nothing more than to help you catch that motherfucker. Is there anything I can do?"

Not knowing Vanessa very well, I was a bit taken aback by her word choice in describing the mastermind behind the bombings, then decided I couldn't think of a more accurate designation. "My husband, who I mentioned earlier, is working on it right now. If you want to help, all I can suggest is make sure you don't tell anyone, and I mean *anyone*, we're here."

"You've got it."

"Now, how about we try to teach Zaron new skills together?" I reasoned I could talk to Ting regarding her sons' myostatin test results later.

Working with Vanessa was like a dream. Intelligent, enthusiastic, yet patient, she was a natural when it came to teaching a tough customer like Zaron. She reminded me of myself when I worked with autistic kids years ago.

Zaron didn't understand prepositions, so we began by teaching some common ones, using discrete trials. I would tell Vanessa to put a cereal box on top of the table, then under the table a few times, as Zaron watched. Then I asked him to do it. If he placed it incorrectly, Vanessa guided him to put the box in the correct position. If he did well on his own, I rewarded him by letting him bounce a tennis ball Vanessa had found in a closet. If I noticed no progress for a while, I changed the way we did it. We spent a solid three hours teaching on, under, in front, and behind.

We broke for lunch around 1:00 p.m. to enjoy the delicious meal Ting and Fung prepared from the remaining contents of the refrigerator. When I retrieved Lim to join us, he looked surprised upon seeing Vanessa.

"No, you're not so overworked you're starting to see things," I said. "Lim, meet Vanessa. She lives here."

Lim's face brightened. "So, you're Ju and Hai's daughter," he said. I wasn't sure which name referred to the mother, which to the father. "I've heard a lot about you."

Vanessa smiled. "Mostly complaints, I'll bet."

"Not at all. I can tell they are very proud of you, although I wouldn't be surprised, knowing your dad as well as I do, if he doesn't let it show when he's with you."

"I'll bet you're the computer wizard my dad has mentioned on numerous occasions."

"Well, I do work with computers."

"Dude, he's really excited about your company. Maybe I'm not supposed to say that. Maybe I'm supposed to be like really cool and say he's hardly given your company a thought."

"You're not giving anything away," Lim said. "I think he's been pretty honest with me. We're working things out. It'll be good for both of us."

"So, let me get this straight. You're this computer wizard at the startup my dad's all jacked up about, and your wife happened upon sweet Zaron here," she glanced at Zaron fondly and stopped to take in a breath.

"Right," Lim said.

Vanessa continued. "Here's where it gets really weird. Zaron is connected to the psychopath behind the baseball game bombings, and you're all hiding from him in my family's house while you work on tracking the guy down. Is that right?"

"That's it," Lim said. "In an eggshell."

"Nutshell," I corrected him, whispering loudly, unable to hold back my laughter.

"Okay, nutshell. Whatever shell."

"This is so exciting," Vanessa said. "What have you found out?"

"Glad you asked," Lim said, looking around. "Since you're Ju and Hai's daughter, I feel like I know you already and can trust you. The emails demanding money from the sports teams originated in the United States but were routed to appear to come from Bucharest. Our murderer went to a lot of trouble to confuse anyone trying to find him, using different IP addresses and VPNs. I can see why the FBI wasn't having much luck. Right now, I'm trying to determine the physical location of the IP addresses he used. I don't know if different computers were involved, or if only one—probably a laptop—was used, and he changed the IP address each time he used it. I suspect the latter."

"I know if anyone can figure this all out, you can," I said.

"Unfortunately, if he's moving a laptop around, I won't be able to locate it in time for law enforcement to catch him before he moves it again. But that's not all," Lim said. "I also made another break in the case."

Ting was quietly translating Lim's words to their parents. All eyes were on Lim as he continued.

"In general, when an IP address is ghosted, it cannot receive return emails because the server would route them to the fake IP address of origin. Not so in this case. Special Agent Williams told me the return emails they'd sent to the bomber had been answered. Knowing that, I traced the routing of the FBI's responses to a computer in Buenos Aires, one that is never used locally. The murderer has been remotely intercepting email received by this computer regularly. We're dealing with someone who is very sophisticated."

"It must have been hard to figure all of this out," I said.

"Quite. This guy's turning out to be a challenge."

"Any idea how long it's going to take you to trace the exact origin of all the messages he's sent?" Vanessa asked.

"Hard to say. If there were ten of me, it would go much faster."

"Can't the FBI help?" I asked.

"Unfortunately, no. They can't use my software. Not only is it proprietary, but I need to cut a few corners they can't. Not legally, anyway."

Once we finished eating, Lim returned to his office. Vanessa volunteered to go grocery shopping and run any errands we needed. I made a shopping list with Ting and asked Vanessa to pick up a few jigsaw puzzles for Zaron. She promised to be on the lookout for anyone who might be following her.

Vanessa left, and I took Ting aside to have the difficult conversation I'd been dreading while Zaron watched a movie on my iPad. I told her that in addition to having genetically engineered DNA resulting in hemoglobin to enhance their stamina, Kang's and Mingyu's genes for producing myostatin had been destroyed, making their muscles destined to grow larger than normal. The good news was there was no known harmful effect from this. On the other hand, this additional genetic manipulation put them at increased risk for unintended, possibly life-threatening, DNA changes. There was no way to know what the future held.

Ting tried to remain stoic in the face of this new information as tears formed in her eyes. I realized we might never know the extent of the changes that had been introduced into these young boys. All we could do was hope they would remain healthy.

Chapter 22

Vanessa returned with several bags full of groceries and three colorful jigsaw puzzles. Zaron put the groceries away, then opened one of the new puzzles. He began putting it together while Vanessa and I watched the news. Several massive fires had erupted in central and southern California. We were in the midst of what had recently become referred to as the "fire season." Fortunately, there were no large fires nearby, although I knew the situation could change rapidly. I heard no mention of the latest NFL extortion attempt.

For the remainder of the afternoon and early evening, I worked with Vanessa to teach Zaron sign language. If he could understand certain simple signs, and I could teach them to Lim's parents, they wouldn't need to use the stack of cards Lim and I had prepared for them.

Zaron learned to read the signs for each letter of the alphabet quickly. Given his excellent memory for concrete information, I wasn't surprised. While he had difficulty forming the letters with his fingers, he could read my fingers after an hour. Next, I taught him to understand the signs for milk, water, rice, tofu, cup, plate, bowl, spoon, chopsticks, laundry, shower, arm, leg, face, and hair. He soaked it up.

While Ting and Fung prepared dinner, Vanessa took Zaron to the basketball half-court in the backyard, where she worked with him on shooting baskets from the free-throw line. I watched TV in the family room, changing from one news program to another. Finally, I found an update about the latest bomb threat. In a joint news conference, the FBI and NFL announced that the fifty-million-dollar extortion fee had been deposited in the bomber's account. There was much discussion about whether they had done the right thing.

The FBI let it be known they were against paying the money, but the NFL had insisted. An NFL spokesperson emphasized how much his organization was concerned about the safety of the public. I understood the viewpoint of those arguing that this was letting the terrorist win but was glad the public wasn't in danger. The safety of the boys, on the other hand, was still very much in question.

No sooner had the station switched to a commercial for a macho truck than Lim burst into the room more electrified than I'd seen him in quite a while. "I just got off the phone with Williams," he began. "Earlier, I found out the Cayman Islands bank account used by the bomber had been emptied of all recent deposits. Only a hundred dollars remains. After Williams told the bank he knew the account was empty, he was able to persuade them to divulge some useful information. I imagine his powers of persuasion involved threats backed by the full weight of the US military."

"Don't keep me waiting! What did he find out?"

"All the money, including the original five million dollars, was transferred out in five-and-a-half million-dollar increments, to ten recipients."

"Where to? Switzerland?" I asked.

"All I know is it wasn't transferred to another bank."

"Was it transferred to individual people?"

"I don't know—they wouldn't say, but I suspect not. Homeland security has already alerted other countries to watch out for large transfers from the Cayman Islands."

"I doubt every country in the world will cooperate with our government," I said.

"True, but any nation with a government unfriendly to the US would likely confiscate the money. I doubt this guy is stupid enough to let that happen," Lim said.

"What if he's actually a terrorist? Doing this under the direction of a group or country to get money to support terrorism?"

"Doubtful. I had a long discussion with Williams. The FBI believes this guy was born here and knew about the real Donald Brock years ago. As you and I know from his visit with us, he has no accent. He's intelligent and educated. Although he could be a so-called home-grown terrorist, there is no underlying political message in any of his emails. His IP address was ghosted through Bucharest, a country commonly used by Americans to hide IP addresses."

"Why is that?" I asked.

"Romania has no agreement with the US government to reveal the source of emails routed through them, and they don't keep logs. If our murderer were a terrorist working for a rogue government, he probably would have routed his emails through the country his organization is associated with, or a sympathetic one."

"Where do you think the money went?" I asked.

"He most likely divided it between ten financial institutions overseas."

"Will you be able to find out, or is this a dead-end?"

"The FBI is trying to get the cooperation of major investment firms abroad. If just one cooperates and confirms they received five and a half million dollars on the day the Cayman Islands account was emptied, we'll have a good foothold into what this guy is doing with the money. That information should help me track the other money and eventually lead us to who he is and where we can find him."

Fung interrupted us and spoke to Lim in Chinese. Lim turned to me and smiled. "Dinner," he said. I hadn't realized till then how hungry I was. We followed Fung back to the kitchen where Ting, Kang, Wang Shu, Zaron, Enlai, and Vanessa were already seated. Mingyu was asleep on a blanket nearby on the floor.

The dinner Ting and Fung made was fabulous as usual. Lim ate such a large amount I thought he would burst. I realized he hadn't eaten much for the past few days. The progress he and the FBI made earlier released some of the pressure he'd been under, and his appetite made up for lost calories.

After dinner, Ting and Wang Shu helped me try to teach my in-laws sign language. After nearly two hours, we hadn't made much progress.

I noticed Vanessa and Zaron outside, shooting each other with water guns. I didn't remember seeing Zaron so happy and playful, running and laughing. I was mesmerized, watching this handsome young man, his hair seeming to glisten in the sun, radiating pure joy.

Vanessa and Zaron didn't come inside until sundown. Both soaking wet, they plopped onto the family room couch, unconcerned about keeping the furniture dry. I was glad to see they'd left the water guns outside but sad thinking Vanessa wouldn't be staying long.

"Wanna see something really cool?" Vanessa asked.

"Sure," I responded.

"Watch this," she said. "I made up this sign for Zaron."

Zaron watched her as she pointed her index finger and bent it back and forth several times. Zaron went outside and returned with one of the foot-long blue and white plastic water guns they'd been playing with. Then I watched in astonishment as she used sign language to spell out my name. Before I could respond, a stream of water from Zaron's weapon hit me in the face. Vanessa was beside herself with laughter.

Maybe it's not so bad she'll be leaving soon.

Chapter 23

Knowing I had accomplished a lot with Zaron, I slept well that night and woke up refreshed. Lim was fast asleep at my side. I didn't remember hearing him come to bed, so I assumed he stayed up late working on his project. I tiptoed out of the room and made a large pot of coffee. I brought him a cup, black, and set it on the nightstand next to his side of the bed. I started to leave quietly when I heard a familiar voice.

"You don't think you're getting off that easy, do you? Just a cup of coffee?"

I turned to see Lim sitting up in bed, sipping his coffee.

"Is there anything else I can do for you, sir?" I asked demurely.

"For starters, you could fuck me until I'm awake and alert. So, I can get back to my important work."

"For my country?"

"Yes. It's your patriotic duty."

There was no arguing with that. Lim and I emerged from the bedroom later—how much later, I couldn't say. The kitchen seemed like Grand Central Station—Zaron was doing one of his new puzzles on the kitchen table while Kang and Wang Shu played Go Fish on the floor. I was pleased to hear them making their fishing requests in English. Ting was feeding Mingyu something that looked like mush while her parents watched a Chinese channel on TV. Vanessa was still asleep, I was told.

Not quite 9:30 a.m., I wouldn't have expected someone of her age to be awake yet.

Lim and I wanted to have a quiet breakfast, just the two of us, so we ventured into the formal dining room. The large room was dominated by a table with seating for sixteen, made of thick glass supported by an ornate gold tree-shaped pedestal. Gold candlesticks—six of them—decorated the center of the table. The white walls were adorned with Chinese scrolls, each with its own light above. A striking black, white, and red rug covering most of the floor was visible through the table, as were the red seats of the thickly padded chairs. I laughed to myself, imagining Lim and me seated at opposite ends of the table as servants served us cold cereal and milk on silver trays. Instead, we sat next to each other at the end of the table nearest the kitchen.

Lim told me he had received word at one in the morning, ten Zurich time, that exactly five and a half million dollars had been deposited in a Swiss investment firm the same day the money had been removed from the Cayman Islands account. "What you call 'our big break,'" he said. "I don't have the name of the person who owns the account, but I'm sure it's our guy."

"It feels wonderful having good news for a change. Where do you go from there?"

"I'd like to find the name on the account. So far, I've run into a wall."

"Will our government ask them to freeze the funds?" I asked.

"Doesn't look like it. Freezing the funds would likely cause him to make more bomb threats and demand more money."

I knew Lim found coordinating with the FBI frustratingly slow, but working with them made perfect sense. The agency had the force of the US government on its side, while Lim had unique access, including a network of international sources and proprietary software that wasn't completely legal.

After breakfast, Lim returned to his office, and I worked with the rest of the gang to teach Zaron to follow my in-laws' sign language commands. At first, the in-laws didn't sign accurately, Enlai being worse than Fung. In time, they became more proficient, and Zaron appeared to enjoy following their instructions. Communicating without language seemed to appeal to him.

Mingyu contributed by sleeping soundly atop a nearby couch cushion on the floor. Time moved quickly, and soon it was lunchtime. Ting and Fung prepared a spicy mixture of vegetables, chicken, and rice noodles. I had to practically pry Lim away from his computer before he joined us. Once safely away from his work area, he exploded with information. Another five-and-a-half-million-dollar deposit had been located, this time in a Finnish financial institution. Almost immediately, the funds had been disbursed into various stocks, bonds, ETFs, REITs, and commodities.

"Dude, that's way impressive," Vanessa said. "Here I am majoring in econ at a not-too-shabby institute of higher education, and I don't have the balls to invest in commodities. Most people don't have a clue about all that stuff."

"That's what Williams and I were thinking," Lim said. "This guy is very sophisticated when it comes to investing. Or he's a total fool and has no idea what he's doing. I suspect it's the former. One more thing we found out. These accounts are not new. They each had about a half-million dollars invested already. He just added to preexisting accounts."

"My god," I exclaimed. "You're telling me this guy already had lots of money? That doesn't make sense."

"I'm sure it makes sense to him. He had a lot of money. Now he has a whole shitload more," Vanessa said.

"Maybe he done," Ting said.

"Done? What do you mean?" Lim asked.

"Maybe he stop. No more threat. No more bomb. He have enough."

Her words sent a shudder down my spine. It's something I'd considered before. If he were done extorting money, the four boys he had would no longer be useful to him. I doubted he would let them go. He seemed afraid of what Zaron might divulge. It would be the same for the others. Lim was about to go back to his computer when my cell phone rang. April. I hoped she didn't have more bad news.

"I wanted you to hear it from me before you saw it on the news," she said. "I heard from the FBI he's asking for another fifty million dollars."

I was somewhat relieved. At least he wasn't about to murder all the boys right away. I turned to the others and relayed what April had just told me.

Lim, Ting, and Vanessa looked at me expectantly as I turned my attention back to the phone. "Another football game?" I asked.

"This guy's clever, all right," April said. "He knows we know he's only got four suicide bombers left. He's not going to want to use two or three of them at once to convince the NFL they'd better pay because once he runs out of them, he won't be able to extort more money. Now he's threatening to blow up one of the five games scheduled for this Sunday. Our murderer has accurately assessed the situation. He knows the FBI doesn't have the capacity to carefully monitor all those games, watching for several bombers at each one. He's got us over a very large barrel."

"What's the FBI going to do?"

"I don't think they've decided. I'm happy to say I'll have nothing to do with that decision. It's a tough one."

Once I'd disconnected, I told Lim and the others what I'd learned from April.

"This is so interesting," Vanessa said. I think she detected our disapproval of her seemingly insensitive comment because she quickly added, "Sorry, I don't mean there is anything good about the whole thing. It's just that I had a class in game theory two semesters ago, and what we have here is a classic game theory problem. The best option is to figure out a way everyone wins. That's game theory. We're playing cat and mouse with this very intelligent guy. He's got four boys he can use to get more money, but if the NFL decides not to pay, he needs to, well, keep blowing them up to convince the NFL executives to meet his demands. I have no doubt he'll figure out ways to prevent even the best behaviorists and FBI agents from spotting his boys at the games. Sorry to sound so callous, but that's how I see the situation. Once he has no more boys, he knows he can no longer leverage them to get more money."

"This may be an interesting game theory problem," I said, "but we're dealing with real people here. It's not a game." I must have sounded irritated, because I was.

"Look," Vanessa responded. "I take this as seriously as you. I feel there's got to be a way to negotiate with him so everyone benefits. Maybe let him walk away with all his money, as long as he lets the boys go."

"Interesting idea. I could sure live with that," I said, "but I don't know if the FBI would go for it."

"I'm just thinking. What would my dad do? I know he'd want a lot of people thinking about the problem. He'd call for a meeting of everyone involved. There's a large conference table in my dad's office he sometimes uses for meetings. You could all meet there—everyone with direct knowledge of the case. That's what they teach us in business school. Get the best minds together, and cooperate. Of course, I know the cooperation part doesn't always work out."

"I'm not optimistic, but I'll ask Williams if we could all meet," I said. "I just wish we had more information about this guy right now."

The mood around the table was somber as we finished lunch. Afterward, Zaron proceeded to clear the plates and put them in the dishwasher.

Lim returned to his office, and Vanessa watched Zaron work on a puzzle, a colorful field with horses running free. I wished I were there, outside in a beautiful setting, carefree. I turned on the kitchen TV and flipped between news channels for a few minutes. So far, nothing about the new threat. The local news was focused on the bad air quality we should expect soon from the large conflagrations south of us. Hot weather was forecast for the next week, and the risk of fires in our area was great. The National Weather Service was issuing a Red Flag warning. Ting played Go Fish with Wang Shu and Kang in the family room while her parents went outside and did tai chi.

A half hour later, Lim came to the kitchen to report the bomber was buying and selling options on many of his stocks.

"Whoa," said Vanessa. "I took a finance class last quarter. It was a real bitch. Options trading is even more ballsy than commodities. This guy must have some serious knowledge and experience in finance."

With those words, an idea popped into my head. I must have subconsciously put together my theory about the murderer faking his death and the realization he had a deep knowledge of financial instruments. At first, I spoke slowly, then sped up as the thought gelled.

"About four years ago, a couple died in a boating accident off the coast of southern California. Their bodies were never found," I said, "but remains, or should I say partial remains, of the crew member on board with them were retrieved. It was assumed sharks ate up the other two, or whatever was left of their bodies floated away."

"It's not unusual to be unable to find bodies of people who die in boating accidents," Lim said.

"I know, but this story was sensational because the man whose body was never found was out on bail, awaiting a well-publicized trial. The possibility he had faked his death was considered but eventually ruled out because the accident—a large explosion—was witnessed by people on two other boats in the area. No evidence the explosion was staged was ever found. Eventually, the case was closed, and the man and his girlfriend were declared legally dead."

"You think this is related?" Vanessa asked.

"You bet I do. The man awaiting trial could very well be our murderer. He owned a very successful hedge fund. By reputation, he was a pretty ruthless financial genius. The crime he was about to be tried for was insider trading. Lots of money was involved. He would have spent at least twenty years behind bars if the prosecutors had gotten their way, but he died, or appeared to have died. Some of his profits—millions— were never recovered."

"What was his name?" Lim asked.

"I can't remember."

"It shouldn't be hard to find out," Lim said.

"And get a picture," I added.

"Wouldn't the FBI have been able to match his fingerprints?" Lim asked. "There were plenty of prints of this guy taken from the group home. And the suitcase he left in our place. Surely, if he'd been arrested, the police would have his prints on file, and they would have come up with a match by now."

"Good point," I said. "But what if, once someone dies, their fingerprints are removed from the FBI database?"

"That would explain no print match," Lim said.

"There must be other places they can look, like databases that never get purged of dead people. But let's not get ahead of ourselves," I said. "Even if we can identify him, it's not the same as knowing where he is, and it doesn't ensure the safety of the boys."

"But it's a good start," Lim said.

I called Williams and told him about my theory regarding the man and woman declared dead in a boating accident four years ago. Then I suggested a gathering of all who might contribute to finding this murderer.

"That would be very unusual," he said. "Perhaps we could all meet at the FBI headquarters in San Francisco."

"It would be easier for people to come here. I wouldn't feel safe going to San Francisco with Lim. Could you at least think about it?" I implored, trying not to sound like a whiney five-year-old.

"I'll call you back."

Williams called me in half an hour. "It's on for tonight," he said. "I'll be there along with April and her chief, one or two officers from the Oakland police department, a colleague from the FBI, and a retired Mossad behaviorist we've been working with. Like I said, such a meeting is highly unusual, but this is a highly unusual situation. We'll arrive at seven-thirty."

"Fantastic. I sure hope we come up with some good ideas."

"Right now, I'm going to search for the identity of the man declared dead four years ago. I'll let you know what I find at the meeting."

I was unable to think about anything else for the next five hours.

Chapter 24

"Are you expecting visitors?" The call from the sentry gate came at exactly 7:30 p.m.

After I gave the okay, I watched as three cars drove up the driveway leading to the house and parked in front—a white Honda Civic, a black Toyota Rav4, and a silver Toyota Prius. The car doors opened almost simultaneously. April and her chief got out of the Civic, two heavyset men exited the Rav4, and Williams, along with two other men, emerged from the Prius. All had agreed to take non-standard law enforcement cars to avoid detection.

Everyone in the house except my in-laws and Mingyu greeted our guests. Williams introduced us to the other FBI agent and the former Mossad agent he'd arrived with, the San Francisco Police Chief, and the detectives from the Oakland Police Department who had arrived in the Rav4. I recognized the Israeli, having seen him on TV after the first bombing. A minimum of pleasantries was exchanged before Ting left to take Wang Shu and Kang to join her parents and Mingyu in the kitchen.

Vanessa escorted me, Lim, Zaron, and our visitors to her dad's office, which I saw for the first time. We entered the spacious, rectangular room through a set of double doors. I hesitated to step on the elegant two-toned parquet floor with inlaid jade squares, until I noticed Vanessa casually walk across it.

Looking up, I saw an expansive window across from me, running almost the entire length of the room. The picture-like view of lush greenery and the rock-lined waterfall leading to a pool holding koi and water lilies emanated peace and tranquility.

At the end of the room to my right, a formidable black lacquer desk faced us. Two computer monitors and a device charging station holding an iPad were on top. Positioned behind the desk was a black leather chair. Matching filing cabinets and bookcases crammed with books were located on either side. A wet bar at the opposite end of the room was made of black lacquer cabinetry matching the desk.

The middle of the room was dominated by a rosewood conference table with inlaid Chinese characters of a lighter wood running lengthwise in the center. I counted between seven and ten symbols, not sure exactly what constituted a complete character.

"What does that mean?" I asked Lim quietly, pointing to what I assumed would translate into a long phrase in English. The sentiment had to be very important to Vanessa's father, given how difficult it must have been to find someone skilled enough to inlay the complex arrangement of lines and curves making up the characters.

"'Rice doesn't cook itself.' It's a Chinese proverb."

I was surprised at the shortness of the translation. "The owner of the house must be a man of action," I said.

"He is."

Ten green upholstered chairs matching the jade in the floor were arranged around the table, with additional chairs lined up against the wall to the left of the entry. Conveniently, there were ten of us, including Zaron. I wanted to include him in case he was needed to identify pictures, or there was something the former Mossad agent wanted to learn by observing him, something that might help him detect an autistic man like Zaron walking in a crowd.

After a few awkward moments of playing musical chairs, we all found a seat. People sat near those most familiar to them, as did I, taking a seat between Lim and Zaron. Not wanting Zaron to be bored and make noises, I handed him my iPad so he could play Word Search. Ting entered and took orders for coffee and tea. Vanessa gave directions to the nearest bathrooms, after which several people excused themselves to use the facilities. As the last person returned, Ting reappeared and served the hot beverages. We were preparing for a long night.

It didn't take long to figure out who was in charge. Williams stood and passed out pads of paper and pens for note-taking, then distributed a printed agenda for the evening. We would start with presentations, progressing in order down the list of speakers Williams had prepared. After all the reports were completed, we would discuss options. I scanned the lineup and noted I was scheduled to be the third to talk.

Once Williams finished his short introduction, he nodded to the San Francisco Chief of Police and yielded the floor. I listened intently as the police chief, then April, presented their information. When it was my turn, I summarized the chain of events leading up to our hiding in the current location. Just describing the horror of the night the sanctity of our home had been breached by the murderer made my stomach tighten and my muscles tense. After I sat, I realized I was sweating. Lim must have realized how stressed I felt and gently squeezed my thigh under the table to comfort me.

I relaxed as the others took turns delivering their reports. I was familiar with most of the material presented, but heard a few things for the first time. Most significantly, I learned that officers had confirmed Brandy's report that a man living near Bright Lights had driven Zaron to a local doctor for a tetanus shot on the morning of the teacher's murder. The neighbor knew Zaron because he'd been paid to take him to the doctor once before and was happy to drive him to make extra cash. After the doctor's visit, the man dropped Zaron off in front of the school, knowing he would walk inside as instructed. It was assumed Zaron entered the building, didn't understand the significance of his dead teacher lying on the floor in front of him, and proceeded to work on a puzzle.

I looked at Zaron several times during the presentations to make sure he wasn't upset by the discussion. Fortunately, he appeared to remain focused on the iPad in front of him, oblivious to the conversation around him. He never looked up, even when his name was mentioned. Nonetheless, I was glad the detective didn't mention the name of Zaron's brother, Zachary.

The last speaker was Williams's FBI colleague, who talked about the latest bomb threat. "The NFL wants to pay. They have a large pool of money and don't want to jeopardize the popularity of their games. We've tried to explain to them they won't be able to meet these huge extortion demands forever, even with their large war chest. The dollar amount demanded might increase any time."

Once he finished, Williams announced, "Now you are all almost up to date on the investigation. Let's take a ten-minute bathroom break. When we reconvene, I'll tell you about some important new information, and we'll decide on a strategy."

I checked my watch and was surprised to find we'd been at it for close to three hours. I was more than a little eager to hear about the "important new information" but resigned myself to waiting a little longer.

I used my cell phone to call Ting and ask her to bring more tea and coffee. "It all ready," she said. "I bring it now."

I left with Zaron and Lim to visit the restroom near Lim's office, where we took turns. Upon returning to the conference room, I noticed Ting had already set pots containing hot beverages on the wet bar counter. Lim, Zaron, and I helped ourselves to tea. As I slid back into my seat, Williams announced we were about to begin.

"Now you have all been brought up to date," Williams said. "Up to date except for what we've found out since Dr. Rosen shared her latest theory with us—that our perpetrator is someone who was awaiting trial for financial crimes when he faked his death. In view of the extensive financial experience this criminal no doubt has, we thought it quite plausible he might be the man she suspected. It didn't take long for one of our agents to turn up the name of the man, and photographs."

My heart was racing with excitement as Williams reached into his briefcase and produced a stack of papers he handed to the San Francisco police chief sitting next to him. "Take one and pass the rest around, please. I want everyone to have this picture of Robert Garrett, declared dead almost four years ago." There was an audible gasp from the group, including me. I recognized the name—it was front-page news at the time. Exactly the man I'd been thinking of, although his name had escaped me. "The picture matches the one found under Brandy's mattress. We were able to find a record of his prints once we searched a database that includes deceased persons. The prints on file for him match many found at the Bright lights crime scene, the group home, and the suitcase found in the Chen and Rosen condominium. I'm convinced that this man, accused of making millions from insider trading, is our killer."

"One moment," I interrupted. "We should get corroboration from the only direct witness we have. Please be quiet and give us your full attention." The room fell silent as I took my copy of the picture and placed it on top of the iPad in front of Zaron. "Who is this?" I asked.

The voice was soft but could be heard by all. "Don."

The room exploded. Zaron covered his ears, appearing distressed by all the noise, which showed no signs of letting up.

"Please keep it down," I said. "You're upsetting him." The noise level dropped, and Zaron went back to playing Word Search.

Williams continued, "You can all read about this man for yourselves, in the pages attached to the photograph." He paused as he took another stack of paper from his briefcase. "We also retrieved a photograph of his girlfriend, Lydia Powell, declared dead at the same time as Garrett." He handed the papers to the police chief for distribution around the table. "As you can see from the description of her, she is petite, five foot one, just like the woman described by Dr. Rosen."

I interrupted as I looked at the picture in my hands. "Yes, this could be her. But given the large sunglasses she wore when I saw her and the long hair in the photo, I can't be sure."

I slid my picture of Lydia Powell in front of Zaron and held up one hand, palm out, signaling the group to be quiet. "Who is this?" I asked, tapping the photo.

"Isabelle." Again, the voice was quiet, the name clear. I looked around the table and saw most people quietly nodding.

"We don't know how they did it," Williams said, "but we believe the two of them survived the boating accident they carefully planned close to four years ago, and are working together now." Williams took a deep breath and smiled uncharacteristically. "It sure feels good to have the names of these scoundrels."

The other FBI agent interrupted. "I look forward to capturing these SOBs, finding out how they pulled off the boat explosion escape, then watching them put Garrett down like a rabid dog, even if that takes twenty years."

"I think most of us here share your sentiments," Williams said, then continued. "While this information is of great help, we still have to apprehend them without bringing harm to the four young men we believe are still with them. We have all-points bulletins out with pictures of the couple, and information regarding the young men, including descriptions of some of the behaviors they may exhibit. We suspect the boys are kept secluded to avoid attracting attention, and the couple have been using disguises. Our next step is to decide what to do about the latest extortion demand."

I stood again. "We have a complex problem here. We need to catch Garrett if we can, limit the amount of money he extorts, and keep the innocent boys he has safe. Vanessa, the young woman you met earlier, is studying economics at MIT and thinks this is a good situation for applying what she has learned about game theory.

"You are dealing with a highly intelligent man," I continued. "I'm most concerned with getting the boys back safely. I think you need to come up with a strategy using the principles of game theory, where everyone wins. Offer Garrett money for the boys. Say, fifty million from the NFL, no questions asked. He gets fifty million free and clear, and in return he transfers the boys to your custody. You give your word that once the boys are safe, you won't look for him. Win, win."

"We don't negotiate with terrorists," Williams's FBI colleague countered. "The people in charge would never approve."

I was angry. "You have the lives of these young men at risk. This man has already shown he is willing to kill them."

"We'll try our best not to let that happen," the agent said, "but we need to bring this guy to justice. Besides, he's not going to turn over the boys until he knows the money's been transferred. What if the NFL transfers the money, but he doesn't release the boys? It's not like there's an escrow company that deals with this sort of thing."

"You can give a partial payment for one of the boys. He gets the money, releases a boy. Then a partial payment for the next and the next," I said.

"What about the last one? Once we give him the last payment, he might keep the last boy."

"Not likely," I said. "I think that's a chance worth taking."

"He might never take such a deal, even if it were offered," the agent said.

"How about making the offer and finding out?" I asked. "He'd have a lot of money, he'd have his freedom, and he wouldn't have to watch after the boys. I imagine he doesn't want to take care of them."

"Before we consider taking such a proposal back to our department head, let's hear from our behavioral expert," Williams said.

Williams was changing the subject. He clearly had no interest in pursuing the solution I proposed. If it were possible, my blood would have been at a rolling boil.

Williams continued, "Looking at the datasheet I passed around, we know a lot about Garrett. Like it says here, he liked chess—was a Grandmaster—and his favorite bands were AC/DC and Guns N' Roses. Maybe these are things we can use. Also, he was very close to his mom. After Garrett was charged, she was very supportive of him, and accused the D.A. of framing him."

"I'd concentrate on the mother for now," the former Mossad agent said. "He's probably staying in touch with her. Cutting ties with family is the most difficult part of pretending to be dead. Most people can't do it for long and get caught because they can't stay away. Find Garrett's mother and get her to help. If she refuses, then wait patiently until she leads you to him. You can also explore other directions. For instance, he probably likes expensive things, but unless we know of a particular type of item he or his girlfriend collects, like rare coins, art, or expensive cars, you can't narrow the search sufficiently."

"I agree with our Israeli consultant. If we could find his mom, Roberta Garrett, that might help a lot," Williams's colleague said, "but it won't be easy. I tried to locate her before we came here, but couldn't find any record of her.

"After Garrett supposedly died, the FBI monitored his mother for a year, with no evidence Robert ever contacted her. Two years after her son's disappearance, she sold her home and has been lost to us ever since. Knowing what we know now, I would guess Garrett bought a new home for her close to where he'd been living behind Bright Lights, and is making sure she's living comfortably, probably under an assumed name. I wish there were someone we could ask—what is Don's mother's address?" He paused, then started to correct himself, saying "I mean Robert Garrett's . . . "

He almost drowned out the voice coming from the young man sitting next to me. Quiet, yet clear, without stopping his progress in Word Search, he said, "Two five two two Kensington Avenue."

Chapter 25

We all stopped and looked at each other upon hearing Zaron recite Roberta Garrett's address. All this time, while we were searching for the identity and whereabouts of the killer, Zaron had known the address of his mother. I had no reason to imagine this critical information was locked up inside his head and wondered what else he knew.

"I know where Kensington is," the San Francisco police chief said. "It's near West Portal Elementary School. My niece is in the second grade there."

Knowing Roberta Garrett's address was a game-changer. Contacting her and getting her help was placed at the top of the to-do list. After much back-and-forth heated discussion, with me and Lim strongly advocating letting Garrett go in exchange for the boys, the FBI decided on a two-pronged approach.

The first prong called for agents going to the address on Kensington to contact Roberta Garrett. The Israeli behaviorist was optimistic that if approached, she might be convinced to help them find her son. Provided she had a conscience, she'd want to stop him from harming more people. Even if Garrett's mother didn't care about others, she would likely be motivated to prevent her son from being hurt or killed by law enforcement. Being close to his mom, there was a chance Robert Garrett would acquiesce to his mother's wishes and turn himself in. If Roberta refused to help, information might be gleaned from monitoring her activities and tapping her phone.

The second prong, exploiting the game theory approach, required convincing Robert Garrett his best option was to let the boys go and refrain from more extortion. The NFL would pay the most recent demand for fifty million dollars, giving him over one hundred million in ill-gotten gains. It would be enough to afford him a luxurious lifestyle anywhere. Garrett had to know his ability to continue extorting money was limited, given that he had only four more trained boys. If he freed them unharmed and refrained from further illegal activities, the FBI would agree to stop actively pursuing him. I was happily surprised to hear them adopt my proposal until reality struck.

"That'll never happen," William's colleague said. "Only a fool would think we'd let him go, but maybe Garrett will fall for it. Instead of a win, win situation, it would be a win, lose. Win for us, lose for him." His comment was followed by a round of laughter.

Williams said he'd ask top FBI negotiators to compose an email to Garrett outlining their proposal. He would tell them to make it sound like a bullet-proof, legally binding promise not to pursue him if he freed the boys.

I was surprised the FBI would blatantly flout a legal document, potentially eroding trust in their word and crippling their ability to make such agreements in the future, but that wasn't my concern. I wanted to ensure the boys' safety.

When our meeting finally broke a little before 1:00 a.m., I was tired. Lim and I escorted our guests to the door, and we watched as the Honda Civic, Toyota Rav4, and Toyota Prius drove away in the same order in which they had arrived.

I went to bed that night feeling encouraged. I hoped the mom route would work. If not, there was a good chance bargaining would break the stalemate.

My optimism died the following morning when Williams called to tell me Roberta Garrett didn't live at the address Zaron had given us. It was Kensington Street, not Avenue, and the young couple with a baby who lived there denied any knowledge of Roberta Garrett, Robert Garrett, Don Brock, or Bright Lights. After searching the small San

Francisco house, the agents found no evidence otherwise. The home was a fixer-upper, not the sort of place one would expect a wealthy man to buy his beloved mother. Nevertheless, the FBI would keep a surveillance team on the house.

I wondered if Zaron had been mistaken, or we hadn't heard him correctly. It wouldn't be like him to remember "avenue" instead of "street." He wouldn't know those two words have similar meanings. I called him over to my laptop and had him sit. "Type the address of Don's mother," I said.

Zaron typed the same address we had all heard the day before—2522 Kensington Avenue. "Avenue" again. I wondered if he misremembered, had seen the address written incorrectly, or was mistaken it belonged to Don's mother. Then again, why would he have seen the address of the young couple? A thought flashed through my mind. "What city?" I asked.

Zaron typed "Richmond." Richmond is a city on the other side of the bay, a short BART ride from San Francisco. Although known for high crime, there are some nice areas in Richmond, and the weather is considered by some to be the best in the Bay Area. I could imagine Robert buying his mom a house in an upscale Richmond area, perhaps on the waterfront. Zaron kept his hands on the keyboard, turned his head towards me, and froze. The expectant look on his face told me he wanted me to ask him another question. My mind went blank, and I couldn't think of one—until I did.

"What state?"

Zaron typed "Virginia."

We had all made the same foolish assumption. Garrett's mom didn't live in San Francisco or the surrounding area. She lived in Richmond, Virginia. It made sense, as she and Robert were from that area. It wouldn't be hard for him to catch a flight and visit her regularly.

I checked Google maps and found Kensington Avenue in Richmond, Virginia. According to the real estate site Zillow, it was in an expensive part of town. I stopped myself. Should I ask Zaron what country? That would be ridiculous. There is only one state of Virginia on the planet. I googled "Virginia" to be sure and confirmed there was no country, state, or province of Virginia outside the US. I hugged Zaron, who tolerated my emotional display. I wanted April to be the first to know, so she could get credit for informing the FBI. My finger was shaking so much I had difficulty pressing the "call" icon on my phone. She answered on the first ring.

Before April had a chance to speak, I said, "Garrett's mom doesn't live at the house they went to this morning."

"I know," April responded. "The house didn't check out, so we're back to bargaining with the psychopath as the only option. Zaron's lead wasn't good."

"Actually, it was—"

"Look, I know you're very fond of him, and you get excited every time he helps us. You're disappointed, but this time, he was plain wrong. Maybe he didn't remember it correctly. It's 'street,' anyway. No one is angry with him. We know he didn't mislead us on purpose."

"He didn't mislead us at all," I said. "When Williams told me about their disappointing visit to the house on Kensington, it got me thinking. I asked Zaron about the address again—only this time I asked him the city. And state. It's Richmond, Virginia."

"Well, I'll be damned," April said. "Richmond, Virginia. We all just assumed it was San Francisco, but he never said it, did he?"

"Exactly."

"I'll let our friends from the FBI know. They can take the team off watching the house in San Francisco and dispatch a team in Virginia."

"How soon do you think FBI agents can get to Virginia?"

"First, I have to convince Williams that Garrett's mom is there. I don't think that will be hard. Then all he needs to do is get on the phone to the Richmond office in Virginia. They can dispatch agents quickly. I'll let you know when I hear something. Should be later today."

April was right about one thing. I had looked forward to Zaron wowing everyone again and providing valuable information. I was like an insufferable mother, ready to brag about her child's ability to win at checkers or shoot a basket from the free-throw line. I'd been looking forward to the oohs and aahs that would be coming after the agents met face to face with Garrett's mom, thanks to Zaron. I was disappointed when it didn't happen, but now I was optimistic again. I just had to wait a bit longer.

While I waited to hear back from April, we all said our goodbyes to Vanessa. She left the keys to her car and gave us permission to use it as needed. After wishing her a safe flight, I made Vanessa promise to call when she arrived in her Cambridge apartment. She wanted to know what was happening with the investigation, so I was confident I'd be hearing from her soon. I had her cell number, but like others her age, Vanessa rarely answered her phone and never listened to her voicemail, so I'd wait for her to call. I was sorry to see her go as the Uber car left with her and two suitcases stuffed with clothes.

April called in the early afternoon. "No word yet from Virginia, but on another note, things are looking up. Garrett replied to the FBI's email. Says he's willing to stop the bombings if the NFL pays him fifty million."

"That's a step in the right direction," I said. "Garrett can hand over the boys and get on with spending all his dirty money. The FBI can continue hunting him down if they want, but I'll be happy once the boys are safe."

"Unfortunately, it's not going to be that simple. For some reason, Garrett doesn't want to give the boys back."

I was silent for a moment. "What does he want to do with them? I can't believe he and his girlfriend want to keep them around forever."

"Garrett claims to have made arrangements for them to live elsewhere where they'll be safe and well-cared for. He doesn't want to turn them over to the FBI or any other law enforcement agency. Claims he doesn't trust 'the system' to do right by them."

"Sounds like a load of crap if you ask me," I said. "That psychopath doesn't care about them. He's murdered three already."

"We all know that. The FBI is trying to get him to say where he plans to send them. Agents will pick them up after they arrive."

"Sounds fishy to me."

"To me, too, frankly. I don't trust that guy—not one bit."

"I hope when they find Garrett's mom, she'll cooperate and at least help the FBI rescue the boys if they haven't been found."

"We should know about that soon."

For the next hours, I oozed anxiety. Would Garrett's mom lead us to her son? Could the FBI convince Garrett to turn the boys over? I kept checking my cell phone. Martha called to update me on some of my patients and ask questions on their behalf.

"I almost forgot," she said. "A woman came by. She wanted to give you a gift. Said you had taken such good care of her niece, she wanted to thank you."

"Who was the patient?"

"She wouldn't tell me. When I told her you were out for a while, she asked for your address so she could mail you the present."

I didn't recall a patient's family mailing me a gift before. Occasionally they brought something to the clinic and left it if I wasn't there, but they never sent me anything in the mail. "What did this person look like?" I asked.

"She was a small lady, with blond hair. I can't describe her much because she wore sunglasses the whole time."

It sounded like Isabelle. Or Lydia Powell, to be more accurate. "What did you tell her?"

"I said I didn't have your address because it's the truth. Should I have called you?"

"No, you did the right thing." Although I didn't expect the woman to return, I added, "If she comes back, call the police. I think she may be someone they'd be interested in."

"Will do."

The news of Garrett's girlfriend looking for me tied my stomach in knots—more than I already had. To get my mind off the danger posed by the bomber and his sidekick, I contacted my mother's care facility to get the latest news on my mom. She was choking on her food more but was otherwise stable. The update didn't make me feel better. Finally, I got a call from April.

My first words upon answering were, "Did they find Garrett's mom?"

"Sorry, there's still no word on that. I'm calling to let you know—I realize you're not going to like this—but remember, I'm just the messenger."

"What? Don't tell me something happened to one of the boys."

"No, not yet."

I felt my chest tighten as I heard the word "yet."

April continued. "The NFL has unilaterally decided to pay the fifty million, no strings attached."

"You mean without a guarantee for the boys' safety?"

"I'm afraid so. Garrett sent an email saying this will be the last demand for money. After he gets the fifty million, he'll have enough."

"I'll say he'll have enough. Enough to buy anything he wants, other than a large country."

"I think he's worried about his image—he says he's not a bad guy. Claims he could have used more C4 and added things to kill and injure more people, but he was only interested in getting the 'bureaucrats,' as he called them, to turn over the money. He seems to want us to think he's not a psychopath, that he doesn't get his kicks killing people."

"Nice to know," I said. "He only kills people to get money. Well, I don't think he knows the definition of a psychopath because he fits the description to a T."

"He also said he doesn't want to harm the remaining boys. I guess that goes along with not being a psychopath. Said the FBI shouldn't waste their time trying to find him, because they have no chance of succeeding. Once he gets his money, he'll turn the boys over to someone else's care. He's adamant about that, although he won't say where they'll be. The way I see it, there's no guarantee."

"I'd say his word isn't worth much."

"I know," April said. "But it was apparently good enough for the NFL. They want to be done with this. I doubt they're concerned about the boys. The bottom line is what's important to them."

"Hell, as I see it, they don't seem to mind wrecking the brains and bodies of their own players. Why would they care about the boys? They feel they're off the hook as long as this psychopath tells them the boys will be okay, even if there's no reason to believe him."

"I agree."

"What do you think will happen to them, really?" I asked, afraid of the answer.

"Probably nothing good, to be honest. We have agents trying to talk the NFL out of paying without a guarantee for the boys' safety, but so far they've been unsuccessful."

I hoped for a last-minute breakthrough in that regard, realizing it was unlikely.

Chapter 26

"They found Roberta Garrett." Williams sounded almost excited over the phone. I imagined him smiling ever so slightly.

I felt the tension in my body, tension I didn't know I had, disintegrate. "Fantastic," I responded. "That should be a real game changer."

"I wanted to let you know as soon as I heard. She's living at the Richmond, Virginia, address Zaron gave you. Nice house, I'm told. Don't be too optimistic, though. We don't know yet if she'll cooperate. She'd been living under an assumed name since selling her old house. At first, she denied her identity, but when confronted with a photo the FBI had on file and told she would be taken to the local police station for fingerprinting, she acknowledged her real name. From what I heard, she was relieved. That's all I know. I'll keep you posted."

I thanked him for keeping me in the loop. "What about the boys?" I asked. "Are you making any progress in finding them?"

"I'm afraid not. The NFL could have helped, but they've made it pretty clear they only care about the success of their games. They say finding the boys is our problem. Once they make the payoff, which will be any minute now, we'll have no leverage."

Shortly after I had disconnected, Lim ran into the room. "Those motherfuckers at the NFL," he exclaimed while making a fist, a sure sign he was mad.

"What now?" I asked.

"I was testing my algorithm, looking at Garrett's accounts. I can see all of them now. He just transferred a total of fifty million into them. The NFL must have paid him, but he hasn't given up the boys, has he?"

"No, he hasn't," I said. "Shit. I was hoping the NFL would change their mind at the last minute and demand the release of the boys, but it's too late for that now."

"I don't think Garrett ever believed the FBI would stop looking for him if he turned the boys over."

"You can be sure Garrett's going to hide now," I said, "and he'll be difficult to find. I can believe he'll stop trying to extort more money, but I can't understand why he'd want to keep the boys. Something's not making sense."

"Although I doubt Garrett intends to leave the boys at a reputable facility, those places need to be told to notify the FBI if they hear of them. It would be nice to have some good news soon."

"I almost forgot. I do have some good news. The FBI located Garrett's mom in Richmond, Virginia."

Lim smiled. "That's what you'd call a big break, right?"

"Sure is."

"Is she going to cooperate?"

"They're not sure yet. I'm keeping my fingers crossed."

"Why would you do that?"

"Sorry, another expression. It's a superstition. You cross your fingers to get a wish. If only it worked."

Lim went back to his office while I passed the time teaching Zaron new sign language words and spelling out words with my fingers. He seemed to like interpreting my finger signs, although he didn't appear eager to make signs himself to communicate.

Vanessa called to let me know she'd arrived safely in Boston. I filled her in on the latest news, and we commiserated about the fate of the boys.

Minutes later, April called. "I just got off the phone with Williams and have an update for you on Roberta Garrett. She says she wants to cooperate, but it's unclear how much she's really willing to help, if at all. The woman is a mess. Lots of crying, and begging them not to hurt

Robert. She doesn't believe her boy did all the terrible things he's accused of, but if he did, it's because he was forced to by his girlfriend, Lydia Powell. According to Roberta, Powell is a terrible person who has been a bad influence on her prince of a son."

"It sounds like this woman will justify anything Robert did and will probably protect him."

"Seems that way. She's seen his picture on the news and knows he's wanted. Claims he hasn't visited her since she moved to the house in Richmond, over three years ago. She swears she hasn't spoken to him or communicated with him in any way. The agents who searched her house report she has an extra bedroom set up very nicely, a place where her son could stay comfortably if he visited. We know there's no mortgage—Garrett must have bought the house with cash before he disappeared in the boat explosion. He probably used money he had kept hidden from government investigators."

"She must be lying about not hearing from him for the last three years."

"That's what we believe. Roberta admits her darling son pays all her expenses, including credit card charges, but claims she doesn't know how. No visits, no phone calls, no letters, no emails. No idea where he keeps his money. All she knows is, he pays her bills."

"What's the plan now?" I asked. "They can't give up on her. She's got to be able to help somehow."

"They're working on it. Roberta says she's giving them her full cooperation, but they strongly suspect she's holding back. They're watching the house 24/7 and are working on getting a warrant to tap her phones, landline and cell. The FBI suspects Garrett has domestic accounts he uses to pay bills, his and hers. Right now, they're looking into the source of money used to cover his mom's property taxes."

"Does Roberta know anything about the boys?"

"Denies any knowledge, other than what she's seen on the news," April said.

"Has the FBI made any progress in finding them?"

"Williams assured me they have agents contacting group homes and other facilities that might have them, but so far, they haven't come up with anything."

"I was afraid of that. Looks like locating Garrett is going to take a while," I said.

"Unfortunately, it may take more time than we have to save the boys."

After the phone call, I felt a sense of urgency. We needed to find Garrett if we wanted to have a chance of saving the boys. I didn't know what he planned to do with them, but I doubted they would miraculously surface at a care facility.

From what I knew of him, Garrett was probably living in a large home in an exclusive neighborhood not too far from a metropolitan area—the type of locale where people would likely keep current with the news via newspaper, internet, or TV. His face was so publicized now, I assumed he had changed his appearance to avoid recognition.

I wanted my husband to spend less time chasing Garrett's money, and more time trying to find the scumbag. Lim was ensconced in his office, looking at the laptop screen in front of him and taking notes, when I entered through the open door.

"Knock, knock," I said, my gentle way of interrupting him and letting him know I needed to talk.

He looked up and smiled. "I was just thinking it was time for a break. I'm getting hungry."

"That's no surprise. You haven't eaten in hours. You want me to fix you something, or would you prefer your mom's cooking?"

"You know how much I love you, but when it comes to cooking, I have to be honest. Mom wins. I'm sure she'd love to make lunch for all of us."

I laughed. "I'll ask her to fix something. Or rather, I'll ask Ting to ask her to fix something. We can talk while we're eating."

I went to the kitchen and told Ting that Lim wanted their mom to make lunch. It didn't take long for Fung to fill the kitchen and surrounding rooms with the aroma of fennel, cinnamon, cardamom, and other spices. Twenty minutes later, I was at the table eating with Zaron, Lim, and the rest of his family. My in-laws ate quickly and left. Mingyu started fussing, and Ting took him to play with some toys, hoping to cheer him up. Wang Shu and Kang followed, leaving Lim, Zaron, and me at the table.

"Garrett's mom probably isn't going to be of much help," I said. I repeated what I had learned from April. "Is there any way you could find out where Garrett is living now?"

"He constantly moves his computer, which I assume is a laptop. Lately, it's mostly been in southern California, but sometimes it's here in the San Francisco area. I doubt he ever uses it in his house—he's too smart for that. I wouldn't be surprised if Garrett drives over fifty miles from his home each time he uses the internet."

"He probably bought a new house in the last few months. Until then, he and his girlfriend were living in the group home."

"What happened to the house Garrett lived in before he was arrested four years ago?" Lim asked.

"I was told the government confiscated it, then sold it. They took everything of his they could get their hands on."

"If there is a way to narrow down the search significantly, it would be helpful," Lim said.

"I think it would be safe to focus on California, mainly the San Francisco and Los Angeles areas. The house would be expensive. Probably north of three million dollars."

"Even limiting the search to those parameters, it would take me a long time to find him," Lim said. "First, I'd need to search for sales of high-priced homes, one area at a time. Then I'd have to track down which ones were paid for in cash, which wouldn't narrow it down much. Very expensive homes are usually cash transactions because buyers rarely take out mortgages for homes over three million dollars. Those homes are usually bought by people who have lots of money to move around. Is there anything else, like the style of home or number of bedrooms, that might help?"

"Maybe that's something Williams can tell me. I'll see if he can find out any details about the house Garrett lived in before he disappeared. I'll call him after lunch."

"I'll keep my fingers crossed," Lim said, a hint of a smile crossing his lips.

"There's another thing I need help with. Is there any way you could find out if Garrett sent the boys to a home?"

"Why don't you ask me to do something easy?" Lim asked. "I don't know anything about those places, like where they'd be registered, and so on. That would be best left up to the FBI."

"Williams told me they're investigating that now, but I know they work slowly. So far, they haven't come up with anything. I'm going to be worried until I know they're safe."

"I suppose I could look into an unusual withdrawal from one of his accounts to pay for them to stay in a facility. I'll see if I can find evidence of a transfer from any of his overseas holdings."

"Do you think it would be safe for us to go back home now?"

"Ask Williams what he thinks. We can't stay here forever, but it doesn't seem like the FBI is going to catch this guy anytime soon."

Lim returned to his office, but not before we kissed. He said he'd work for an hour, then get a workout in the gym. While Zaron played Word Search on my iPad, I called Williams but only reached his voicemail. I left a message, asking if it would be safe for us to move back home. I also inquired about details of the house the government had confiscated from Garrett.

While waiting for Williams to call back, I tried to relax. There wasn't much I could do right then to help with the search. My phone rang, and I was glad to see Martha's name on the caller ID. I needed something to distract me from worrying about the boys, as I was completely impotent to help them.

"I've got some bad news," she said.

Not what I wanted to hear, but probably trivial compared to the other things I was dealing with. "What happened?"

"A process server came by looking for you a little while ago. You're being sued."

Chapter 27

It took me a moment to shift gears and register what Martha had just told me. "Shit. I'm being sued. That's the last thing I need now."

"I know. There's never a good time, but I feel especially terrible telling you this now."

"Who's suing? What's it about?"

"He wouldn't tell me. They never do—I've been asked to find doctors for several process servers over the years, and they've never told me a thing. When I said you weren't in, the guy wanted to know where he could find you so he could serve the papers today. Seemed very insistent."

"What did you tell him?"

"I told him the truth. I didn't know where you were, or when you'd be back. He yelled at me and said you can't hide forever, and you'd be held in contempt of court."

"He sounds very unprofessional. A real jerk." I had an unsettling thought. "What did he look like?" I asked.

"Well-dressed, average height."

"What color was his hair?"

"I guess I didn't mention it. He was a Black guy, so he had dark hair."

I was relieved it wasn't Garrett. Even so, I ended the call feeling utterly overwhelmed. Not knowing who was suing me or what it was about, unnerved me. I started thinking about cases in which parents may have blamed me for their child's plight. There was the kid with cellulitis who needed an operation to debride his leg because his mom waited so long to bring him in. I thought of the girl with diabetes who had kidney damage because her parents didn't manage her diet properly. Then I remembered a five-year-old boy who died a few months earlier after a long battle with leukemia. He'd had the best treatment from our pediatric oncologists, but the parents might have been lashing out at all who treated him.

It was clear I could drive myself crazy trying to figure out who was suing me. I wondered for a moment if Garrett had hired someone to pose as a process server in order to find me and lead him to Zaron. I dismissed the idea as wishful thinking. There was no denying I was being sued, and I was shaken. Someone was accusing me of being sub-par, incompetent. My head would be filled with self-doubt at least until the matter was resolved. If I lost the suit, I'd never feel the same again. I found a bottle of Riesling in the refrigerator and poured myself a glass. Then I did something I'd never done before. I drank it—alone.

By the time I finished, I felt calmer. I took out a set of multiplication flashcards, shuffled them, and began quizzing Zaron. I held up the first one, six times seven.

"Forty-two," Zaron said.

"Good job," I answered.

The moment was interrupted by a loud knock at the front door. My heart raced. So much for the calming effect of the wine. Had Garrett found us after all? I remembered seeing a video monitor in the kitchen, with a view of the front door. I looked at the screen and was relieved to see one of the guards. I took my time, moving the camera remotely, making sure there was no one behind aiming a gun at him. I opened the door.

"I'm sorry, ma'am, but I think I must warn you," he said.

Damn. Garrett must be out front with a gun pointed at the head of the other guard. "What's happening?" I asked.

"The Gulch fire, which you probably heard about earlier, is getting close. You may need to evacuate. For now, I suggest you pack your suitcases and get ready to leave."

I hadn't heard about the Gulch fire but was strangely relieved knowing our biggest imminent threat right then was a fire closing in on us, rather than a murderer at our gate. Looking around, I became aware of the haze in the air and the smoky smell. "How close is it? Should we leave now?"

"No, it's just a precaution for now. Currently, the fire isn't moving in this direction, but the wind could change. I will, of course, keep you posted if it gets closer."

I thanked the guard and got busy. I explained the situation to Ting, who told her parents. Within a half hour, our bags were packed and piled up near the front door. I was glad we had use of Vanessa's Prius, but we would need two cars to accommodate all of us. I called the guardhouse to ask about the availability of another car should we need to leave quickly. I was assured one of the guards would be happy to drive us to our destination in San Francisco.

My neck, shoulders, and chest were tight as I attempted to calm myself by closing my eyes and breathing slowly. Between the danger from Garrett, the fire nearby, my mother's condition, my risk of inheriting her disease, and now the lawsuit, I felt my head was about to explode—I was near my breaking point despite the glass of wine. I tried to get my mind off the situation by quizzing Zaron with more multiplication flashcards. We'd gone through no more than five when Ting ran in, crying. I hoped that whatever was upsetting her wouldn't send me over the edge.

"Something wrong with Mingyu, I know it," she said. She was cradling her son, who was crying inconsolably. "He no eat or drink, and he cry and cry. Not like him. He not crybaby. Something not right with him."

"Maybe he's just teething," I said, trying to comfort her. "It's most likely nothing. Sometimes babies cry a bit for no clear reason."

I knew Ting was aware of that, having two older children. Looking in her eyes, I sensed immense distress. I doubted there was anything wrong with Mingyu, but Ting needed to be reassured. Then again, he was the victim of embryonic stem cell gene editing.

"Here, let me look at him," I said, taking the baby from Ting. Although he'd recently begun to walk, he now appeared listless, unwilling to stand. As soon as I held him, I noticed something wasn't right. "He feels like he has a mild fever. Don't worry, it's probably just a cold. I'll examine him to be sure."

His eyes looked a bit sunken, consistent with mild dehydration. As Mingyu continued to cry, I detected no wheezing or difficulty breathing, despite a stuffy nose. His skin appeared pink and well-oxygenated. I felt his chest and determined his heart, while beating a bit rapidly due to his distress, manifested no outward signs of dysfunction. All my findings were consistent with a cold. When I assessed his abdomen, I switched into clinician mode and refrained from blurting out something I would regret.

Ting must have noticed a change in my expression. "What is it?" she asked. The anguish in her eyes made the situation even more difficult. "What wrong with my baby?"

The problem wasn't teething. Or a cranky mood. Or a cold, although he almost certainly had one. "His liver is enlarged," I said. I couldn't, for the life of me, stop a few tears from trickling down my cheeks.

Chapter 28

Enlarged liver in a baby. The list of possible reasons for this is long. It includes a number of potentially deadly conditions such as primary or metastatic malignancy, inflammation, metabolic disease, and biliary obstruction. The last possibility was unlikely since I saw no evidence of jaundice, such as yellowing of the eyes. Mingyu would need to undergo a battery of tests, including imaging studies, blood work, and probably a liver biopsy. I worried that an unintended consequence of the genetic manipulation he'd been subjected to was about to declare itself. He might be suffering from something unimaginable, something never described before.

I didn't know what significance Ting gave to my saying "enlarged liver," but she wasn't taking it well. She grabbed Mingyu from me and held him close as she cried, the pain in each wail self-evident. Wang Shu and Kang came to comfort her, only to wind up crying, too.

I found Lim in the gym, running hard on the treadmill at maximum incline. His earbuds were in, so he was likely listening to a podcast, *Pivot* and *The Economist* being among his favorites. Keeping in top shape was important to him, and I hated interfering with his exercise more than I disliked interrupting his work. He didn't notice me until I was standing directly in front of the treadmill. He took the buds out of his ears.

"What's up?" he asked, without slowing down.

"It's Mingyu. There's something wrong with him."

I think it was then he noticed the tears welling in my eyes. He stopped the machine and jumped off. "What happened? Did he have an accident?"

"No." I couldn't keep from crying. Lim put an arm around me. It was sweaty, yet comforting.

"Talk when you're ready."

It took a few seconds for me to gain my composure. I explained that Ting had been concerned about Mingyu fussing and crying a lot. Although I had initially discounted her concern, upon examining him, I discovered Mingyu's liver was enlarged. It was a significant finding, likely portending something ominous. I could see Lim was shaken.

"What do you suggest we do?" he asked.

"He's going to need some tests. We could take him to Stanford Hospital. It's close by."

"If Garrett is still out there looking for Zaron, going to Stanford might lead him back here if we're not careful."

"I tried to get in touch with Williams earlier," I said, "but he didn't answer. I'm less worried about Garrett right now. He's done with the bombing—if we can believe him. Right now, Mingyu needs our help. That has to be our priority."

"I agree. We can take Ting and Mingyu in Vanessa's car. My parents can take care of Zaron and the other kids."

Realizing Lim hadn't heard about the fire threat yet, I brought him up to date. "All our things are packed, by the door, in case we need to leave. If an evacuation is ordered while we're gone, one of the guards will take the others back home to San Francisco."

Lim grabbed some clothes from his suitcase and changed quickly. Under a darkening sky heavy with smoke, Ting, Mingyu, Lim, and I loaded into Vanessa's Prius. We stopped at the sentry booth and explained we were leaving five people in the house who needed to be evacuated should the fire become a threat, and gave the guards our condominium address. It felt strange leaving the premises. None of us had dared step off the property for days. I felt free. I didn't see anyone follow us as we merged with traffic on I-280, nor when we exited at Sand Hill Road. We parked near the entrance to the Stanford Hospital Pediatric Emergency Room. Unlike the overcrowded emergency rooms

I was used to at county hospitals, this ER was sparsely populated. We walked past rows of empty chairs in the waiting area and approached the reception desk.

I explained to the clerk that I was a pediatrician accompanying my sister-in-law and her son, the latter appearing to be ill and in need of evaluation. Within minutes, after filling out several forms, a woman escorted us through a set of double doors, and down a corridor flanked by glass sliding doors opening into small exam rooms. Staff, mostly wearing surgical greens, milled around or sat at nursing stations we passed. We were led to a room like the others, with a treatment bed, several chairs, a sink, and the usual supplies and equipment. Our escort left our door open and spoke to a clerk sitting at the nursing station across from us before leaving. We remained standing while we waited for a physician to arrive, as Mingyu continued to fuss. Ting held him close.

I tried in vain to distract Mingyu with some of the colorful toys in the room, but he was too uncomfortable to be consoled. Finally, a man with thick glasses, around forty years of age and wearing a white coat, entered.

"Dr. Weston," I exclaimed.

The man seemed temporarily surprised as he looked in my direction. "Why, if it isn't Dr. Rosen."

By serendipity, Mingyu was about to be tended to by a previous head resident I had trained under, Jared Weston. I'd had a great deal of respect for him, and we'd gotten along well. Too well, I thought, when I'd sensed he was trying to work up the nerve to ask me on a date, something I was not interested in. I managed to defuse the situation by mentioning an old boyfriend I was seeing, which was a complete lie. He backed off, and we remained friends with no awkwardness in the way.

I made introductions, and we caught up for a minute, often needing to speak loudly over Mingyu's wails. Then we got down to business. I explained Mingyu's situation—the crying, most likely because of a cold, and the enlarged liver, an inadvertent finding, probably unrelated. I mentioned my trip to China and Mingyu's medical history, which included embryonic stem cell gene editing, resulting in abnormal hemoglobin and myostatin deficiency. I wondered if Mingyu's enlarged liver was the result of an additional genetic alteration, accidental or intentional.

"I remember hearing about the gene editing on the news," Jared said. "I didn't realize you were the doctor who had investigated the facility in China."

"I was on the local news a few times but did my best to keep my name out of the media. Unfortunately, Ting still gets harassed by journalists looking for information about the children."

"Well, they won't find out anything from me or my staff, that's for sure."

He got Ting's permission to evaluate Mingyu, who appeared tiny as Jared placed him on the bed big enough for an adult. While Mingyu continued to cry, Jared took his temperature, and looked in his eyes, ears, and mouth. Then he removed the stethoscope from his pocket and listened while moving it from Mingyu's chest to his abdomen. He picked up a small hammer from a nearby tray table and checked his reflexes. Lastly, Jared felt Mingyu's abdomen. As he pressed down, Mingyu screamed louder.

Jared turned and spoke to Ting. "Your son does have an enlarged liver, as Dr. Rosen indicated. Other than a viral infection, a cold, I don't see any other abnormalities at this time. It is important to find out why Mingyu has a big liver. If it weren't for Dr. Rosen examining him because of his cold, we might not have found out about it for quite some time. It's good we discovered it relatively early."

Lim put an arm around his sister, I believe to comfort her as well as hold her up. She appeared to be on the verge of collapsing under the weight of the information about her son's condition.

"With your permission, I would like to admit him to the hospital for tests," Jared said.

"Can I stay with him?" Ting asked.

"Certainly, you can stay in his room as long as you like. We'll have a bed brought in for you."

"Then okay."

"We'll have some blood drawn, and then someone will take him to his room. You can all follow."

I told Jared I'd been checking Mingyu and his siblings often, worried about collateral damage from the gene editing. Mingyu's labs had been normal, and his liver wasn't enlarged the last time I checked, less than a month ago.

"Whatever this is, it looks like it's been caught early," Jared said.

It seemed like a long time before Mingyu's blood was drawn, and we were settled in his room on the third floor of the main building. A nurse gave him Vicodin orally for his pain, and he drifted off to sleep. We were all relieved when the crying finally stopped. Jared came by to inform us he had scheduled an ultrasound for the next morning and reserved a time for a liver biopsy in the afternoon. If the ultrasound showed a biopsy wasn't warranted, he would cancel it.

Meanwhile, Mingyu would continue to receive medication to control his discomfort. Ting gave Jared permission to provide me with all the test results. Lim and I left Ting in the hospital room, hovering over Mingyu. As we walked to the car, Lim phoned the guards at the house and inquired about the fire situation. No evacuation had been ordered yet, so we drove back to our temporary residence in Woodside.

By the time we walked through the front door, it was after 11:00 p.m. All was quiet, and I thought everyone was asleep. Lim and I sat at the kitchen table and shared a pot of herbal tea as we went over the day's events. Within a few minutes, Fung appeared in her nightgown. She spoke to Lim in Chinese. I knew she was asking about Mingyu. With tears forming in her eyes, she left us alone.

Lim told me he wanted to get more work done before retiring for the evening and headed towards the study. Exhausted, I decided not to wait up for him and went to the bedroom, where I lay in bed thinking about Zaron and how much he meant to me, before falling asleep. I dreamt I was watching Zaron jump around in the sunlight, smiling and laughing as he played with a water gun. All the while, the sunlight seemed to make him glow. I was awakened when Lim came to bed later. It seemed like hours had gone by, but I didn't know. I thought about adopting Zaron. Although unusual, I knew adults could be adopted. I wondered what Lim would think of the idea, then fell asleep.

The next morning, I awoke to a dark sky and the strong smell of smoke. I checked with the guard out front and determined there had been no evacuation order yet. Given the conditions outside, I wondered if we should leave anyway.

Williams called as I was mulling that over. He apologized for taking so long to return my call, but he'd been in back-to-back strategic meetings the entire previous day. He'd heard about the fire danger on the news and that some areas near us had been evacuated.

"We've been warned we might have to leave any time. Our bags are packed by the door," I told him.

"I think you should be safe going back to your home now," Williams said. "Since Garrett just got another fifty million, the last payment he said he would ask for, he'll probably stay under the radar and get on with his life of obscene riches. Although there's been no agreement from the FBI not to hunt him down because he didn't give us the boys, he's got no obvious reason to harm you or Zaron."

"That's good to hear. What about his mother?"

"She hasn't given us any more information. She's clearly holding back, but the FBI got a warrant to tap her phone. Nothing on that yet, and nothing from the team watching her house. We did locate the bank Garrett used to pay her property tax and other bills. It was set up under a fictitious name. Unfortunately it's a dead end in terms of leading us to him. We've seen no evidence in that account that he made any unusual payments, nothing to a facility to house the boys."

"What about Garrett's previous house? Did you look into that?"

"He had a house in Pacific Palisades, a ritzy area in west Los Angeles. It was large, with lots of windows and a view of the ocean. He had a four-car garage and a doghouse. Nothing else distinctive."

"And the four missing young men? Any news about them?"

"Sorry, nothing. We are looking for them in residential homes, but there are an awful lot of them. It's going to take a while before we know one way or the other whether he turned them over."

I was getting ready to disconnect the call when I heard a loud knock at the front door. I checked the monitor and saw one of the guards. I opened the door while still holding the cell phone to my ear.

"You've got to go now!" the guard yelled. "Everyone needs to evacuate. The winds have changed, and the fire is coming quickly. Some of you take Vanessa's Prius, and I'll drive the others."

"Did you hear that?" I said into the phone.

"I did. You better get going."

I disconnected and rounded up the others. Once we stepped outside, I noticed an orange glow rising above the treetops and became aware of the fire's ominous roar, sounding like a powerful beast coming after us. Fear overwhelmed me, smothering me with thick smoke.

We were on the road in minutes. I was in the Prius with Lim driving and Zaron in the back seat, while my in-laws, Wang Shu and Kang rode in the guard's car, a black Taurus. We followed the guard down the winding road, flanked by a dense growth of trees on both sides. Visibility was limited due to the heavy smoke. Large ash particles lay on the ground and bombarded the windshield as we drove. Breathing was uncomfortable. I asked Zaron to get a shirt for each of us from the suitcase on the backseat next to him. Once he'd done that, we each held the clothing over our mouth and nose in an attempt to filter the air. The Taurus we were tailing suddenly slammed on the brakes. I looked up to see a wall of flames crossing the road a hundred yards in front of us. I became aware of an intense heat and began shaking uncontrollably. Sweat dripped from every pore, a reaction to the heat and primal fear. *Is this the way it all ends?*

Lim placed a hand on my knee. "Don't worry. I'll get us out of here."

He wasted no time putting the car in reverse and, tires screeching, made a three-point U-turn, narrowly missing the car coming up behind us. As we headed in the opposite direction, Lim gunned the engine and raced away from the approaching fire. I turned around, relieved to see the Taurus close behind. A car with a lower center of gravity would have been nice, as Lim sped down the narrow, curved road. He made a sudden turn down another road, knocking me against the door, as an airplane roared overhead.

"The guard behind us signaled to turn," Lim explained. "He knows where to go—he's listening to someone on the front line of the fire with his radio."

We were silent as our vehicle sped past the lush greenery. We'd driven ten minutes, and I was beginning to feel safe, when we came to a halt behind a long line of stopped cars. The air was black with smoke, as several more planes passed over us. One dropped a pink substance on the inferno below. Cars piled up behind the Taurus, and I turned to look at Zaron. He was still, and looked calm as he held the shirt over his mouth and nose. I wondered if he had any concept of the danger approaching.

The guard driving the Taurus got out of his car and approached us. Lim lowered his window. "There's a tree down ahead," the guard said. "Rescuers are sawing through it so they can remove it. They should be done in a few minutes. We're close to the freeway onramp. If they get the tree out of the way in time, we'll all be fine."

He turned and walked away as I yelled out, "What if they don't? What if they can't remove the tree in time?" The man didn't answer.

Chapter 29

"You're not going to like this," Lim said, "but if the flames catch up to us—if I see them coming from behind—I'm carrying you out of here. I'll run around these cars until I reach safety. I'll try to get Zaron, my parents, Kang, and Wang Shu to run with us. The guard should be able to help. I'll do what I can, but I can't save everyone if the fire gets close."

The world was closing in on me. An incredible pressure enveloped me as I tried to think of the best response—wondering if we should all die together in the flames if it came to that, or if I should let Lim carry me out, knowing some, if not all of us, might perish. Could I go on if I survived and the others didn't?

The brake lights on the car in front of us went off. As quickly as we had come to a stop, we were on the go again, and the traffic began moving swiftly. My thoughts recalibrated as I realized there was a good chance we would all escape. In several minutes the trees on the side of the road became more spaced out, then almost non-existent. The freeway, packed with bumper-to-bumper cars, came into view, then the freeway onramp. We made it.

From then on, the drive back was uneventful. We joined the slow-moving freeway traffic, leaving the terror we had just faced behind. It was several minutes before I could speak.

"Zaron," I said. "Were you afraid?"

Silence.

"Did you see fire?"

"Yes."

"What else did you see?"

"Airplane. Cars. Trees."

I tried asking more questions, but they were all met with silence. By the time we reached San Francisco, the air, while smoky, was much cleaner than it had been close to the fire. Lim found parking in front of our building, and we all exited the vehicles. I looked around but saw no one nearby. I felt relieved, having survived the fire, and finding no one obviously looking for us.

We entered the building, where our mailbox was stuffed with the usual advertisements. Lim's parents took Wang Shu and Kang to their apartment. I thought it best if Zaron stayed with Lim and me, as my in-laws would be watching Wang Shu and Kang full-time while Ting was in the hospital with Mingyu. When we got to our front door, a pile of San Francisco Chronicles greeted us. I picked them up as Lim unlocked the door, and we all entered.

Dorothy was right. There's no place like home. Despite spending the last few days in a spacious, opulent residence, it was good to be back. Zaron seemed edgy until I explained he would be sleeping on our sofa bed that night. That settled him. I'd left our place a bit of a mess, but Zaron wasted no time straightening the kitchen and taking the malodorous garbage to the chute. Once the condo was cleaned up, he found a puzzle, poured the pieces on the kitchen table, and began putting it together.

I told Lim what Williams had said about Garrett's previous home.

"That information could narrow down the number of houses to look for Garrett in," Lim said. "But the list will still be long. I'm going to concentrate on following the money for now." He headed to the study to get back to work.

I hadn't seen much of the news recently, so I decided to relax on the living room couch and read a few newspapers. Reports on the fire, gun control, the economy, and the Middle East were prominent. I was distressed to see a front-page article on Preston Sallow, a pathetic failure, who had recently inherited a large fortune when his mother, his last living parent, died.

A short, homely, overweight man in his mid-thirties, Sallow was an only child who had dropped out of college and, by all appearances, diligently pursued a career of doing nothing. He had not followed in his parents' philanthropic footsteps but instead supported white nationalist hate groups. In the past, these organizations struggled for money, supported mainly by low-income, poorly educated losers who blamed their misfortunes on others. With this wingnut Sallow infusing these groups with money, they were becoming more empowered—a sad state of affairs.

I was reading a more uplifting article about a man who had risked his life to pull a woman from a burning car when Lim interrupted me.

"He got more money," he said.

"Who?" I asked, my mind still occupied by the good Samaritan story.

"Garrett. He has a new deposit of ten million dollars."

"You sure?" I realized it was a stupid question the moment I raised it. Lim wasn't one to make statements of fact if he wasn't certain.

"Yes, I'm sure."

"Where's it from?"

"I don't know yet, but it looks like a direct wire deposit from an account not linked to him previously."

"Damn," I said. "He must be extorting money from another source. I'll bet that scumbag still has the boys."

"See if Williams knows anything. Meanwhile, I'll try to track down the source of the money."

I phoned Williams, who was dumbfounded by the news. "This is potentially a very bad turn," he said. "I'll get back to you or Lim once I learn something. It might be a while."

After I prepared a salad from the contents of the refrigerator, Lim, Zaron, and I sat together for lunch. When we were finished, Zaron cleared the dishes as I read more of the newspaper, then checked my watch. 2:00 p.m. I felt insecure taking Zaron outside for a walk. I wasn't convinced we were safe in San Francisco, and the air quality was deemed unhealthy, so I spent the afternoon doing flashcards with him and teaching him more sign language. Despite the smoke outside, Enlai went shopping so Fung could cook for all of us. Around 6:00 p.m. Lim, Zaron, and I went to my in-laws' unit for dinner. The meal was delicious as usual but less joyful without Ting and Mingyu. Concern for the baby's health hung in the air.

Following dinner, I returned to my condominium with Lim and Zaron. I read as Zaron played Word Search on my iPad. After he was asleep on the sofa bed, I retired for the evening, too emotionally exhausted to wait for Lim who was still busy in the office. I thought about going back to work on Monday and hoped Lim would be able to find the source of Garrett's money quickly. Then I thought about Zaron, and what would become of him after all this was over. The next thing I remember was Lim waking me up, holding a cup of coffee. It was 8:30 a.m. I noticed the sunlight rolling into the bedroom was fainter than usual, a consequence of the smoke and ash suspended in the air.

"For sleeping beauty," Lim said, handing me coffee.

"I don't remember hearing you get into bed. Did you go to sleep last night?" I asked.

"For a few hours. I got a call from Williams earlier and just got off the phone with him. He was very interested in the information I had about the money transfer to Garrett's account."

"I bet he was. Did he have any idea where it came from?"

"No. Said he wasn't aware of other extortion attempts."

"Do you believe him?"

"I do. He seemed very upset. He's worried Garrett extorted money from someone else who hasn't come forward yet. It could be very dangerous if there are more bomb threats the FBI doesn't know about, especially if a victim decides not to pay. The public, and of course, the boys, could be in danger. Williams is going to investigate the transfer on his end, but he wants me to continue looking into it, too."

"I want to talk to him myself," I said as I dialed Williams on my cell. He answered quickly. Before he could ask why I was calling, I asked for an update on the search for the boys.

"I'd tell you if we had any news. We have staff right now working around the clock, checking on all the facilities where Garrett might have placed them, but they've come up empty so far. There are a lot more facilities to check, though."

"I don't suppose you've gotten any more useful information from Garrett's mother, have you?'

"No. We're monitoring all her calls, but none have been from him. Besides a stakeout near her house, we have an agent staying with her in her house throughout most of the day in case Garrett tries to make contact in some other way. She hasn't objected to the agent's presence yet, probably because she's trying to convince us she's fully cooperating. However, she seems to be getting more nervous as time goes by. I think she knows her son's going to call soon. She's probably trying to figure out how to protect him when that happens, without raising suspicion. Sorry I don't have more to tell you."

After our call ended, I had breakfast alone since Lim and Zaron had already eaten. I was reading about the recent interest rate hike expected by the Feds when my cell rang.

"Jared," I answered. "I hope you don't have bad news for me this morning."

"And how are you?" Jared asked.

"Sorry. I don't mean to be antisocial, but as you know, I'm terribly worried about Mingyu."

"I know, so I'll give you what we have so far. The ultrasound doesn't show any tumors or masses in the liver, or anywhere else we checked, for that matter."

I breathed a sigh of relief. "Thank you so much," I gushed. "That's been my number one concern."

"I'm still worried he has another serious condition."

"Of course.

"His labs are fairly normal, just a mild elevation of liver enzymes, likely related to his enlarged liver. I've discussed this with our liver experts. The general thinking is we're dealing with a metabolic disorder, probably a glycogen storage disease."

"But the glucose level is usually low with glycogen storage diseases. His glucose levels have been normal," I said.

"That's true. His glucose is normal even now, which would be unusual in a glycogen storage disease. But he has an enlarged liver, mild liver enzyme abnormalities with no jaundice, no other masses, and no evidence of tissue infiltrates anywhere else, all of which are typical for those disorders."

Something wasn't adding up in my mind. As far as I knew, Mingyu's DNA had been edited the same as his brother's, yet Kang showed no signs of having the same disease.

"Why do you suppose Mingyu's brother doesn't have this problem? He has the same altered hemoglobin and myostatin genes."

"I can't answer your question, but whether Mingyu's problem is from gene therapy or normal inheritance, I hope to have a diagnosis soon. I expect the biopsy we did will show increased glycogen in the liver cells. The first slides will be out tomorrow. Assuming we see increased glycogen as expected, we'll do more tests to determine which type of glycogen storage disease he has. That may take up to a week."

"What are the treatment options? I'm not current on that."

"Neither was I, but I've been brushing up. It's rare, as you know, and depends on the type. I'll discuss it with our experts once we know more."

"Have you explained all of this to Ting?"

"I have. I'm not sure she understood everything I said, but she got most of it, at least. She's very distraught. I suggested she go home and get some rest, but she refused."

"That sounds just like her."

I remembered Ting checking the ID badge picture of everyone who tended Kang when he was hospitalized in the pediatric ICU after being hit by a car. At the time, I'd thought she had paranoid ideations—until a man entered the ICU wearing a stolen ID. He would have killed Kang with his hidden knife had she not alerted us.

"Has she been checking everyone's ID tag?" I asked.

"How'd you know?"

Chapter 30

I was thinking about how glad I was to be back home when Shanika, the geneticist, called. "Your test result is in."

"So soon? I wasn't expecting it to be done for a week."

"I had my best tech work overtime this weekend. I've just gone over the results."

"Well? Don't keep me waiting," I was trying to hide it, but I probably sounded irritated. *Give me the results already.*

"Like I told you before, I don't give these results over the phone. You need to come in."

"I thought you'd make an exception for me." I stopped myself from continuing. If the result were negative, she wouldn't have hesitated to tell me over the phone, I reasoned. I must have tested positive. I would get Huntington's disease. I was doomed.

"I told you before. No exceptions. Now I see you didn't believe me. Can you come in tomorrow?"

"I don't know. I'm pretty busy these days."

"Erica, I don't want you to start thinking crazy. Just because I want to have a face-to-face conversation with you doesn't mean you have the disease. I can tell that's what you're thinking."

"What time do you want me to come?"

"Let me know when you're free. I'll make time. And, as I tell all my patients undergoing this sort of testing, whatever the result, I suggest you bring your husband."

When I finished the call, I wasn't sure what to believe. I probably had the disease, but there was still room for hope. She might have been leveling with me, and if so, I might be negative. I'd ask Lim to go with me. I gave Zaron a puzzle to work on and was on my way to Lim's study when I received a call from Williams.

"He called," he said.

Who called? His words disoriented me. Then I realized what he was talking about. "Garrett? He called his mother?"

"Yes. He called when an FBI agent was there. Roberta pretended to be talking to someone else, and said she didn't need a walk-in tub, then told the caller she had already given to their charity. She was nervous as hell and couldn't manage to keep her conversation consistent. She was flustered, but loyal to her son."

"Damn. I take it the conversation didn't last very long."

"Probably less than a minute. Unfortunately, it could take days to completely trace the call."

"Why so long?"

"The call was forwarded from a SIM card which is in the middle of nowhere, near the Mojave Desert. It pinged off one of the few cell phone towers in the area. Several calls have used the same SIM card to forward calls to Roberta Garrett in the last month. The card doesn't appear to have moved, so the phone it's in was probably abandoned in the desert someplace where it won't be disturbed. Agents are looking for it now, but finding the phone is unlikely to help us find him. I'll say it again—this guy is smart."

"Can't you find the phone that forwarded the call to the phone in the desert?"

"It's not that simple. We think he's got several phones, each one forwarding to another one, forming a path that will be hard to follow. They need to get warrants to trace the calls to each one. Even if they get to the location of the originating call, it will undoubtedly be miles from where Garrett lives, and won't help us get any closer to finding him."

"Are they going to at least try?" I asked, disappointed.

"I don't think they've made a decision on that yet, but probably not. All is not lost, however. The FBI had Roberta's phone tapped."

"How will that help? They hardly spoke, you said."

"True, but when Garrett's mom answered the phone, a dog was barking. She asked what the sound was, and he answered that he'd gotten a new dog, the kind his girlfriend had always wanted, a Löwchen puppy."

"Never heard of those. Is that important?"

"Absolutely. Löwchens are a very expensive, rare breed. Hard to get. There aren't many breeders around, so our agents can contact all of them, starting with those on the west coast. I'm told these breeders can be very picky. They only sell to what they consider to be good homes and usually like to meet the buyer, or at least have a video chat. There's often a long waitlist."

"You think they've been on a waitlist for a dog all this time?"

"Doubt it. It's more likely they bribed one of the breeders to move them up in the queue."

"That might help if the breeder would admit to taking a bribe."

"Whether or not the breeder owns up to taking a bribe, this gives us something to explore."

"Did the agents learn anything else useful?"

"I don't think so. Garrett didn't say anything to let us know where he is and, like I said, didn't talk long. He likely figured out someone was with his mom by the way she was talking, but probably didn't suspect her phone was tapped. I feel sorry for his mom, knowing what her son has done. Of course, she still loves him. Seems to be rationalizing his behavior by blaming the girlfriend."

I was guardedly optimistic the trail of the adopted Löwchen might lead to Garrett. At that moment, however, I wanted to speak to Lim right away about my test result. I entered the study while saying, "Knock, knock." I assumed Lim was in the middle of an important train of thought, as he momentarily ignored me, striking the keyboard in front of him while looking at the screen. "Shanika has the results. She wants to see me tomorrow," I said.

Lim stopped typing, shoved his chair back, and looked at me. "Well, this is what we've been waiting for, isn't it?" he said.

"I'm not optimistic. She wouldn't give me the results over the phone. She says you should come, too."

"She already warned you she always insists on giving the results in person with the significant other present if possible, whether good news or bad."

"I know, but I thought that if it were good news, since she knows me, since I'm a friend, she'd tell me over the phone if the test was negative."

"Honey, I don't think she would do that, break with her usual way of doing things. You're overthinking this. We'll go together. We'll hope for the best. If it's not good news, we'll face it together. I love you. No matter what. Don't forget it."

"I love you, too, Amazing Husband," I said. I hoped he didn't detect the shakiness in my voice.

"Remember, no matter what, I want us to have kids. This is the first step. One way or the other."

The thought of finally having children of my own brought a smile to my face as I left the office and allowed Lim to get back to his important work.

I sat on the couch to catch up on my medical journal reading, as Zaron completed his puzzle and Lim worked in the study. My concentration was not what it usually was.

Ting called Lim in the early evening to say she was in an Uber, coming home with Mingyu, and would arrive in a few minutes. Lim and I took Zaron downstairs to my in-laws' condo to welcome them. It was good to see them. Kang and Wang Shu wrapped their arms around Ting's legs as soon as they saw her. She squatted and hugged them both while holding Mingyu, who was fast asleep. Ting looked exhausted but insisted on carrying Mingyu around with her.

Fung prepared dinner, and we all ate together. With Ting back, Zaron could stay with my in-laws, so I decided to return to work the next morning. I would break away at lunch to visit Shanika. If the news were bad, I wouldn't have time to dwell on it right away, as I'd need to return to the clinic.

After dinner, Lim and I enjoyed a quiet evening together, having a glass of wine on the balcony. I was mesmerized by the grandeur of the Bay Bridge, with its thousands of lights lining the vertical cables shimmering in the blackness of the night. I momentarily turned off the traffic running through my head. I'd worry about Robert Garrett, my test results, my mother, Mingyu's biopsy results, and my lawsuit the next day.

I slept surprisingly well. I called Shanika first thing to tell her Lim and I would be in a little past noon. After a quick breakfast, I was off to work. Martha was glad I was back but wasted no time before presenting me with a stack of papers I needed to sign. Soon she was busy scheduling patients for me to see later. "Let me know right away if the process server shows up again," I said. "Interrupt me if I'm with a patient. I need to find out what this is about."

"He left me his card so I could call him right away if you came in later that day," Martha said. "You want me to call him and tell him you're here?"

I thought a moment. "No, I want to speak to him myself right now. I'll call."

Martha fished in her pocket momentarily and produced a professional-looking business card for J & E Process Service. My chest tightened as I dialed the number.

A man's voice answered. "Yeah?"

I was surprised at the casual salutation. "Is this J & E Process Service?"

After a long pause, the man responded, "Aw, shit. Is this about that doctor?"

I wasn't sure whom I was speaking to or how much I should say. "I'm calling to notify your company that you can deliver your papers to Dr. Rosen. She's in today."

"It's too late. I only had a day to find her."

I was confused. "I don't understand. You don't have to deliver papers immediately, just as soon as possible. Sometimes it can take weeks if someone's out of town."

"Well, I was given a new suit and two hundred bucks to try to deliver the papers. I'd get an extra five hundred if I actually found the doctor. But the offer was only good for that one day, so I don't give a crap where she is right now. I get no more money."

"Are you saying you weren't really delivering papers for a lawsuit?"

"It was just an envelope with some blank papers in it."

"Who hired you?"

"Some lady. I didn't get her name. Paid me in cash."

"What did she look like?"

"Nice lookin' blond. Always wore her sunglasses. Tiny thing—not much more'n five feet."

Chapter 31

I should have been relieved I wasn't being sued, but I found no comfort knowing Garrett and Powell were looking for me. On the other hand, they were only interested in knowing my whereabouts on the day the process server came to the clinic. I concluded that meant they had left town the next day, and we were safe.

The rest of the morning passed quickly, with the usual assortment of sore throats, diarrhea, lacerations, and parents concerned about trivial matters. Lim texted me at noon that he was waiting outside to accompany me to my appointment. I met him in front of the clinic building, and we walked the short distance to find out my fate. Thankfully, the air had cleared up somewhat and was now deemed only unhealthy for sensitive individuals.

Lim and I took the same route we'd walked the previous week and entered the Golden Gate Genetics suite. We started to take a seat in the empty waiting room when the receptionist said, "Sorry, but we're closed. Did you have an appointment?" She stood, holding her purse, and appeared to be on her way out. Remembering the time, I figured it was her lunch hour.

As I was about to answer, Shanika appeared through the same side door she had used previously. "Come on back," she said, waving us through the doorway.

Lim and I followed my friend to her office once again. After we were seated, I noticed the office looked unchanged, with the exception of several picture frames which had been added to Shanika's desktop.

"I've got your test results right here," Shanika said as she picked up one of the stacks of papers on her desk.

"Before you give me my results," I said, "how about some baby pictures? I still haven't seen any. Carter must be over eight weeks by now."

Shanika smiled. "Ten weeks, to be accurate." She put down the papers in her hand. "Okay, I'll show you some pictures, but I know you're only trying to delay finding out your test results."

She turned one of the frames on her desk to face us. "Cute baby," Lim said, then watched as I picked up the frame and oohed and awed over the cute pictures in the collage.

"Times up," Shanika said after a short while. "No more putting this off."

About to receive my sentence, I returned the photo collage to Shanika's desk. My muscles stiffened and I became aware of my heart racing. I imagined my feelings were similar to those felt by defendants in court when their verdict is about to be read. Lim put an arm around me and drew me close. As Shanika started to speak, my mind wandered to thoughts of my mother. The first word I heard my friend say was "Unfortunately." Damn. Shit. I was doomed. Negative thoughts and profanities swirled around my head. After the initial shock, my mind joined the conversation again.

" . . . so I doubt you will have the same course as your mother. But, as I said, I can't be completely sure."

What had I missed? Lim's eyes were closed as he took in a deep breath, a smile on his face. He looked relieved as he squeezed me around my shoulder.

"I'm sorry," I said. I must have looked dazed. "I think I missed something. Could you repeat it, please?"

"Sure. It's a lot to take in. Again, as you know, Huntington's disease is caused by an increased number of CAG sequences in the Huntingtin gene, where the DNA building blocks cytosine, adenine, and guanine recur in that order many times, one after the other. People with thirty-five or fewer of these sequences, called repeats, are normal, and will not get the disease. People with Huntington's disease typically have forty or more repeats, sometimes over a hundred. The number of repeats has been shown to correlate with the age of onset. The more repeats, the younger the onset of disease. Your mom has fifty-five repeats."

I was getting impatient. *Get on with it.* Shanika continued with her prepared explanation, one I was sure she had given before.

"What we know now is about one in four hundred people, and that's a lot of people, have thirty-six to thirty-nine repeats. That's considered a gray area. Most of those people will never get Huntington's. Unfortunately, you have thirty-six repeats, which puts you in the gray area. With your mom having so many repeats, it appears you didn't inherit your mom's harmful gene. You probably inherited the gene with thirty-six repeats from your dad, who, as I understand it, never had any signs of Huntington's."

"Yes, but he died at an age before it's usually detected."

"I know. But there's no reason to think he had it. Huntington's disease is rare.

"What do you think? Do you think I'll get Huntington's?"

"Your only risk is from the slight increase you have of repeats. I can't say at this time what your actual risk is, but I'm certain that if you do ever develop the disease, it is likely to be mild, and at an advanced age. I wish I could say you have absolutely no risk at all, but all things considered, this is a lot better than inheriting your mom's highly abnormal Huntington's gene."

I felt my stomach relax, and my heart slow. "I'll have to learn to live with the uncertainty," I said. "We all have some uncertainty in our lives. I have a slightly increased chance of coming down Huntington's, but my risk for contracting some other horrible disease is still the same. Overall, my prognosis hasn't changed much."

"That's a good way of looking at it," Shanika said. "I, for one, am very optimistic about your chances of escaping Huntington's altogether. That's not even taking into consideration treatments that might be developed over the next twenty years."

"What about kids?" Lim asked.

"You can still do IVF and screen the embryos," my friend said.

"That's right," I said. "Just like we planned to do if I knew I was doomed. We should only take the ones with less than thirty-six repeats. The lower, the better."

"I agree," Shanika said. "We'll screen for the lowest number of CAG repeats since we now know the number of repeats can increase in the next generation."

"We'll do IVF, but no gene editing," Lim said.

"Of course," Shanika said. "We don't edit the genes of embryos in this country. But my lab can do the screening and guarantee you have embryos without risk for Huntington's. Let me give you the name of a fertility clinic I work with. I think they're the best."

I left feeling upbeat. On the way back to the clinic, Lim and I ordered lunch from a food truck and ate while we walked. Once inside the building, I made an appointment with the fertility clinic. Lim and I were both eager to get started.

My afternoon was booked solid. With Martha's help, I was able to breeze through the first five patients. A call from Jared came in mid-afternoon. I excused myself for a moment and took the call in an empty exam room.

"I just finished speaking to the pathologist about Mingyu's liver biopsy," he said.

"Well? Don't keep me waiting. What'd it show?"

"Just as we thought. No malignancy or inflammation. The hepatocytes are swollen with PAS-positive material which is removed by diastase."

"Am I supposed to know what that means?"

"Sorry. All that means is the liver cells are filled with glycogen. As we thought, Mingyu has a glycogen storage disease."

"Shit."

Glycogen is a large molecule formed by joining together many molecules of glucose, a sugar which serves as the body's main source of energy. Enzymes release glucose from glycogen when the body needs energy. If there is a deficiency in one of the several enzymes that normally free up glucose, glycogen accumulates abnormally, predominantly in the liver, heart, or skeletal muscle. This buildup of glycogen ultimately causes a multitude of problems, resulting in a glycogen storage disease. People with these disorders tend to have low glucose blood levels and weakness, as the body is unable to liberate sufficient glucose for its energy demands.

The importance of sufficient levels of glucose in the blood is appreciated by many long-distance runners, who sometimes practice "carbo-loading," eating a large carbohydrate meal before a race. This causes the liver to store excess glucose as glycogen, which can be broken down into glucose late in a race when it's needed.

"It's probably the best diagnosis we could have expected," Jared said.

"I know. It's just . . . it's just so unfair. Ting and her kids have been through so much. And now this. I can't imagine this disease was given to Mingyu intentionally. It certainly wouldn't make him a better athlete. It must be the result of a mistake introduced when his hemoglobin or myostatin was altered. We'd know by now if Kang had the same disorder. I don't understand why the gene editing affected only one of the boys in this way."

"Maybe there was a difference in technique, or another of Mingyu's genes was edited, one we don't know about. Yet. I'm sure there's a logical explanation."

"Now that we have a diagnosis, what's the next step?"

"I sent a blood specimen for genetic testing yesterday. The most common mutations for glycogen storage diseases affecting the liver will be tested for. Once we know which gene is affected, we can direct treatment."

"When will you have the results?"

"The test turnaround time is usually about a week. I've asked the lab to expedite it. I hope to have the report tomorrow or the next day."

"Thanks. Ting is taking all this pretty hard, as you know. Once there's a definite diagnosis and plan, I think she'll be able to cope better."

I told Jared I'd visit Ting and explain the situation to her after I got home from work. I'd present the information in the most positive light possible, spin doctor that I am when necessary. My afternoon was packed with patients, which made the time pass quickly. I finished all my computer work, reviewed lab results, and left around 6:00 p.m.

I visited my mom who looked as if she'd aged five years since the last time I'd seen her. Lying in her bed, she was in constant motion, grimacing while moving her arms and sometimes her legs, seemingly randomly. I spoke to her, told her I'd been out of town for a few days, and had a busy day at work. I described what I'd had for dinner the night before and for breakfast that morning. I kept the conversation simple and held one of her hands, preventing her from flailing the arm on that side. I didn't know if she understood anything I said, but I sensed she enjoyed hearing my voice. I hugged her tight, feeling tenseness in her muscles. I left for home, depressed as I usually was after visiting her.

Lim had dinner ready by the time I walked through the door to our unit. I discussed what Jared told me earlier, and we agreed to visit Ting together while I explained what was known about Mingyu's condition so far.

Ting was her usual emotional self when I explained the findings. While previously these diseases were often fatal, new therapies were changing the prognosis, and it was likely Mingyu could be treated successfully. There was every reason to be optimistic. Lim and I spent over an hour trying to comfort Ting and her children before returning to our unit, emotionally spent.

I turned on the TV and flipped the channels, trying to find something uplifting to get us out of our funk. News of a devastating earthquake, food shortages in central Africa, and police cam footage of a Black civil rights lawyer in Alabama being shot dead by a police officer didn't make me feel better. Lim returned to the study while I continued to flip channels. I finally found a story about a five-year-old immigrant girl from Guatemala who was a chess champion. Despite living with her family in a homeless shelter, she played chess every chance she got and was winning all the local contests, beating kids twice her age. She loved the game and was looking forward to the state championship. Sitting between her proud parents, she was loveable. A truly uplifting story. It got me thinking about chess, and the fact that Robert Garrett loved chess. I went to bed wondering whether he loved it so much, he hadn't given it up. Maybe the game he had such a passion for could lead us to him.

Chapter 32

I didn't remember hearing Lim get into bed. It seemed to be getting commonplace for us to go to sleep at different times. I didn't like that and hoped it was temporary. The next thing I remembered was Lim serving me coffee in bed. That, I liked.

"How much sleep did you get?" I asked.

"Enough. You'll be happy to know I was mostly working on developing an algorithm to narrow down the search for Garrett's new house. As of three this morning, by eliminating properties that didn't fit the general description of Garrett's previous home, I shortened the list to around eight hundred houses. Still a lot, but I hope to have the number halved by the end of the day."

"I have an idea that might help. Garrett was very interested in chess. I had a friend in college who played chess a lot. She was even ranked—a master, I think. I remember she had a subscription to *Chess Life* magazine."

"Was she what you would call a nerd?"

"I suppose you could say that. But she had a great sense of humor."

"Is that what you say about me?"

"I would if you didn't have other attributes I find so interesting."

"Like what?"

"I think you know. We can explore that later if you wish, but right now, I'm wondering if you could compare the addresses on your list to the subscribers of the chess magazine. That would narrow the list down."

"Are there other chess magazines?"

"Probably, but *Chess Life* is what my friend read. I think it's the most widely read one."

"You mean it has over ten readers?"

I laughed. "Probably even more than twenty."

"You could ask the FBI, but they'd probably waste time with things like court orders to get the list of subscribers. If you want, I could try hacking into their system. Organizations like that usually don't have the best security. Still, I'd rather not spend my time looking into it unless we knew for sure if he subscribed."

"Maybe Zaron could help with that."

I went to my in-laws unit and asked Zaron, "Did Don read a chess magazine?"

No answer.

"Did Don read *Chess Life*?"

No answer.

"What magazine did Don read?"

No answer. I was getting nowhere. On the spur of the moment, I called Martha, told her I'd be late, and took Zaron for a walk to a large bookstore that carried a variety of magazines. We arrived just as the store was opening, and were the first customers to enter. I found *Chess Life* in the magazine rack, and held up a copy for Zaron to see.

"Did Don read this? *Chess Life?*"

"No."

There went my theory. He didn't read *Chess Life*. I didn't know anything about the three other Chess magazines there but figured I should ask Zaron about them anyway.

"Did Don read this? *British Chess Magazine*?" I asked, holding the magazine in front of him.

"No."

I picked up one of the remaining chess magazines. "Did Don read this? *American Chess Magazine*?"

"Yes."

Excited, I hugged Zaron, who stood motionless. I was happy he didn't pull away. To be as sure as possible Zaron wasn't giving me random answers, I needed to confirm what he told me. I held up the last chess magazine displayed. "Did Don read this? *New in Chess*?"

"No."

I asked Zaron about all four magazines once more, in different order. Again, he answered "Yes" only when I held up *American Chess Magazine*. I bought a copy and headed back to my building with Zaron, feeling energized.

I left Zaron with my in-laws, then returned to my unit and handed the magazine to Lim. "Zaron said Don read this one. He was consistent, so if you can hack into this magazine's subscriber information, you might find Garrett's address. Just don't tell me how you do what you do. I don't want to know."

Lim smiled, as he usually did when he was going to do something a little bit illegal and knew I wanted no part in it. I left for work slightly optimistic that we'd be able to find the slimeball Garrett and, hopefully, the missing young men. While finding them before the FBI did would be satisfying, I didn't care so much about beating the FBI at their own game. I wanted to save the boys and have Garrett face the consequences of his actions.

Upon arrival in the clinic, Martha informed me I had a full schedule with sick and injured kids as well as a meeting about a staff dispute requiring my intervention. Behind already, I didn't have time to think about Mingyu, the missing boys, Garrett, Zaron's future, my mom, or my uncertain medical situation, which is what I would have done were I not running around putting out fires. By the time I left work that evening, I was mentally and physically fatigued. Lim had texted me earlier to let me know he had to go to his work office for a meeting, so I knew he would be tied up there for a while. As I walked home, I had time to think and become preoccupied with worry. I entered my empty condominium feeling anxious.

In need of a distraction, I turned on the news. Unfortunately, the first thing I saw was that degenerate Preston Sallow. He was standing at a podium in front of a large and scary-looking group of pierced and tattooed white nationalists—mostly incels, I figured. He was making thinly veiled threats against a Black Lives Matter demonstration scheduled soon in Montgomery, Alabama, to protest the recent shooting of the Black civil rights attorney. Hate and warnings of bad things about to happen spewed from his mouth. His aim was to run all African Americans and others he found unworthy, most likely most of the population, out of the country. I didn't know what his lineage was, but I wouldn't have been surprised if it wasn't pure whatever he thought pure white was.

I was just about to turn the channel when Lim came home. I shut the TV off.

"How was work?" I asked.

"I met with some Google suits where I helped present information about the capabilities of our software."

"So, you had to put on a dog and pony show?"

Lim was confused. "There were no animals."

I laughed. "Just another expression."

"I should have known."

"It means you had to keep their interest by showing all the wonderful things your company can do."

"I see. Well, the software is so fantastic, it was more of a white tiger and panda show."

"How'd it go?"

"They were very interested. Unfortunately, I had to stay with them and answer so many questions, I didn't have much time to work on tracking down who gave Garrett that ten million dollars."

"I understand." I'm sure Lim detected disappointment in my voice which I was incapable of hiding.

"I did have enough time, though, to narrow down the search for his house some more. I compared the subscribers to *American Chess Magazine* with the recent buyers of homes that fit my algorithm. I cut the list to just fifteen."

"That's fantastic, Amazing Husband. If he's at one of those, we should be able to locate him in no time." I felt I was getting close to the end of a long, dark tunnel.

"We need to decide," Lim said, "if we should hand my list over to the FBI, or if we want to find Garrett without their help. That would mean going to the houses ourselves and seeing who goes in and out. It might take some time, especially if Garrett and his girlfriend don't go out much. It might even be dangerous. On the other hand, the FBI could storm any house they see fit."

"That's the best way to go," I said. "No brainer. Let the FBI handle it."

"That worries me, though. I know we'd make the boys' safety a priority. But I don't trust the FBI to do the same."

"They're trained in hostage negotiations and kidnappings. They know how to protect the victims."

"Maybe it's different here. In China, the police want to arrest the guilty. The safety of the victim is not as important."

"I see why you're worried. It's the opposite here, though. The FBI will do whatever they can, even let Garrett escape, to be sure the boys are safe. I think you should give your list of addresses to the FBI. They have the resources to do what's needed."

"Okay. I'll call right away."

As Lim spoke to Williams, I heated up leftovers for dinner. Mingyu's diagnosis lay heavy on my mind, and, I was sure, Lim's, too. I hoped to have some results the next day. We mostly talked about Lim's company, and what he would do once it sold. He was considering setting up another business using some of the proceeds as seed money. On the other hand, he didn't want to start something that would require a lot of his time. He hoped to be well on his way to fatherhood soon.

It was nice going to bed at the same time, for a change. We'd been married for a while now, and the flame was definitely still there, but I didn't want it to start flickering in the winds of life. Happily, the fire was red hot that night. I slept soundly. The coffee Lim brought me in the morning seemed better than usual. I left for work with a smile on my face.

The morning was hectic. When I finally sat down for lunch, I noticed Jared had tried to call me several times. I called him back, hoping at last to hear the final diagnosis for Mingyu.

"Sorry, Erica, it's going to require more testing," Jared said, foregoing the usual greeting when he answered.

"What does that mean?" I asked.

"Mingyu was negative for all the mutations tested. We even expanded the testing to all the known mutations for glycogen storage diseases."

"Now what?"

"We're going to skip ahead and go directly to whole genomic analysis. This will take several days, but they'll hopefully find the mutation resulting in Mingyu's condition."

I thanked Jared, despite being disappointed we'd all have to wait longer. I should have known this wouldn't be simple.

I made it through the remainder of the workday, anxious about the evening, knowing Ting would be upset upon learning the final diagnosis would be delayed yet again. I told Lim I'd have dinner with Zaron that night. He could have dinner with his parents, his sister, and her children. It would be easier for him to explain everything to them in their native language while they were all together. I wouldn't be needed, as there wasn't anything medical to explain. All they needed to know was that the tests so far were inconclusive, and more tests were being done, with results expected in a few days. I knew Lim could explain that much.

I was busy with computer entries, completing my notes and ordering tests, when I checked my watch. It was almost 7:00 p.m. I was tired and hungry, so I did something I resorted to only when necessary. I ordered a pizza at a local Italian hole-in-the-wall, worked for another fifteen minutes, and left. The pizza was ready when I arrived to pick it up. Ten minutes later I was home. I knew Lim was with Zaron, his sister, and other family members in Ting's apartment. I called and asked Lim to bring Zaron to our unit. When they arrived minutes later, Lim and I kissed. He told me he was just about to update Ting and the rest about Mingyu. He returned to his relatives and left me with Zaron and the pizza. After closing the door behind Lim, I turned around and saw Zaron had already set the table. A slice of pizza was on each plate. His piece was half-eaten.

I asked Zaron questions about his day but, as usual, he gave one-word answers or remained silent. I was able to learn that he had gone shopping with Lim's parents and had put together his one-thousand-piece Island Vista jigsaw puzzle. Zaron cleared the table and put the dirty dishes in the dishwasher. We went through a few boxes of flashcards before he poured another jigsaw puzzle onto the table, his way of telling me to stop talking.

I turned on the TV and surfed the channels, stopping at a news stations, when I saw that creep Preston Sallow giving another hate speech. He was saying basically all non-whites and non-Christians should leave the country, and the Black Lives Matter leaders would call off their assembly tomorrow if they knew what was good for them.

I saw Zaron look up and say something. It was hard to understand. Was it "Bubba" or "Bubble?" I asked him to repeat it, but he ignored my request. He returned to his puzzle, as I wondered what he had seen. I forgot all about it when Lim walked in after his family meeting.

Chapter 33

Lim brought Zaron back to his parents' unit, then returned to describe his evening. It seemed Ting was all cried out. She was able to accept the uncertainty about Mingyu, at least for now. Mingyu was already feeling better, having recovered from his viral illness, and was fairly active, toddling around and playing with toys his siblings gave him. There was joy in the household as the children laughed at his baby antics. They enjoyed carrying him, especially Kang, who seemed to find it easier to lift his little brother than his older sister did.

Lim worked in his study, and I read on the couch. An hour later, Lim emerged to tell me he traced the ten million dollars Garrett had received to a clothing company in Bangladesh.

"That doesn't make any sense," I said. "I can't see why he would want to lower his price by eighty percent and start extorting money in Bangladesh."

"When we learn more about it, I'm sure it will make sense," Lim said.

"Did you call Williams?"

"I did. He's perplexed. There have been no more bombing threats from Garrett that he knows about, here or in Bangladesh."

"What now?"

"He's going to try to find out more about the clothing company. That should be pretty straight forward for him—he doesn't need my help for that."

"So now we just wait?"

"That's all we can do for the moment."

We both retired—at the same time. That was two days in a row. Again, I slept well—after confirming that our relationship was as intense as ever. The next morning, I heard Lim get out of bed quietly. I pretended to be asleep, not wanting to interfere with his important responsibility, namely bringing me coffee.

After my morning caffeine fix, I dressed and had breakfast with Lim. He needed to attend a morning meeting at work, and I left for the clinic twenty minutes after him, on foot. Across the street from our building, I noticed someone dressed in a Mickey Mouse costume. It was a professional get-up, the kind you might see in Disneyland. I thought it odd. I often saw strange things in San Francisco, but they were more in line with decked-out drag queens, people talking to themselves, or junkies shooting up in doorways. Never a Disney character.

Work was a breeze, and my thoughts drifted to Mingyu and the hunt for Garrett and the boys. I wasn't expecting a call about Mingyu's latest test results, knowing I wouldn't find out anything until the following day at the earliest.

Lim called while I was eating lunch, a falafel sandwich Martha had grabbed from a local food truck. He informed me FBI agents had found a breeder of Löwchens in California who recently sold a puppy to a couple in the Malibu Beach area, a location bordering the Pacific Ocean. It's known for its beautiful beaches and magnificent homes, many owned by celebrities. The breeder didn't have the buyers' address because he had delivered the dog to a woman in a parking lot near Malibu Beach. The woman, a small blond wearing sunglasses, went by the name Mary Smith and paid in cash. Two of the fifteen homes on Lim's shortlist, those that fit his algorithm and received *American Chess Magazine,* were in the Malibu Beach area. Agents planned to visit both houses to look for Garrett and the boys soon. They'd make the safe return of the boys a priority.

One of my afternoon appointments failed to show up, and I managed to leave work by five-thirty. I let Lim know I'd be home early, and suggested he leave work soon, so we could take a neighborhood walk and chat about trivial things. Something a couple might do on a date. It had been some time since we'd done anything so normal, so carefree. As I approached my building, I noticed Mickey Mouse still hanging around across the street. I wondered if he was a drug dealer or pimp. Maybe he was someone who genuinely wanted to cheer up the few kids who lived in the neighborhood. Whatever the reason, I didn't give it much thought other than to sense he was someone to avoid.

I went upstairs to my condominium and made a cup of tea. A half hour later, Lim came home. With nothing pressing, we indulged in an afternoon—or should I say early evening—delight. A while later, we were about to leave on a neighborhood walk when Fung called Lim. After a short conversation, Lim explained to me that his father was suffering from allergies. His mom wanted to take his dad to an herbalist in Chinatown, one who had been recommended by friends. The herbalist had evening hours, but Fung was afraid there would be a long wait and wondered if Zaron could stay with us until they returned. How could we refuse?

We stopped by their unit and got Zaron before leaving the building. As soon as we stepped outside, I noticed Mickey again. He was looking our way, so I turned my head to avoid eye contact. We'd taken only a few steps when Disney music started blaring from a boom box across the street. Mickey started moving to the music and motioning for us to come to him.

No way am I getting near you. I forged ahead as Zaron made a happy sound. Before I could grab him, he stepped between parked cars and into the street, apparently wanting to get close to Mickey. No sooner had he taken two steps into the road than a gray truck parked a short distance from us peeled away from the curb and accelerated in his direction. I turned to face the noise from the revving engine and screamed as the vehicle continued toward Zaron, obliviously crossing the street. He would have been killed had Lim not sprang into action. He grabbed Zaron, and pushed him out of harm's way as he landed on top of him, beyond the truck's path. The vehicle missed Lim by no more than an inch. I caught a glimpse of the driver—a heavyset man with a shaved head and a face tattoo or large birthmark. I didn't get the truck's license plate or make.

As the vehicle sped away, Lim stood and helped Zaron up. Zaron had a scrape on his left arm but otherwise seemed okay. Mickey started running down the street. Although he had a head start, Lim chased after him and gained ground quickly. Mickey removed his large head and dumped it on the sidewalk as he ran, turning slightly to see who was chasing him. He looked around twenty years old, with long, scraggly brown hair and a patchy growth of beard. He kept running, turning his head nervously every few seconds, looking incredulous as Lim gained on him. Finally, Lim tackled him to the ground. I imagine the impact of the fall was cushioned by Mickey's belly.

I grabbed Zaron's hand, and we walked together towards Lim, who had lifted Mickey up and secured him in a headlock. Lim clenched his fist and looked like he was about to punch the ensnared man hard.

"Don't hurt me! Don't hurt me!" Lim's captive yelled.

Zaron rocked back and forth, making sounds of distress. I yelled, "Don't hurt him. Zaron's upset. He doesn't want you to hurt Mickey."

Lim relaxed his fist, but kept a tight hold on the young man.

"What were you doing out there?" I shouted at Mickey. "You could have gotten us killed."

"Sorry, sorry, man," he said. "I didn't know that car was gonna come after you guys."

"Oh, really?" I asked sarcastically. "Then what were you doing out there all day? Were you waiting for us?"

"Hey, man, I was just doing what I was told. It was just a job."

"What the hell kind of job was that? Who told you to dress up in a Mickey Mouse suit and hang out there all day?"

Lim was on his cell phone.

"Hey, man, don't call the cops. Please," he said, looking at Lim.

"Why shouldn't I? You'd better tell me who hired you quick or I'm telling the police all about this."

"Look, I just answered an ad on Craigslist. I ain't never saw no one. They said I'd get five hundred bucks. They paid two-fifty already. I'm s'posed to get the other two-fifty when I'm done. Please don't call no cops. I've, well, I've got some oxy and ecstasy on me. If I get busted again, I'll go to jail. You can have it—all of it."

"What were you supposed to do for the money?" Lim asked.

"They dropped off this Mickey Mouse suit with a picture of him," he said, nodding at Zaron who was then standing only a few feet away. "I picked the stuff up under a bench in Golden Gate Park yesterday. Never saw who left it. I was s'posed to hang out in this suit across the street from the building you came out of. As soon as I saw the young guy here, I was s'posed to turn on the music and wave for him to come see me. Then I was s'posed to give him this."

He reached into a pocket on the Mickey Mouse suit and produced a birthday card. "They said he's retarded, and it's his birthday today. They wanted to surprise him. Like one of them singing telegrams people used to send. I have a nephew with brain damage. A really sweet kid—the only kin I care about. I figured he'd like something like that. I kinda imagined I was doing this for someone like him. Then that bat shit crazy car came out of nowhere. I had no idea it was there. Honest."

"Let me see the picture."

The man reached into another pocket and produced a headshot of Zaron, the kind that might have been in the binder at Bright Lights.

Lim, still holding the man around the neck, loosened his grip. "When were you supposed to return the Mickey Mouse costume?"

"They didn't want it back. Said I could keep it or throw it away. I figure the guys that hired me must be rich."

"What's your name?" I asked. "Do you have any identification?"

"Name's Mike Towns. My ID's in my pants pocket. Under all this Mickey Mouse shit. If you let me get out of this suit, I'll show it to you."

"Okay, but don't try to run or I'll catch you and beat the shit out of you," Lim said.

I was looking at Lim adoringly. Usually the perfect, refined gentleman, he could act like a street thug when the situation called for it. He always made me feel safe.

Lim let go of Mike and helped him out of the costume. The man then reached into his back pocket and produced a wallet with his license, identifying him as twenty-one-year-old Mike Towns from Topeka, Kansas. Lim took a picture of the license and rifled through Mike's wallet, finding around six hundred dollars in cash. Then he patted him down and discovered a cell phone as well as baggies with pills. Lim found the number of Mike's cell phone and entered it as a note on his own phone.

"I'm going to let you go," he told Mike as he took a picture of him, "but if your story doesn't check out, or I catch you doing something—anything that might harm someone—you'll be sorry."

"Don't worry, I ain't gonna bother you again," Mike said. "Thanks, thanks a lot, man." He backed away slowly, then turned and hurried away.

"I see it's not safe here after all," Lim said.

"Let's go back inside. I need to clean up Zaron's arm."

"What about me?" Lim asked. "I scraped my left hand here on the asphalt."

"I didn't see that. If you promise not to cry, I'll wash your hand off, too, and even put an antibiotic on it. But honestly, I get the feeling you can take care of yourself."

As Mike turned a corner and disappeared from our view, I hugged Lim and Zaron, putting one arm around each of them. I drew our group into a tight circle, thankful no one was seriously hurt. Then we headed back to the condominium.

Once inside, I tended to their wounds. When finished, I went to the bedroom and called Williams to tell him about the failed attack on Zaron. I withheld the information we had on Mike, the dufus in the Micky Mouse suit, not wanting to add to his problems. Without the truck license plate or even the make and model, law enforcement had no way to find the driver. Williams said he'd see if he could get a police car to keep an eye on our place, but we should consider leaving again. I told him I'd discuss that with Lim later. I doubted they'd be able to organize another attack right away.

Before disconnecting, Williams told me FBI agents were chasing down ownership of the Bangladesh clothing company that had given Garrett ten million dollars, and had determined it was owned by a series of shell companies, one of which was American. They expected to have a clear picture of who owned it shortly.

Zaron was doing a puzzle on the kitchen table when I went to the living room and turned on the TV. Ten minutes later, the regular programming was interrupted by breaking news. Lim and I watched in stunned silence. The sight was too familiar. Distant video of the Black Lives Matter rally in Montgomery, Alabama, showed a suicide bomber explode, annihilating those around him. This bombing looked bigger and more destructive than those at the baseball games.

Chapter 34

Is this what Preston Sallow had been warning about? Was he responsible for this horrific act? In addition to Sallow's rants, had there been other credible warnings? Was the FBI there, looking for suspicious characters?

All these questions darted around inside my head in the aftermath of seeing the latest bombing. I couldn't shake the feeling that Garrett was somehow involved. I called Williams and got his voicemail. I left a message which contained a few expletives. Then I called April. She answered but didn't know any more than me. All her information was from the same live news coverage I was watching. We both felt it was likely this bombing was related to Sallow, and possibly to Garrett.

I stayed glued to the TV as reporters updated viewers on the death toll, which stood at twenty-two, including the bomber. This bomb had contained objects—screws, nails, razors, and metal fragments, inflicting painful injuries on those not killed immediately. The coverage segued to Sallow's previous rallies, where violence had been erupting and seemed to be escalating. Protestors outside his rallies had been roughed up, and minorities had been randomly attacked by Sallow's supporters. Three victims were recently hospitalized for injuries. One was currently in a coma from head trauma suffered two weeks prior. Any reasonable person would conclude that the recent Black Lives Matter bombing was related to Sallow's movement, although law enforcement presented no definitive evidence.

With no more news of the incident being divulged, I turned off the TV so Lim and I could discuss the pros and cons of staying where we were. The pros included being comfortable in our own home, not missing more work, and being near my mother. The con—the only one I could think of—was that all or some of us might wind up dead. We decided to go into hiding again the next day.

Once the decision was made, I turned the news back on. The shocker came two hours later. Although I hadn't appreciated it on the grainy footage, it had been verified that the suicide bomber was a young Black man. A perfect bomber for a rally filled with Black people. He would certainly be under the radar if anyone were panning the crowd for suspicious activity. But what Black person would do such a thing at a Black Lives Matters rally? Of the many hypotheses being put forward, the most popular one was that the bombing was pulled off by Boco Haram, an Islamist group based in Nigeria. This could be their way of showing disapproval of African Americans in the US who have adopted Western ways. The second most popular theory was that Sallow's followers had threatened the lives of a Black man's family if he didn't carry out the deed.

Zaron looked up from his puzzle-making at one point and looked at the TV. A video of Preston Sallow flanked by two of his associates, filmed several days earlier, was playing.

"Bubba," Zaron said.

This time I heard him clearly. I jumped up, but by the time I reached the TV, the three men were gone, and scenes of the bombing aftermath were being shown. When another clip of Sallow ran, this time with him alone, I touched the screen over Sallow's image.

"Is this Bubba?" I asked.

"No."

"Who is this?"

No answer.

"Who is Bubba?"

Silence. I became unsure about what Zaron had said. Or maybe Bubba was one of the men standing next to Sallow in the video. Why in the world would Zaron know him? Was he someone Zaron knew before he became a ward of the state? That would be quite a coincidence, I thought. I was tired. It was getting late. I wanted Zaron to sleep in our apartment that night. After the Mickey Mouse incident, I felt he would be safer with us than with Lim's parents. I would call Williams in the morning.

I didn't sleep well, being worried about our security and ruminating over recent events. Why did Garrett want to harm Zaron now? Who was driving the car? I knew it wasn't Garrett. Why would a Black man kill himself in order to kill his brothers and sisters? Lying in bed, contemplating the fate of the world, every noise, from the sound of the refrigerator I didn't remember hearing ever before to the faint din of traffic outside, jarred me to a state of alert. I don't know when I fell asleep, but as usual, I was awakened by Lim bringing me coffee.

"I found out the Woodside house we'd stayed in survived the fire," he said. "I'm sure being made of glass, metal and stucco helped. We can go back there and stay until it's safe."

"That could be forever."

"Not forever. Maybe a week. I don't think it will take long now to find Garrett's house."

"I hope not," I said.

"I'll get my parents and Ting ready while you phone whoever you need to. Let's leave in a half hour."

I called Martha to let her know I'd be away again until further notice. She couldn't have been happy she'd again have to beg the other doctors to see some of my patients and reschedule the rest. Next, I phoned Williams. I told him about Zaron's possible identification of someone associated with Sallow.

"Which video clip?" he asked.

"The one on CNN last night around nine. A man standing to Sallow's right had a Swastika armband and a confederate cap. The guy to his left wore black leathers and had a teardrop tattoo on his face."

"I'll check into it, but to be honest, I suspect this is some sort of misunderstanding. I find it hard to believe Zaron would know who any of those guys are. Nevertheless, I'll get a copy of the video and shoot it over to you. If you can get a positive ID from Zaron, we'll look into this further."

We were heading back to the South Bay house before 9:00 a.m. I drove Zaron, Ting, Wang Shu, and Mingyu in my mother's car, while Lim drove his parents and Kang in Vanessa's Prius. After we exited the freeway near our destination, we passed numerous charred houses, blackened trees, and piles of debris.

When we reached the first segment of the driveway to our hideout, I was momentarily taken aback by the ash and blackened remains of trees all around us. The misshapen remnants of the iron gate that had guarded the house lay on the scorched earth near the pilasters from which they had been secured. I should have expected nothing else, but was nonetheless unprepared mentally. A guard exited the still-standing sentry booth and welcomed us. We drove up the last part of the driveway slowly, Lim leading in the Prius. It felt surreal as the house came into view, blackened with soot but otherwise appearing unscathed, even as all surrounding vegetation had been destroyed. I felt like Scarlett O'Hara in *Gone with the Wind* returning to Tara towards the end of the Civil War.

Leaving the car, I became aware of the smell of smoke hanging in the air. We entered the house which appeared unchanged, although it had been cleaned, and the garbage emptied. As fantastic as the house was, I missed my life and my own place. I hoped this nightmare would be over soon.

I expected Williams when my phone rang, but it was Jared. With all that had happened, Mingyu's condition had all but slipped my mind.

"We have an answer," he said.

Chapter 35

I had only a moment to mentally prepare for what Jared was about to tell me. "I hope it's not bad news," I said. "I don't know if I can take it right now."

"We're pretty sure Mingyu's condition is the result of intentional gene editing," he said.

His words gave me a ray of optimism. "Does that mean it's beneficial in some way?"

"I'm afraid I can't say that. I think the mutation they introduced was intended to improve his athletic performance, but it backfired."

"Backfired? What does that mean? What is the mutation?"

"It's never been described before, so we can't be sure about the prognosis. The metabolic change introduced is related to glycogen storage diseases."

"What do you mean, 'related?' Does he have a glycogen storage disease or not?"

"He has an abnormal buildup of glycogen in his liver. But it isn't caused by an enzyme deficiency resulting in the inability to break down glycogen. There is a unique mutation in the gene coding for glycogenin-2."

"Glyco what? I've never heard of it."

"To be honest, neither had I. Our next-generation sequencers located a mutation in the gene that codes for one of the two glycogenin enzymes, glycogenin-2. This enzyme is found in the liver and heart. So far, it looks like Mingyu's heart is fine, so the mutation may not be deleterious there."

"What does this enzyme do?"

"Glycogenin, rather than breaking glycogen down, initiates the formation of glycogen molecules. Other enzymes subsequently take over, adding more glucose molecules to make the final, large glycogen molecule. It's not well understood how it's regulated, but apparently, this mutated glycogenin-2 of Mingyu's causes the production of more glycogen molecules than normal. Too many, it seems. That's why his liver is distended."

"You're saying he's making too much glycogen, rather than being unable to break it down?"

"Precisely. In contrast to glycogen storage diseases, his body is able to break glycogen down into glucose appropriately, so his serum glucose level is normal, and he has enough glucose to meet his energy needs. You might think of it as being super carbo-loaded. We believe the Chinese scientists thought the extra glycogen would give him an edge, especially in endurance sports. He wouldn't run out of glucose, probably ever. They didn't count on the extra glycogen being a problem. At least that's our best guess. We discussed this for quite some time and agree this is the best explanation."

"I can't say I suspected that, but it makes sense. Whatever the intentions, what should we do next? Did the team come up with a treatment plan?"

"Nobody knows what the best approach is. This is uncharted territory, but the general thinking is we should observe him for a while. If his condition deteriorates, which it may, then we need to consider a liver transplant."

"I hope he doesn't need one, but can he be put on a transplant list now, just in case?"

"Sorry, but no. That would be premature. There will be plenty of time to consider a transplant if he starts showing significant liver damage. That day may never come, so I don't think many doctors would recommend a liver transplant at this time. It's possible that when he's older and more active, especially if he trains like an elite athlete, the glycogen won't accumulate."

"We all have to live with more insecurity than we'd like," I said, thinking of myself as well as Mingyu.

I found Lim getting ready to work out in the gym and explained what I'd just learned. He agreed to be present when I explained the situation to Ting.

Ting was in the family room reading a book to Wang Shu, with Mingyu sleeping on her lap. Kang was nearby, engrossed in an exciting Superman DVD. I didn't enjoy interrupting Ting's precious time with her kids, but Lim thought it best to tell her now, without her children around. He told Kang and Wang Shu to play with their grandparents.

Lim sat next to Ting as I explained the findings. I told her it was good we knew what the problem was, but the best treatment wasn't clear. Then I mentioned a liver transplant might be the best option if he showed deterioration as he grew older. Only time would tell if he would need one.

"If Mingyu get liver transplant, that mean other child must die?" Ting asked.

"Unfortunately, that's true," I said. "But these organ donors are already dead. Braindead. It's not as if anyone kills them."

"How you be sure?"

"I understand why you might be skeptical. There are stories of people being killed for their organs in China. But I can assure you, that's not how we do things here. We have a lot of oversight. It wouldn't be possible."

"Not possible for someone to run over child with car to get organ?"

"I suppose that would be possible, but nothing like that would ever be organized by the government or any member of the transplant team. We surely wouldn't plan on killing any children so Mingyu could get a liver."

"Maybe someone from Chinese government would. They know what they did. Maybe they have spy at hospital, know Mingyu sick from gene editing. Maybe they want him to get transplant, so they know what to do if there are other children in China with same gene edit."

As farfetched as her idea seemed, I didn't have a good argument against it. "Although I doubt that could happen, I can't guarantee it's totally impossible."

"I know babies not die often. Not many baby organs available for transplant. Mingyu have to wait long time for liver if he need it. All that time I have to hope another baby die. I not want that. No way to be."

Again, I had no good counterargument.

"I give my liver," Ting said.

"You can't give your liver. You would die," I said.

"Is okay. I know you and Lim take care my children."

I wasn't terribly worried about Ting giving her liver to Mingyu. No surgeon in this country would remove the liver of a healthy adult. But her plan gave me an idea.

"Healthy adults can donate part of their liver to children. I don't know if that would work in this case. It's just an idea, but I'll ask the team at Stanford."

I left Ting with Lim, the two of them speaking furiously in Chinese, and went to the kitchen. I opened my laptop to Google information about partial liver transplantation but found nothing relevant to Mingyu's situation that I didn't already know.

While I was there, I decided to check my email. I saw a message from Williams and opened it. I clicked on the link he sent, and saw the video of Sallow flanked by the two associates I'd described earlier. I called Zaron over and played it on the full screen. With all three men visible, I froze the picture.

"Who is that?" I asked.

"Bubba."

"Touch Bubba."

Zaron put his finger directly on the image of the man to Sallow's right, the one with the Swastika armband.

"Who is that?" I asked, pointing to Sallow himself.

No answer.

"Who is that?" I asked, pointing to the man on the other side of Sallow.

No answer.

"Who is that?" I asked, again pointing to the man to Sallow's right, the man Zaron had just identified.

"Bubba."

That was enough proof for me. Zaron knew this guy, or at least someone who looked an awful lot like him, and knew him as Bubba.

"How do you know Bubba?" I asked.

Silence. Of course. I knew the question was too complicated as soon as I'd asked it.

"When did you see Bubba?"

"Monday, August twenty-third."

Was this a coincidence? Zaron said he saw this man shortly before the first bombing.

"What did Bubba do?"

Silence. The question was too open-ended.

"Who did Bubba talk to?"

"Don."

I began hyperventilating as I felt a knot form in my stomach. Zaron was telling me there was a connection between Garrett and a man close to Sallow. This was important information. Important enough, I figured, that Garrett or Sallow wanted Zaron dead before he told anyone.

I tried to appear calm as I thought about other questions to ask. Simple questions, questions Zaron would understand.

"What did Bubba wear?" That wasn't useful information, I was only trying to come up with something, anything to ask while I thought of something more useful.

"Blue shirt, brown pants, white shoes, white socks."

Okay, okay. Now I know what he was wearing. What else should I ask? I don't know what possessed me to ask the next question. Desperation, I suppose.

"Did Bubba give something to Don?"

"Clay."

Holy shit. Clay. Zaron didn't know the difference between clay and a plastic explosive.

I was excited, ecstatic, nervous. I hugged Zaron. I wasn't sure what this all meant. I needed a little time to think. I gave Zaron some sesame fritters Fung had brought with us. I didn't often get what I consider quality thinking time, but I really needed it then. I went into the bedroom Lim and I were using and sat at the writing desk, facing a blank wall. Sallow's man Bubba supplied Garrett with the plastic explosives.

Now Bubba was working with Sallow, using explosives to murder people they hated and draw more members into their hate group. I wondered if Garrett himself was connected to the recent bombing. Although a horrible human being, there was nothing in Garrett's history that indicated he was a hate-filled racist. Everything he'd done so far had been focused on getting money. Like a bolt of lightning from somewhere in the universe, I had the answer.

Chapter 36

I was hyperventilating as I reached for my phone. I thought about discussing this with Lim before telling anyone else but decided against it as he was comforting Ting. This couldn't wait.

My chest felt tight as I pressed the call icon next to Williams's name on my phone. I feared I would burst if he didn't answer quickly. Fortunately, he did.

I began speaking before Williams finished saying his name, as was his custom when answering a call. "You're not going to believe this," I blurted out. "Zaron identified one of Sallow's men as the guy who supplied Garrett with the C4."

"He said that?"

"Not exactly. He didn't say it like that, but I played him the CNN video you sent me. Zaron identified the man to Sallow's right as Bubba, and gave me the date he visited Garrett. It was two days before the Oracle Park bombing. And, get this, he said Bubba gave Garrett clay."

"Clay?"

"Yes, that's what he said. Clay," I screamed into the phone. "C4 type clay, I'm sure."

"Damn," said Williams. "I'm not sure this fits together with—"

"I've got this figured out. Now I see it clearly. Sallow's guy Bubba supplied Garrett with the C4 used in the baseball game bombings. Then, less than a week ago, Garrett received ten million dollars from a company in Bangladesh. I'll bet you can trace that company back to Sallow. Money is no object for him. He paid Garrett ten million dollars, not as an extortion payoff, but to buy the four remaining boys. That's two-and-a-half million for each one. He's already started to use them to bomb people he hates."

There was a moment of silence before Williams spoke. "Seems a bit far-fetched, but you might be right. Could explain why Garrett wouldn't turn the boys over, and we haven't been able to locate them. And why people are trying to kill Zaron even now. They're still afraid that young man knows things that could help us."

"Exactly. And that brings me to another question which I think I know the answer to."

"What's that?"

"Has there been any progress in identifying the bomber at the Black Lives Matter rally?"

"Unfortunately, no. You think–"

"I do. Can you get a picture to show Zaron?"

"I'll get to work on it right now. It may take me a little time to arrange."

"We're not going anywhere."

I found Lim in the exercise room. He had finished talking with Ting and was about to start his workout regimen. I told him what Zaron had just helped me figure out.

"I always knew you were as brilliant as you are sexy," he said, kissing me on the cheek. His expression turned serious. "We've got to find those boys. There's probably only three left now."

"I agree. We'll know more after Zaron sees a picture of the latest bomber."

"It may be harder to find the boys now. I doubt they're in Garrett's house. Sallow's probably got them well hidden."

My phone rang. It was Williams, telling me he was coming over right away with a picture of the bomber. "One other thing," he said. "It recently came to my attention they found a letter "A" pendant they believe the bomber was wearing. I spoke to April, who thought you might be able to recognize it."

The next hour was torture while I waited for Williams. He finally arrived, bringing several photos with him. First Lim, Zaron, the agent, and I sat at the kitchen table with my laptop, and I demonstrated how Zaron had identified the man standing next to Sallow.

Then Williams showed me a photo of the pendant that had been found—a bent yellow metallic "A." It looked like it had been covered with rhinestones, but many of them had fallen off. A film of what appeared to be soot was layered on top. "Recognize this?" he asked.

"Looks like the pendant on the necklace Arthur Purcell wore when I saw him in clinic."

"It was found in the debris after the bombing. A video from someone at the event, taken a few minutes before the bombing, showed this around the neck of the person we believe was the bomber. We'd like a confirmation of the identity, though, either from you or Zaron."

"Of course," I said as I pushed my laptop out of the way. The agent placed six photos of African American males fifteen to twenty years of age on the table. Two of the images were very close up, showing just a face—no neck visible. The expression on one didn't look normal. I couldn't identify any of the young men, and held out hope that none were Arthur—or any of the other boys from Bright Lights.

After all the photos were laid out, Williams asked me if I recognized any of the young men. After I told him I didn't, I turned my attention to Zaron.

"Zaron, who is this?" I inquired, touching the first picture.

No answer.

"Zaron, who is this?" I asked, pointing to the next."

No answer.

"Zaron, who is this?" I touched the third photo, the close-up of the face with a strange expression.

"Arthur."

I took a closer look. Now he looked vaguely familiar. His hair was longer than when I'd seen him, and he had a beard, but I recognized him as the boy Brandy had brought to the clinic last year. My chest tightened and I had to wait before I could continue speaking. Arthur was such a sweet boy. Despite my efforts, I hadn't been able to save him from this horrible fate. Time was running out to save the others.

"Zaron, who is this?" I asked, pointing to the next photo, the other closeup.

No answer.

No answer to the fifth or sixth photo, either. We had our answer. The bomber at the Black Lives Matter rally was one of Zaron's fellow student, Arthur Purcell. I was glad Zaron had no idea what had happened to him.

Now I wondered about the other three. Could they all be Black? If so, they could easily mix in at other Black Lives Matter rallies.

I turned to Zaron and mentioned the names of the other students at Bright Lights who were still alive, and asked if they were Black. Zaron didn't answer. I asked him if Arthur was Black. Again, no answer. I asked if they were African American, then if they had dark skin. No answer. Zaron didn't recognize race.

"What now?" I asked. I was sure I sounded desperate, which I was. "This lunatic Sallow, or one of his guys, has the three remaining boys."

"This certainly changes things," Williams said. "I think you're right, and we can assume the boys are not with Garrett any longer. On the plus side, that gives us more latitude in arresting Garrett at home, not having to worry about the boys' safety. Agents have determined there is a dog living at one of the two homes in Malibu on Lim's list. Although the names of the registered owners are not Garrett or Powell, I strongly suspect that's where they live. We have agents in the area who will get a warrant tonight so they can search the house first thing in the morning. We need to find the boys quickly."

"I doubt Sallow's guys are taking good care of them and probably want to get rid of them quickly. The way I see it, the boys are in danger of being blown up and blowing up others any minute."

"Arresting Garrett may help us find them, but we'll also have agents follow Sallow and look into the whereabouts of this Bubba fellow. This is top priority."

"Where does Sallow live?" I asked.

"Sallow has three residences in the South. Atlanta, Miami, and Charleston. He moves around frequently. We don't know anything about the other man, Bubba, though I can assure you, it's only a question of time. If he has a record, if he's out on parole, he may be easier to track down."

"Who do you think has the boys?" Lim asked.

"Probably this Bubba character. I doubt Sallow has the patience to deal with them. Bubba has at least met them before and may have received some training from Garrett regarding managing them."

"I'm worried there will be another bombing before they're found," I said.

"Me, too, ma'am. If we only knew where they plan to attack next, we could at least monitor the crowd. It was easier when the bombings were being used to extort money."

The agent left with me feeling no better than before he came.

"I know I won't sleep tonight," I said to Lim. "I'm glad Zaron is safe for the time being, but there's danger to so many others out there, and there's nothing I can do about it. Let's hope they find Garrett at his house tomorrow and get him to cooperate. I'll bet he knows where the boys are."

"That would be wonderful, but I have a feeling it's not going to be that easy."

It was late. Everyone in the house was asleep except Zaron, Lim, and me. I told Zaron to get ready for bed. Lim and I each had a cup of herbal tea and went to bed shortly after Zaron. I was wrong about one thing. I fell asleep quickly. But it wasn't a restful sleep. My nightmares were so intense I felt fatigued in the morning, even after finishing the coffee Lim brought me.

I wanted to hear soon that Garrett had been found and put under arrest. Then, at least, we could all go home. Zaron would no longer be in danger, and Garrett might lead the FBI to the remaining three boys. I could return to work and a semblance of a normal life.

Lim and I ate breakfast with our cell phones close by. We didn't want to miss a call from the FBI or April, should it come. I felt startled with every sudden noise. After breakfast Lim and I drank more coffee and talked about what we'd do once Garrett was in custody. Zaron proceeded to clear the table as usual, then began working on a puzzle. I watched him, mesmerized by his almost otherworldly ability to put a puzzle together, and couldn't imagine not having him around. I thought about telling Lim I'd been thinking about adopting Zaron. I started to speak, but was interrupted.

It was 10:30 a.m., almost on the dot, when both my phone and Lim's rang simultaneously. I jumped at the sound and took the call. It was Williams. While he spoke, I overheard Lim speaking to another agent.

"I thought you'd want to know. We located Garrett's house," Williams said. A sense of relief washed over me. "Garrett's girlfriend, Lydia Powell, is now in custody. Unfortunately, Garrett wasn't there."

"Do you know where he is?" I asked. *Shit. Won't I ever be able to go home?*

"We haven't been able to nail that down yet, but the girlfriend is cooperating, answering all our questions, even volunteering information on her own. I was told she broke down and started blaming Garrett as soon as the agents identified themselves. Said she was forced into going along with him. Claims she didn't think he meant it when he started talking about his plan. When the bomb went off at Oracle Park, she realized he was dead serious, but by then she couldn't leave. We'll probably never know the complete truth. She had to know about the boys' training and the burns on their arms."

"I'll say. I don't see her as a victim."

"That'll be for a jury to decide, I suppose. You might be interested to know how they pulled off their escape from the boat explosion."

"I think a lot of people would like to know."

"According to Powell, Garrett rigged up explosives. He threw in some paper mache arms and legs so witnesses would see them go up in the blast before they burned up. Several minutes before the explosion, Powell and Garrett escaped in a small submarine, a toy Garrett had bought a few years earlier. Powell said she felt bad leaving the crew member behind."

"It's a little late for that. Does she know where Garrett is now?"

"Says he's helping out a guy named Bernard Crawford, known as Bubba. She confirmed Bubba's the guy with the C4."

"Looks like everything Zaron told us was accurate."

"Remarkably so. We owe him." Williams paused a moment before continuing. "Apparently, the boys are with Crawford. Garrett was pissed when Crawford asked for help with one of the boys. Something about shoes. Before he left, Garrett said this was the very last time he'd help. After this, he was through with Crawford and his people, their crazy ideas, and the boys. Powell figured this guy Crawford isn't experienced with all the ins and outs of managing young autistic men. She doesn't know what airport Garrett flew to, but it's someplace in the south. Shouldn't be hard to track down. She told us he's using the name Robert Stone now. He's shaved his head, grown a beard, and wears large black glasses."

"Do your agents believe everything she's telling them? It seems she's been surprisingly talkative. Aren't they a bit suspicious, with her spilling all this information?"

"So far, it all fits together and agrees with what Zaron has told us. One thing I didn't mention—Powell said Garrett's got a temper and beat her before he left. She had a fractured wrist and a black eye."

"Forgive me for not being sympathetic."

Chapter 37

I received calls throughout the morning updating me on the investigation's progress. It didn't take long for the FBI to learn Garrett had flown to Birmingham, Alabama, and hadn't returned. Lim and I felt it was safe to go back home, with Garrett thousands of miles away. The arrest of his girlfriend was kept under wraps, so he'd have no way of knowing.

Old photos of Garrett, and mug shots of Bernard Crawford taken eight months prior after his arrest for an unprovoked assault on an African American male, were distributed to law enforcement departments throughout the state of Alabama. The photos were accompanied by an artist's rendering showing Garrett with the changes Powell had described. Finding Garrett, now going by Robert Stone, and Crawford was a top priority.

Sallow was planning to hold another one of his hate-filled rallies that evening, this time in Birmingham. Agents were optimistic they'd have Crawford in custody soon, as he had been a constant presence next to Sallow at the rallies. They would hold off on arresting him until they followed him to the boys after the rally. Arresting Sallow, a wealthy man with almost infinite lawyering-up capabilities, would be more problematic. So far, there were no direct ties between him and the bombings, as Zaron hadn't identified him.

At 12:20 p.m. I got a call from Williams. "Are you watching your TV?" he asked.

"No, I'm sitting here with Zaron going over math problems."

"You might want to turn it on. There's been another bombing. It was really bad. Lots of metal fragments were used."

"One of our boys?" I asked, my voice cracking.

"Probably. The information is just coming in now. It happened less than ten minutes ago."

"Where?"

There was a moment of silence. "Birmingham."

I understood his hesitation. Everything had been pointing to something about to take place there. Garrett had flown to Birmingham, and another Sallow rally was scheduled there that evening. Even knowing that, the FBI had been unable to prevent the bombing.

"Where did it happen? What sort of event?"

"Noon prayers in a large mosque."

"Another hate crime, but I wasn't expecting a mosque would be hit next."

"Frankly, neither were we. We were getting ready for Sallow's rally in Birmingham this evening."

I thought a moment. Now I understood the comment about shoes. "Garrett probably went there to teach one of the boys to take off his shoes before entering the mosque."

"Makes sense."

Still connected to Williams, I turned on the TV and flipped channels until I found live coverage of the event. "Looks terrible," I said, seeing images of bodies lying around, people with bloody wounds, and fragments of plaster and wood scattered on the floor. There was no estimate of casualties yet. "What's your next step?"

"This time, we want to show Zaron a picture of the bomber as soon as it's available. There's no point going through our normal procedures first. We just received word about the Bangladesh clothing company that paid Garrett. It's owned by Sallow. You were right about that. The FBI is sending a photographer to the site of the mosque bombing now. Once they send me the image, I'll print it and bring it to you. If it's one of the boys, which I suspect it is, we'll know pretty quickly."

"Then what?"

"We have to find the boys right after Sallow's rally this evening. I'm pretty sure Sallow is planning another bombing very soon. There's a Black Lives Matter rally scheduled for later tonight."

"Where?"

"Birmingham."

"Damn."

"We're trying to stop the Black Lives Matter rally as we speak. Our agents are talking to the people organizing it."

"Although I'm sure the FBI isn't their favorite organization, they've got to cooperate with you."

"That's what I'm hoping. It may take some time, though, to convince them the FBI is on their side. I hope to get the picture soon and see you in the next sixty minutes."

I spent most of the next hour watching the news as the numbers rolled in. At least sixteen dead, twenty-eight injured, some critically. I was relieved when Williams arrived and interrupted the horror on display.

I had Zaron sit next to him at the kitchen table, while I stood behind Zaron's chair. Williams took out a single close-up photo of a dark-skinned young man with a partially swollen face and wavy black hair. I was so overwhelmed by nausea, I had to wait a moment before I could speak.

"Who is that?" I asked, reaching over Zaron's shoulder and touching the picture.

"Martin."

In his usual even, unemotional voice, Zaron had just identified the bomber as another of his classmates—this time Martin, the one with the incredible memory for baseball scores. I broke into tears and took a chair at the table as Zaron sat passively.

Williams said, "If there was any doubt before, I think there's none now—the boys have been turned over or, to be more accurate, sold to this white nationalist group." He took a folded piece of paper from his shirt pocket and opened it. There I saw a list of the eight students who had been enrolled in Bright Lights. A line had been drawn through four of the names. He clicked his pen and, shaking his head, drew a line through the name Martin Rich. That left only Zaron Johnson and two other names not crossed off, still alive as far as we knew. He folded the list and returned it to his pocket.

Lim entered the kitchen, surprised to see me sitting next to the agent, crying. "What happened?" he asked, taking the empty chair next to me and wrapping an arm around my shoulder. I hadn't interrupted his work to tell him about the bombing. I didn't feel I could speak without breaking down, and I knew he'd find out eventually.

Williams explained what had transpired, and Lim looked visibly upset.

"There's two boys left in addition to Zaron," Lim said. "You need to find them."

"We're trying. We've alerted all the Alabama airports to notify us if Garrett, or Robert Stone as he's known now, checks in. We have agents standing by to arrest him immediately."

"What about this guy Crawford? And Sallow?" Lim asked.

Williams explained the plan to follow Crawford to the boys after Sallow's rally that evening. "With the boys safe, there will be no bombing at the next Black Lives Matter rally."

"So, you don't think they need to call it off?"

"I didn't say that. Our plan is to rescue the boys before the rally takes place. We can't count on that happening, so we're trying to get the leaders to cancel. It would be dangerous to have the rally before we have the boys."

"Once you have the boys and arrest Crawford, then what?" I asked.

"We should be able to apprehend Garrett soon. Zaron can identify both Crawford and Garrett. His identification may not hold up in court, to be honest. A good attorney will most likely try to convince a jury he's an unreliable witness. But his identification is enough for us to arrest both of them and start collecting evidence, even if Powell stops cooperating, and the boys we hopefully rescue can't tell us anything. Since we don't have any direct evidence Sallow is involved, we hope Garrett or Crawford will implicate him."

"What about the ten million Sallow paid Garrett?" Lim asked.

"Circumstantial only. No way to prove what the money was for with what we have now."

"So, we wait? Until Sallow's rally tonight? Or Garrett shows up at the airport?"

"That's right. Whichever happens first, we should have the boys tonight."

Williams promised to keep us informed and left. Lim and I kept our phones close. I was optimistic we could return home the next day. Meanwhile, dividing my time between Zaron and playing with Ting's children kept my mind distracted. Some of the time. At 2:30 p.m., April called.

"Williams wanted me to tell you that Garrett, using the name Robert Stone, recently checked in at the Birmingham-Shuttlesworth Airport to catch a plane to LAX. Agents are on the way to make the arrest."

I felt almost lightheaded, and started to laugh. The relief was hard to describe. "One down, two to go," I said, thinking of Crawford and Sallow still out there, in need of being put behind bars. "Let me know when that bastard Garrett is actually in custody. I hope he tells them where the boys are quickly. They could get them before Sallow's rally."

"That would be ideal," April said, "but he probably won't be inclined to cooperate. From what I can tell, he hates the government, the FBI, and anyone who gets in his way."

I told Lim about Garrett's impending capture, feeling this news was important enough to interrupt his work.

"What's your expression?" he asked. "Don't count your chickens before they hatch?"

"Why do you say that?" I was surprised he'd gotten that expression right.

"A lot could go wrong. Let's wait to celebrate until after Garrett's in custody."

Fifteen minutes passed slowly, and I still hadn't heard anything. Then a half hour. Finally, a phone call, this time from Williams.

"I'm afraid I don't have good news," he said.

I didn't think I could handle bad news right then, not when they were finally on the verge of rescuing the boys. "What does that mean?"

"He got away." My chest tightened. "There's no sugarcoating it. Garrett had a plastic gun hidden under his clothes."

"You mean a toy gun?"

"No, plastic. Probably made on a 3-D printer. They didn't pick it up with the metal detector at the airport. No metal parts. The bullets weren't picked up, either. We suspect they were special, contained no iron."

The explanation was making me crazy. I didn't care why he'd gotten away, I only wanted to know where he was. "Where did he go?" I yelled. "Is he on the loose again?"

"Yes. Two agents tried to arrest him at the gate, but he took a pregnant female hostage with his gun. Shot one bullet in the air so they'd know the gun was real. It was a long, drawn-out ordeal. Swat teams were called in as he made his way out of the airport. Sadly, they couldn't get a clear shot. The hostage was hysterical. He forced her into a cab with him and escaped. The woman was later found a half-mile away. She appears to be okay, but we don't have him."

"So now he knows we're onto his new identity."

"Yes, you can be sure of that."

"Do you think we need to stay here, or is it safe for us go home?"

"Good question. Garrett knows we don't need Zaron anymore. He knows we know who he is and what he looks like. I'd say there's nothing more Zaron, you, or your family members can do to endanger him. You should be safe at home."

"Wonderful. Is there any way I can watch Sallow's rally this evening? I'm sure it won't be covered on live TV."

"I'll email instructions to stream it live."

I told Lim it was safe to go home, and we began packing our things. My in-laws insisted on sweeping and vacuuming the areas we'd used. We were back in our condominium a little after 4:30 p.m. Lim and I decided to keep Zaron with us until bedtime.

It felt good to be sitting on my own couch, with my feet on my own coffee table. I balanced my laptop on my thighs and turned it on. Sallow's event was set to start in twenty minutes. Zaron sat at the kitchen table and played Word Search on my iPad, while I followed the instructions Williams had emailed me and logged into the video streaming service covering the rally. Cut off from Facebook and YouTube, Sallow had found a small live-streaming service, Burst, with no scruples. For all I knew, he owned it. I registered using a Gmail account under the name "secondamendmentforever" and began watching.

I'd never seen a more menacing crowd. Mostly men under the age of forty, all white. There were piercings, tattoos, swastikas, confederate flags, beer bellies, muscles, and a good amount of leather. I saw a lot of drinking from beer bottles and flasks, as well as many a shared doobie. Small squabbles broke out but were quickly resolved. Some rally participants brandished weapons—guns, chains, all sorts of knives, blackjacks, and brass knuckles. There was a general rowdiness to the crowd. I imagined it wouldn't take much to set Sallow's supporters off on a rampage. Looking at them, it struck me that someone associated with this group was probably the driver of the car that tried to run over Zaron.

Finally Sallow, wearing khaki pants, a white shirt, red tie, and blue blazer, took the stage. Loud cheering followed. My chest tightened when I didn't see his sidekick, Bernard Crawford. Instead, he was surrounded by three men I didn't recognize. I could only hope Crawford was somewhere in the crowd and the FBI was watching him.

Sallow started by quieting his adoring fans, waving and motioning downward with outstretched arms. When the time was right, he began to speak, and the crowd quickly settled down.

"I want to thank you all for coming here tonight. We have some very important business in front of us. Our nation needs us badly. We're on the brink of ruin. You know it, and I know it."

Sallow ranted on about baby-killing liberals and groups of people he referred to in the most hateful, base, manner. He used all the racial epithets against Blacks, Hispanics, Jews, Muslims, Asians, and members of the LGBTQ community I knew, as well as some I'd never heard before. People in the crowd began echoing his cringeworthy racial slurs as they continued to drink and smoke weed.

"These animals want to destroy our way of living, but the good citizens of our community are fighting back. We've seen what's happened lately—death and destruction at a Black Lives rally and a carpet-kissing ceremony. I'm sure nobody here had anything to do with those events—" Sallow paused while the crowd erupted in laughter— "but given the deplorable state of our once great nation, it's no surprise things like this are happening. There will be more to come. The public is fed up with these liberals and their hate of good, true American white folks like us."

The crowd hooted and cheered loudly, as Sallow scanned the crowd, a pleased look on his face.

"See? You know what I mean, and you know it's true. Now, talk is easy. But I have a strategy that's sure to help. Tonight, I'm going to tell you about my plan. It's all going to start in this beautiful state of Alabama, where the state motto is, 'We dare defend our rights!'"

Sallow waited a full five minutes before continuing as the crowd cheered and got more drunk, high, and raucous.

"We're going to start local where things that matter most to folks on a daily basis are decided. See these fine men up here with me?"

More hoots and cheers.

"Each and every one of them has agreed to run for local office under the new political party I am now launching. It's called the Righteous Party. Remember that name because you're going to hear a lot about it. The Righteous Party." Sallow stopped as he was handed four red baseball caps from someone who had been off-camera. He put one hat on his head, displaying "Righteous Party" in white lettering under an American flag on the front. As the crowd clapped and cheered, he handed matching hats to the three men standing by him, all of whom smiled and waved as they donned the hats. "History is being made now, and you'll be able to proudly tell your grandchildren you were here when this all started. You're all a big piece of history now."

The crowd roared with excitement. Sallow waited patiently for the noise to subside, then went on to introduce the men beside him. A middle-aged man with a shaved head, wearing a T-shirt and sport coat closed tightly over his pot belly, was running for school board. A red-headed man looking around thirty years old, wearing a long-sleeved white shirt and holding a long gun by the barrel in his left hand, was a candidate for city council. The third man, a muscular older individual, wore a Hawaiian shirt revealing forearms covered with swastika and Confederate flag tattoos. He had his sights on the state legislature.

After each man was introduced, members of the crowd registered their approval loudly. Then Sallow read the names of more men who were also planning to run for office. The platform was simple. Non-whites and non-Christians weren't welcome. Members of the LGBTQ community needed to get the hell out of their state.

Sallow ended the rally by predicting more violence would come to unwelcome intruders. While being careful not to say anything to tie him to past or future atrocities, he said violent acts were inevitable given the dire situation they were in. Sallow's whole rally lasted only a little over thirty minutes, but it left me shaken. Less than five minutes after it ended, Williams called.

"We're in deep shit," he began. "Crawford didn't show up at the rally."

Chapter 38

My chest felt heavy as I made an effort to breathe. "What now? We were counting on that."

"I know. We have to come up with a new plan. And the rally—it was bad, really bad."

"I know. I saw the whole thing."

"So, you know Sallow is on a rampage against every minority group in this country and is starting a new political party with a grass-roots campaign to put party members on local ballots. I'm sure the two recent bombings were timed to generate enthusiasm, and he's planning to add to the frenzy by using the two remaining boys to set off more bombs in the near future."

"Clever. After setting off a total of four bombs in quick succession, he'll probably gain supporters who will follow him anywhere."

"Meanwhile, the Black Lives Matter organizers don't even have metal detectors set up, and we don't have time to get them—not that they've helped in the past. We'd like to bring in bomb-sniffing dogs, but they won't allow that, either. Cops with dogs doesn't go over well with this crowd. The leadership here is refusing to cancel or postpone their rally. They feel we are using the threat of a bombing as a ruse to suppress them."

"Damn. There's no doubt in my mind Sallows's planning to bomb it."

"That's what we're thinking. We have no choice but to try to stop the next bomber from entering the rally. We'll try, but I'm not sure we'll be able to pick him out in tonight's crowd. The rally starts in thirty minutes, and we don't have a good plan. If we suspect someone and physically restrain him, I imagine it will turn ugly, especially if that person turns out not to be our bomber."

"I have an idea," I said. "See if the rally organizers will allow you to have agents speak to every male attendee who appears to be between the ages of twelve and twenty-five. Have them ask questions about Spotify, or Facebook, or Drake's latest song. Open-ended questions. See if they can talk like a normal person. Or tell a joke and see if they laugh. If someone doesn't respond normally, if he remains quiet or gives a one-word or meaningless answer, have agents standing by to quickly look for a vest under his clothes, prepared to neutralize a bomb if need be. In addition, set up a live video feed for me so I can have Zaron watch. I'll see if Zaron can identify anyone as they're being questioned."

"That might be our best chance. It's highly irregular, but so is this whole case. I'll see if the organizers will let us set up tables for interviewing and videoing males in the appropriate age group. Already, I'm told, there are white nationalists causing trouble outside the rally site. I'd better hurry. Bye."

I was left wondering if what I set in motion would work. I began to unpack but didn't get very far when my phone rang. Williams again.

"Okay, we're getting things in place," he said. "Fortunately, the Black Lives Matter organizers have agreed to our plan. The local police have formed a wall and are preventing everyone from entering the rally venue. The screening area they're setting up isn't visible to the crowd waiting outside, so no one will know about it until they enter. The situation is very tense. The crowd of white nationalists and legitimate rally goers outside is growing."

"Mixing those groups together can't be good," I said.

"You're right about that," Williams said. "I'm told there have been several fights already, with two knifings. I heard an ambulance siren over the phone moments ago. I'm going to send you a link and password to our VPN network as soon as we hang up. Sign in and have Zaron ready to look at people. Once you log in, be aware that I or one of my associates will be listening to the audio coming from you."

"Okay, I'll try not to say anything too embarrassing," I said chuckling slightly.

Williams responded in his usual, humorless manner. "That would be good." He paused a moment before continuing. "We have a lot of agents here. We're setting up six screening stations. An agent will be seated behind a table at each one, and will be prepared to ask questions. They're discussing the best way to do that with a behaviorist right now. I've got lots to do in the next few minutes. Any questions?"

"No."

"Okay. Just make sure Zaron stays there. Keep him focused."

"Got it."

"Bye."

I found Williams's email and followed the VPN login instructions. Once done, I had a live feed of the rally venue. It was stomach-turning to watch, as whoever had the camera was moving it around randomly. I sat next to Zaron and asked him to watch with me. I told Lim to see if his mom had any sesame fritters.

Finally, the camera was still, and I saw a row of six tables set up, an agent sitting behind each one. The computer screen suddenly split in two, as live feed from a second camera came into view. Within seconds, I was looking at the real-time streaming from six cameras. I heard someone yelling in the background, what sounded like doors opening, then people rushing in. Several loud voices directed individual members of the crowd to either enter the rally through a large space to the left, or stand in one of the lines in front of tables set up on the right. Some people argued when asked to stand in the queue, but tempers remained calm as someone who identified herself as one of the rally organizers instructed everyone to cooperate.

The agents holding cameras took positions behind the agents staffing the stations and focused on the faces of the young men opposite, standing in front of the tables. With the cameras shooting over the heads of the seated agents, Zaron and I had unobstructed views of the faces of all the young men being interviewed. I could hear what they were saying, although, with multiple simultaneous conversations, it was sometimes difficult to follow.

One young man after the other conversed with the agents, who asked questions about sports, movies, school, and music. Some looked angry, while others were expressionless or had confused expressions on their faces. I tried to imagine how strange it must have seemed to be forced into a meaningless conversation with an FBI agent before being allowed to enter the rally venue.

As each young man was waved through and allowed to pass between the tables after a short assessment, the next one stood in his place. With each new face, I touched the screen and asked Zaron the name. He remained silent.

The screening was moving along quickly when Lim arrived with a plate full of sesame fritters and placed it on the table. Zaron seemed content as he ate the treats and looked at the faces on the screen.

It took twenty minutes for Zaron to finish most of the fritters. With only two left, I would soon need to think of something else to keep his attention. A young Black male in dreadlocks, wearing a tattered Harvard T-shirt stood in front of a table, his face expressionless. The agent asked him what his favorite car was. No answer. Then he asked what his favorite TV show was. Still no answer. Did I detect a hint of annoyance in the boy's demeanor, or was he trying, yet unable, to speak? I couldn't tell.

I tapped the screen wildly. "Who is that, Zaron?"

No answer. My pulse quickened. *Shit, that's got to be the bomber. What should I do?*

Then the agent asked, "What's the hypotenuse of a right triangle where one side is four and the other is three?"

The youth sneered, and said, "Easy. It's five. You're so full of shit. I bet you thought I was too stupid to know that."

The agent let him through. It was annoyance I'd seen in his face after all.

A few minutes later, as Zaron ate the last fritter, another Black youth with an expressionless face approached an agent. The boy had unkempt hair and wore a dirty green T-shirt with the name of a sport's team on the front. The agent's questions about sports and music were ignored. I tapped the screen and Zaron looked up.

"Who is it?" I asked. I'm sure I sounded like an anxious crazy person.

"Derrick."

I recognized that as the name belonging to the extraordinary artist at Bright Lights. I screamed into my computer, "Did you hear that! That's him! It's Derrick! Zaron identified him!" I kept yelling until the young man was grabbed and brought down. It seemed like an eternity although, in fact, it only took seconds. I didn't see any more of the youth as people swarmed around, although agents ordered them to back up. Many in the crowd were yelling and taking videos on their cell phones, in keeping with the common practice of videoing police activity for evidence of brutality. My chest was tight, my stomach in knots, and I was hyperventilating. All I knew was, so far there had been no bomb detonation. Minutes of pandemonium followed, the jerky video streams showing parts of random people at strange angles, with so much noise I could only understand an occasional spoken word.

Finally, an agent faced one of the cameras and spoke to me directly. He was breathless and had a slight smile on his face. Good sign, I thought.

"Thank you both," he said. "Zaron, you're a real hero." Expressionless, Zaron got up and walked away from the table, looking for something more interesting, now that the sesame fritters were gone. He found a red ball lying on the floor and began to bounce it.

"What happened?" I asked.

The agent was breathing a little slower when he answered. "The young man Zaron identified, well, he was wired up with a vest containing bricks of a substance, most likely C4. Our bomb team deactivated the bomb, and the boy is fine. We're keeping him under tight security, where he'll be safe."

People continued to stream into the venue behind the agent. "Fabulous," I said, feeling the tension leave my body. "But don't forget, you need to keep screening the crowd. There could be another bomber."

"Don't worry. They're still screening at the tables, but most are already inside the auditorium now. Hang on for a few more minutes. I don't think we'll see a second bomber tonight. I doubt this guy wanted to shoot his whole wad in one place."

I called Zaron back to the table, where he took up Word Search again. I directed his attention to every new face on the screen, with no reaction. Ten minutes later, we were done. The doors to the rally were closed, and nobody else was let in. I heard the muffled voice of the rally master of ceremonies in the background.

I kissed Zaron and thanked him. He tolerated the gesture without interrupting his Word Search. Lim, who had been standing behind me the whole time, poured two glasses of wine.

"I think you need this," he said, handing one to me. "Even if you don't, I sure do."

I took one of the glasses and smiled. "Thanks, honey," I said. I drank slowly, appreciating the flavor more than usual. "How about another," I said after I'd finished my glass. "After all, I'm going to be starting the IVF process soon. If all goes well, this will be one of my last tastes of wine for a while."

Lim smiled as he poured me another glass.

I was relieved the rally was kept safe and they had one of the boys safely tucked away. But Crawford was still out there, as was the one remaining boy, Kyle. I wondered what Crawford would do once he saw footage of Derrick on the ground surrounded by FBI agents. I hoped Derrick had information to help them find the other boy. He would have to be approached with skill and care.

I realized the need for me to protect Zaron from Garrett and his associates was coming to an end. I had some decisions to make.

Chapter 39

Thirty minutes later, my cell phone rang. Williams. I answered, hungry for news.

"I thought you might like to know how things are developing," he began.

No shit. "Of course," I answered, politely.

"Derrick is scarfing down a burger and fries at a diner a mile away from the rally. He's with three FBI agents and a behaviorist who works at Open Vistas, a residence for developmentally disabled adults a few hundred miles from here."

"I've never heard of it."

"It's a really nice place, they tell me. Lots of space, horses, walking and biking trails, good food, and nice apartments. The staff is huge with two speech pathologists, three behaviorists, and I don't know how many teachers, so the people who live there continue to learn. Basically, you have to be the kid of someone very rich to live there."

"Sounds lovely. I didn't even know such places existed." I wondered if Open Vistas might be the perfect place for Zaron. He might even do better at a place like that than if I adopted him. I set that thought aside, certain it was financially out of reach.

"We had contacted them earlier today and were told one of the behaviorists happened to be in Birmingham, so we called him. I'm told he's been a big help."

"That's wonderful," I said. I was glad they weren't expecting me to try to get Derrick to talk over a phone connection. "Has he said anything yet?"

"He answers 'I don't know' to everything they ask."

"That means he doesn't want to talk. It's his way of saying, 'Get out of my face.'"

"That's pretty much what the behaviorist told our agents. Progress with Derrick has been slow. So far, he hasn't said anything of substance, but they were able to get some useful information from the cameras they'd set up outside before the Black Lives Matter rally. Derrick is wearing a green shirt, which was a big help because it made it easy to trace his steps. We saw him get out of a car as close to the event as anyone could drive. The car double-parked and a man got out with him. He kept his face low, but I think it was Crawford. He directed Derrick toward the entrance, waited to be sure he went in the door, then left."

"Could you tell what kind of car it was?"

"Better than that. We got the plates."

"That's great. How soon till you can find him?"

"We put a rush on tracing the plates. The car was stolen two days ago. Now we've got cops all around the city and surrounding areas looking for it. So far, zilch."

"Nothing about this case has been easy," I commented.

"Unfortunately, that's usually the way it is. The pieces don't fall neatly in place like on TV. We need to sift through all the information we have and decide what is useful, what isn't, and how to use what we have to solve the case and catch the bad guys."

Just like medicine. Once a diagnosis is made, in retrospect, the information makes for a compelling conclusion. But while you're working up a case, you need to decide which symptoms or history are relevant, which are not, and what tests may be a false positive or negative. Then you need to decide on a treatment.

"Can I see Derrick?" I asked.

"Hold on. I'll have one of the agents with him Skype you."

Within a minute, I received a message from Skype telling me John Doe was trying to contact me. I accepted and was greeted by a middle-aged man who identified himself as a Special Agent. He introduced me to the two other agents and the behaviorist sitting around the table. The agents, a man and a woman each around thirty years old, had short hair and wore dark suits. They contrasted sharply with the behaviorist, a balding man with a ponytail, wearing a beige T-shirt.

The agent turned his camera to Derrick, hurriedly stuffing fries into his mouth between gulps from a Pepsi can. I basked in the joy of seeing this sweet-looking young man seeming so happy after weeks of being in the hands of monsters, where, I imagined, he was probably deprived of all but the barest of necessities.

"His shirt," I yelled. "What does it say?"

Someone's hand straightened out Derrick's shirt, crumpled against his thin body, revealing the inscription "Alabama Buckhorns" over a picture of a bat and ball.

"I'll bet that's a shirt from a local team," I said. "Maybe it's from a high school."

"I suppose it could be."

"Crawford could live in the area where the team plays. Can you find out where that is?"

I heard the agents speak among themselves before one spoke up. "Seems like a good task for a rookie."

There was more muffled speaking in the background, which I hoped was the rookie making calls about the Buckhorns.

"Where is Derrick going to stay tonight? I asked.

"He'll stay with me," said the behaviorist. "I'm crashing with friends, and there's plenty of room."

Derrick continued to eat as I heard more indistinct voices in the background.

The agent turned the camera back to himself. "Gardendale," he said, "a small town about ten miles outside of Birmingham. That's where the Alabama Buckhorns used to play some years back. Their colors were green and yellow. We're sending more cars out there. I'll be in touch with Williams."

Before I could say goodbye, he disconnected the video chat.

Lim and I decided it would be best if Zaron slept in our condominium on the sofa bed that night in case we needed him to identify his remaining classmate. After he went to sleep, I tried to read my medical journals at the kitchen table but had difficulty concentrating. Lim worked in the study.

At 2:00 a.m., Lim emerged to tell me Garrett had transferred a third of his wealth to banks in Qatar. He kept his voice low to avoid waking Zaron. "He's out there somewhere," Lim said. "Probably planning to get to Qatar. I checked. The US doesn't have an extradition treaty with them."

"Sickening if he gets away with everything."

"On the other hand, he'll be stuck living in Qatar," Lim said.

"There's a lot of money there. I'm sure he'll be able to get what he needs to live a comfortable life. Very comfortable."

Finally, at 3:00 a.m., the call I'd been waiting for came. I realized I'd fallen asleep while reading, my right cheek stuck against the page of the journal in front of me on the kitchen table. As I lifted my head, I saw Zaron stir, but the call didn't wake him. The light in the study was on, meaning Lim was still hard at work.

"We've got 'em," Williams said.

"Kyle?"

"Kyle and Crawford."

I didn't remember ever feeling so excited. "Is Kyle okay?"

"Kyle is fine and Crawford's in custody. When our agents broke in, Crawford was asleep. He didn't put up much of a fight. Didn't even try to pull out the handgun under his pillow."

"All talk and no action," I said.

"That's often the case with these losers. The stolen car was parked in the carport, right where they could see it. Not the brightest bulb, as they say. Before our agents broke into the house, they had Derrick confirm it was the house where he'd stayed with Crawford and Kyle. The behaviorist helped with that."

"I'm sure that removed any doubt you had the right place. Especially given Derrick's memory for drawing buildings."

"Absolutely. Turns out Crawford's been renting a nice house in a good neighborhood. We learned he'd been laid off from his middle-management job about three years ago. That's when his wife left him, took the kids, and moved to another state. Crawford got the house but hasn't had a job since."

"You think that's why he started making bombs?"

"Hard to say. He may have decided he didn't have time for a job after he became involved with fringe groups and learned how to make bombs. Or maybe he started making bombs because he couldn't find work. Not sure which came first. The old chicken and egg problem. At any rate, his house was foreclosed on two years ago. He's been renting in the same neighborhood but was about to be evicted."

"I imagine he blames all sorts of people for his troubles."

"That wouldn't be surprising, but our agents haven't questioned him yet."

"I'll bet his house is full of evidence."

"Agents will be sifting through everything tomorrow. In plain site, on his dresser, were several rechargeable cigarette lighters with coils on one end that get red hot. From the description, I'd say they were used to make those burns on the boys' arms."

"What about Kyle? Where was he?"

"Kyle was in a small bedroom with the windows covered. He was chained to a bed, wearing only underwear. Soiled underwear. I've seen pictures and can tell you the conditions were pretty pitiful. Poor kid was filthy. There was another bed in the room where, we assume, Derrick had been chained."

"Will Kyle be able to stay with the behaviorist too?"

"They're calling him now. I think the behaviorist will be fine with that. He's already arranged to take Derrick to Open Vistas tomorrow. They offered to put him up for a few days there. I'm hoping they can do the same for Kyle. But first, they're looking for a twenty-four-hour hamburger joint. This kid looks hungry. He probably hasn't eaten for a while."

"It's over. Finally, over," I said. "Thank you, thank you so much."

"Thank *you*, for all your help. We still have to find Garrett, but the boys are safe, and you've been a huge part of that."

"Don't forget, Zaron's really the one who led you to finding these boys and preventing another bombing."

"You're right. I'm sure none of us will forget his role. Now, finding Garrett will be up to us. Looks like we're on our own to get that done."

I paused a moment, then said, "Don't be surprised if Kyle removes all the lettuce and pickles on his hamburger. He won't eat anything green." I visualized Kyle carefully picking out all the green items from his burger and putting them on the side of his plate.

"We'll tell them to leave the green stuff off. Least we can do."

"Finally, I can sleep," I said to Lim as soon as the call ended. I filled him in on how they'd found Kyle, and about the offer by Open Vistas to put Derrick up for a few days. Hopefully they'd do the same for Kyle.

"I know what you're thinking," Lim said.

"How could you know that?"

"How could I not? I see those wheels turning in your head."

"Okay, what am I thinking?"

"You're thinking Open Vistas might be the perfect place for Zaron and the other boys, and you'd like to find a way for them to stay there forever. I'm right, aren't I?"

"Damn you, Lim. I hate it when you do that."

"No, you don't."

Although I did think Open Vistas might be the perfect place for Zaron, I hadn't given up on the idea of adopting him. I put thoughts of Zaron and the other boys aside as Lim grabbed me and led me into the bedroom. I didn't resist as he locked the door. We didn't get to sleep for at least an hour. I slept very well.

*

The next morning, Monday, Lim and I slept late. Lim woke me with a cup of coffee around nine-thirty. I was glad I hadn't told Martha I'd be in to work. By the time I was up and dressed, Zaron had already eaten a bowl of cereal and was busy looking at flashcards. Lim and I had a leisurely breakfast, and he left for work. I was feeling relaxed and thought about bringing Zaron downstairs to stay with my in-laws.

Instead, I called Daisy and invited her over to spend more time with Zaron. Daisy said she'd be over at noon, when she planned to take a break from her work and have lunch. I made sandwiches and had just finished when Daisy rang from the entrance of the building. I buzzed her in and turned to Zaron.

"We're going to have a visitor."

Zaron continued his flashcards without looking up. When Daisy was at my the front door, I let her in. We hugged—it had been an unusually long time since we'd gotten together. Daisy walked over to Zaron and smiled.

"Hi, Zaron," she said.

"Hi, Daisy," he responded without looking up.

We both laughed. "That's what happened the first time we met," Daisy said.

"Not exactly," I said. "This time he said 'Hi' right away, and he didn't cover his ears."

We ate our sandwiches, Zaron scarfing his down, Daisy and I eating at a leisurely pace as we chatted about recent events. When we were done, Zaron cleared the plates, and put them in the dishwasher.

"Wow, I'd sure like a guy like that," Daisy said.

"I know. I would miss him if he weren't around."

Zaron poured a three-hundred-piece jigsaw puzzle on the table and began to put it together. Daisy and I talked for the next thirty minutes as we watched him work on the puzzle.

"What else does he like to do?" Daisy asked after Zaron had placed the last piece of the puzzle in its place.

"Zaron, what would you like to do now?" I asked as Zaron began to disassemble the puzzle and place the pieces back in the box.

No answer. I don't know why I asked him that. The question was too open-ended, but I suppose I wanted to pretend Zaron could and would respond normally. I thought about the red ball he played with the night before. I didn't know where it was, but I was sure Zaron could find it easily. "Get a toy," I said.

To my surprise, Zaron didn't get the ball but instead went to the suitcase containing the clothes he'd brought from the Woodside house, and retrieved one of the blue and white water guns he and Vanessa had played with. I could see that bringing it to the condominium was no accident, as he had wrapped it in several T-shirts and hidden it amongst his things.

I laughed and turned to Daisy. "I had no idea he'd brought the water gun with us. I guess he really liked shooting it. Too bad we don't have a good place to play with it in here." I noticed it was still full of water. "Zaron," I said. "Take the water gun and shoot the plant on the balcony."

Zaron carried the gun to the outside balcony and aimed at the one plant we had there, a half-dead philodendron. He fired, splashing the plant with water, jumping and making his happy sounds. Afraid he might decide to spray me with water, I told Zaron to put the gun in the kitchen and watch a video on my iPad. After he was engrossed in a Disney cartoon, Daisy and I continued talking.

"He seems like a remarkable young man," Daisy said. "What will happen to him now?"

"I'm not sure. With all that's been happening, I haven't discussed this with Lim, but I've been thinking about adopting him."

"I can't see how you could take care of him. It's just not practical. Even if Lim's parents watch him during the day, it won't be long before you're overwhelmed trying to enrich Zaron's life.

"Deep down, I know you're right," I said. "As you know, Lim and I are planning to start making a baby of our own, and I don't know how Zaron would react to a new baby. He's okay with Mingyu but—"

"With a new baby, you're not going to have time to take care of Zaron properly. He needs a lot of attention if he's going to grow."

I let out a deep breath and relaxed. "You're not telling me anything I don't already know. I just needed to hear it from someone else."

"So, that's settled. No adoption. Have you thought about alternatives?"

"I think Zaron should move to a facility for developmentally disabled adults." It felt good hearing myself say it out loud. "There's a wonderful one in Kentucky I recently found out about. It's expensive, though. I want to start a GoFundMe page so he can stay there, at least for a while."

"That's a great idea. I've been wanting to help you ever since you got involved in this whole bombing thing. I'll set up the GoFundMe page. It shouldn't take me more than a few minutes. It's the least I can do." I thanked Daisy, who left shortly to get back to work.

After Daisy left, I answered calls from several journalists who wanted information about Zaron and the role he had played in stopping the bombings. I spent the rest of the afternoon with Zaron, grocery shopping and preparing dinner. Lim, Zaron, and I had a quiet dinner together, and Zaron slept on the sofa bed.

Before going to sleep, I followed the link Daisy sent me. The GoFundMe page she'd set up had one hundred dollars so far. The single donor was Daisy. Hopefully, more donations would follow. A lot more.

It had been a good day. I should have known better than to think my troubles were over.

Chapter 40

The next morning was hectic, but I took a few minutes to read the article on the front page of the San Francisco Chronicle about Crawford's capture and the rescue of Derrick and Kyle. A large picture of Zaron I had taken a few weeks earlier was above the fold, with a caption giving him the credit he was due. The article was tagged "Associated Press," so I knew it was distributed nationally. I smiled like a proud mother and hugged Zaron. Lim was preparing to leave for a meeting with investors, and I was planning to drop Zaron off at my in-laws before going to the clinic. Later that day, I would have my first appointment at the fertility clinic. I'd told Lim I was fine going alone as it was a short walk from where I worked, but he insisted on accompanying me. Zaron was dressed and busy folding the sofa bed into a couch when there was a knock at the door.

"I'll see who it is," I shouted to Lim as I went to the door.

There was another knock, as an impatient voice shouted, "Maintenance."

"Maintenance? What's this about?"

"Didn't you get the notice from the condominium board? We need to inspect the ceiling sprinklers in all units."

"I don't remember getting any notification about that."

"Here's a copy." He slid a sheet of white paper under the door, which I picked up and examined. Everything looked in order, with the usual logo and signature. I figured Zaron had thrown the original away without my seeing it, as he'd done before. Since I no longer felt the need to be wary, the letter was more than I needed to assure me the man at the door was legit.

"Maintenance is here," I yelled to Lim, warning him not to enter the living room in an indecent state. Not that he had anything to be ashamed of without his clothes on.

"Let me know if you need me for anything," Lim said, walking out of the bathroom and into the living room, a large towel wrapped around his waist. He disappeared into the bedroom and shut the door.

I looked through the peephole and saw a man with wire-rimmed glasses and curly blond hair in a brown uniform. He was carrying a large toolbox and was looking down as he smoothed out his shirt.

I undid the chain, which Lim had installed after our visit from Garrett, and started to open the door when it was thrust open, pushing me back. I regained my balance and looked at the man before me as he stepped into the living room, slammed the door shut behind him, and dropped the toolbox. He was pointing a gun at my head.

Despite the disguise of blond hair and glasses, I recognized him. Garrett. I reflexively screamed. Lim ran into the living room, wearing a pair of tighty-whities and a half-buttoned white dress shirt. Garrett turned the gun to aim at Lim.

I was speechless, but Lim found his voice immediately. "What are you doing here?" he yelled.

"You have something I want."

"What do we have that you could possibly want?" Lim asked. He was doing all the talking for the two of us.

"I want that," Garrett said, pointing toward Zaron, who was sitting on the couch playing Word Search on my iPad as if nothing were happening.

"Why do you want him?" I asked, finally able to speak.

"Zaron, come here," Garrett said.

Zaron got up from the couch, still holding the iPad, and walked toward Garrett.

"No, Zaron. Sit on the couch," I said.

Zaron abruptly stopped, then turned around and sat on the couch.

"I see you're in the mood for games," Garrett said. "No matter. He'll come with me after I kill the two of you."

"Why kill us?" Lim asked. "You successfully extorted a fortune. You can take it and live very well someplace where no one will find you."

"I intend to do just that. But to be clear, I have merely replaced all the money the government confiscated from me. If I hadn't been arrested for so-called insider trading bullshit, none of this would have happened.

"That insider trading bullshit you did is against the law," Lim said.

"It shouldn't be. Our members of congress make money all the time with their inside knowledge. I'm good at networking. Why should I be penalized because I make important connections and get information? Information I used to make a profit? It's not as if I stole from anyone."

Garrett looked like he was becoming incensed, the veins in his neck standing out as his face reddened. I wanted to deescalate the situation if at all possible.

"Why hurt us?" I asked.

"That's the only way I'll be sure you won't interfere with my plans anymore."

"The FBI already knows you're going to Qatar," Lim said.

I knew Lim hadn't informed anyone in the FBI yet about Garrett's latest money transfer. He was bluffing. It caused Garrett to pause, but just for a few seconds.

"No matter. The US government can't touch me there."

"How will you get there? Everyone's looking for you," Lim said. "There's no way you'll get on an international flight."

"Not that it's any of your business, but I'm taking Zaron with me to Miami on Preston Sallow's private jet. My mom's on a train right now, and I'll meet her in Miami this evening."

"You'll be caught there."

"I have several good disguises. But the real ace up my sleeve is Zaron. He's the perfect hostage. I've got a vest and everything I need to rig him up with a bomb. It's all here in this toolbox. If I'm recognized, I'll threaten to blow him up. No one would do anything to endanger him.

Not since the story of his heroism has been on the front page of every newspaper. Everyone loves him. Thanks to the two of you, he's an American treasure. To me, he's my get-out-of-the-US-free card, in case I need it. Once I get to Miami and meet my mom, with Zaron's help, we'll get to the marina where Mom and I will board the large yacht waiting for us. Then we're heading out for a new life in Qatar."

"What will you do with Zaron?" Lim asked.

"I won't have any more use for him. You should thank me—by killing both of you now, I'm saving you from the pain of having to mourn after I dispose of him."

As Lim and Garrett were entrenched in a conversation, the type seen in movies when the bad guy reveals all his motives and future plans just before killing off his nemesis, I was thinking of an angle. Garrett planned to kill Lim and me. I had no reason to think he would get softhearted or squeamish at the end. He would surely kill Zaron once he was safe on the yacht.

Unnoticed, as women often are when alpha males are having it out, I slowly turned and gestured to Zaron, still sitting on the couch. Did he still remember? It had been days since I'd practiced with him, but it was worth a try. He seemed to focus on my hands as I gestured.

Zaron put the iPad down and rose from the couch, as my heart raced. *Yes! Yes! He got it!*

Garrett glanced at Zaron. *Shit.* I didn't want him to pay any attention to Zaron. Garrett quickly turned back to Lim, the only real threat in the room, as I'm sure he saw it.

My chest was about to burst. I could hardly breathe as I watched Zaron follow my instructions and methodically move toward the kitchen counter.

Lim was speaking forcefully. "You'll be dying to get back to the US in a matter of weeks. And your mom, how do you think she'll enjoy living in a country with Sharia law? The way they treat women?"

"She'll be with me, her perfect son," Garrett said with a smirk. "She won't care about anything else. Anyway, as soon as we get there, I'll start working on new identities and fake passports. We'll be back in the US in less than a—Hey!"

A stream of water from the water gun hit Garrett squarely in the face. He turned sideways, dropped his gun-bearing arm, and sputtered. Enough time for Lim to pick up the decorative red steel apple sitting on the living room coffee table and hurl it at Garrett's head, hitting him in the temple with a loud thump. Garrett stood expressionless for a second, then was forced to the ground as Lim leapt over the coffee table and tackled him. Before Garrett had a chance to react, Lim rolled him over, removed the gun from his hand, and slid it a safe distance away.

"Get me one of the ethernet cables from the box in the study bookcase," Lim yelled. Followed by, "Please."

I ran into the study, located the box, and grabbed an ethernet cable, neatly folded and held by a wire twist tie. I unfastened the tie and handed the cable to Lim. He used it to secure Garrett's hands, then lifted him up like a rag doll, plopped him in a chair, and held onto his shoulders.

"I need some duct tape," Lim said. "Call my parents, and ask them to bring some up. I know they have a roll."

"How about you call them?" I asked. "We don't exactly speak the same language."

"Sorry, I forgot." I reached into Lim's pocket and pulled out his phone. Still focused on Garrett, Lim grabbed the phone with one hand, while maintaining his hold on Garrett with the other. I heard him speaking Chinese. Garrett started to stir.

"Don't move if you know what's good for you," Lim said, returning the phone to his pocket.

Garrett struggled to stand up and Lim punched him in the face—hard—just before a knock on the door caught my attention. Blood trickled from Garrett's nose as I swung the door open and ushered Enlai in. At first appearing to be taken aback, he rushed to his son's side and began unwrapping duct tape from the roll he was carrying. No words were spoken as the two men secured Garrett to the chair. When they were done, Lim turned to me.

"Who do you want to call? I'll leave it to you to decide who gets credit."

I looked around the room for a moment. Lim and his father embraced, Garrett looked miserable as a large bruise formed around his left eye, and Zaron sat on the couch, engrossed in Word Search.

I called April.

Chapter 41

I've always considered myself a pacifist and humanitarian advocate, someone who believes in everyone's right to due process and a fair trial, but I would have been in favor of taking Garrett out to a field someplace and shooting him immediately. I would have volunteered to shoot him myself. After seeing him with his hands cuffed behind his back, escorted outside between April and another police officer, and secured in the back of a police car, I had time to reflect on what had just happened. My rational mind took over and I decided it was best to let the government figure out what to do with him. I was confident he would be going away forever.

I called Daisy and thanked her for inadvertently saving our lives. If she hadn't visited the day before, I wouldn't have known Zaron had brought the water gun back to our condominium.

April called the following day to tell me that despite hiring an expensive attorney, Garrett was denied bail. He'd be left to rot in jail until his trial.

I visited Open Vistas with Zaron four days after Garrett was captured. The GoFundMe page had raised a fair amount of money already, enough for Zaron to stay there for a while. I wanted to look the place over, and if it seemed suitable, leave Zaron there at least temporarily to see if it was worth considering Open Vistas as a permanent home.

The flight to the largest city close to the facility, Louisville, Kentucky, and the drive through the beautiful rural countryside, were uneventful. Throughout most of the trip, Zaron focused on the new iPad I'd recently bought him. Driving down the long, tree-lined driveway leading to Open Vistas, I felt optimistic. The expansive surroundings of fields with scattered clumps of trees were peaceful and calming. I parked in the asphalt parking lot in front of the sprawling two-story Georgian-style building. It was formidable yet welcoming, with a border of bright flowers. The sunshine and blue sky dotted with cottony clouds added to the optimistic feeling I had as I entered the building.

We were greeted by a friendly receptionist sitting behind a desk facing the entrance. She took the small suitcase with Zaron's things I had brought with me. "We've been waiting for you," she said. "Zaron, I'm so glad to meet you." She extended her hand, and Zaron gave it a quick, listless shake as he looked around. "Charles will take you to the dining room where Derrick and Kyle are waiting for you." She entered something on the computer in front of her, and a young man with a warm smile appeared shortly. Charles introduced himself, welcomed Zaron, and escorted us to the dining room, a short walk down a hall.

We entered the large room with around twenty-five rectangular tables, each surrounded by six comfortable-looking chairs. Derrick and Kyle were seated at the nearest table, together with the behaviorist who had taken them in during their stay in Birmingham. Against my wishes, journalists were there to witness the reunion. They were standing off to the side, and I noticed them getting their pads, pencils, and recording devices ready. If the press had been expecting the young men to jump up and down excitedly and rush to hug each other, they must have been sorely disappointed. Zaron looked at the boys and they looked back. The behaviorist walked over to Zaron and handed him a ball.

He asked Derrick and Kyle to stand up, then coaxed Zaron to walk toward them. When they were around twelve feet apart, he asked Zaron to throw the ball to Derrick. Derrick caught the ball and threw it back. Following more instructions from the behaviorist, Zaron threw the ball to Kyle, who returned it. Lights flashed as the press photographers took pictures. The reporters erupted in hoots and applause. Almost immediately, the boys let the ball fall to the ground as they covered their ears in discomfort from the noise. The clapping stopped, the behaviorist ushered Zaron to a seat at the table with the other boys, and turned to the press. "I think you need to wind this up soon. Take your photos, but keep the noise down."

The journalists murmured amongst themselves. Lights flashed as more photos were taken, and they departed.

I left Zaron in the dining room and met with the director of Open Vistas, an athletic-looking middle-aged man. "First, let me show you this place. I'm very proud of it," he said.

I was glad I didn't have to ask if they could spare someone to take me around. I wanted to see as much as possible.

The director escorted me around the building we were in, then walked me outside to tour the grounds in a golf cart. Set on a hundred acres or so, the facility included spacious living quarters for the residents, a modern kitchen, classrooms, a computer lab, a shop for assembling things such as furniture and bicycles, rooms for crafts and puzzles, a gym, bowling alley, basketball court, swimming pool, vegetable garden, horse stables, and paths for walking and running. I was reminded of the beautiful residential facility in Rain Man, the 1988 fictional movie about an autistic man played by Dustin Hoffman, and his con artist brother, played by Tom Cruise. Having seen it, I now knew—this was what I wanted for Zaron.

When we returned to his office, I chose my words carefully. I desperately needed his support. I started by telling him about the GoFundMe campaign Daisy had started so Zaron, Derrick, and Kyle could stay at Open Vistas. The boys had been made famous by the press, with Zaron considered a hero. The public was generous, with over eighty thousand dollars raised in three days. That was enough for the boys to stay there almost two months.

"The money is still coming in briskly," I said. "I'm hoping that when the enthusiasm dies down, there will be several hundred thousand dollars in the fund, enough to last a year. In the meantime, I want to set up a charitable fund so these boys might remain here in perpetuity. Given all they've been through—"

"I understand how you feel," the director interrupted. I was prepared to hear a few comforting words before being told that regrettably Open Vistas was not a charitable organization, they had bills and salaries to pay, and would not be able to keep the young men once their funding ran out, which it surely would. While they were there, though, the staff would look for the best state-funded facilities they could find for the boys to be transitioned to. When he didn't say what I expected, I was not disappointed by my failure to correctly predict the future.

"A number of our clients' parents are sympathetic," the director said with a smile. "As you have probably deduced, the parents of our clients have means. Some are quite wealthy. They all understand the needs of our most vulnerable people. They have formed a committee to assure that Zaron, Derrick, and Kyle have funds to enable them to stay here for the remainder of their days."

I cried. Amazed, happy, relieved, appreciative, all rolled into one. Finally, I was able to speak. In a weak voice I hardly recognized, I said, "I can't thank you and the wonderful parents of your residents enough."

"I'm sure the boys will be happy here."

"I have no doubt."

Before I left, I hugged Derrick and Kyle. Then I hugged Zaron long and hard. I would miss him, but I knew this was the best place for him. As I left, he followed me.

"No, Zaron, you need to stay here," I said.

I turned to leave, and he began to follow me again. A staff member spoke quietly to me. "Don't worry, ma'am. This is normal. I'll take him to the cafeteria and get him something good to eat. I know he'll adjust."

She grabbed Zaron's hand and tried to lead him away. He let out an ear-splitting squeal of despair, similar to the sound he'd made months earlier when April tried to take him from my condominium. Then he broke away.

"Please go, ma'am," the staff member said. Then she yelled out, "Gary, come help me, here."

A muscular young man in a gray uniform ran up and gently held onto Zaron. "You can go now," the woman repeated.

With tears in my eyes, I walked out of the main building, hearing the soothing voices of the staff as Zaron continued to squeal. I reached my rental car and waited for my eyes to dry so I could see. Then I left.

Two days later, I went to the fertility clinic. I'd missed my previous appointment due to the need to go through multiple interviews with police regarding Garrett's capture. A week later, my mother passed away after choking on a piece of chocolate the caregivers were unable to dislodge in time to save her. Her death left me sad but thankful that any suffering she'd experienced was over.

Within a month of her arrest, Lydia Powell worked out a plea deal. In exchange for her testimony, she agreed to serve twelve years in prison.

Bernard Crawford escaped the death penalty by accepting a sentence of life in prison without the possibility of parole and agreeing to testify against Garrett and Sallow.

Preston Sallow was apprehended while trying to board a yacht docked at an exclusive Miami marina. I wondered if it was the same yacht Garrett had planned to take to Qatar. None of his high-priced attorneys lasted long, and he ultimately decided to represent himself. He is currently awaiting execution at the supermax facility in Florence, Colorado, although appeals are pending.

I heard Robert Garrett was unpopular with the other prisoners and was placed in solitary after a group of their best savagely beat him. His trial was delayed multiple times by his team of attorneys and probably wouldn't take place for over a year. Roberta Garrett moved to a small apartment near the jail and visited her beloved son often. Maternal love overlooks a lot of faults. I wondered how I would react were my child a mass murderer.

I've visited Zaron several times at Open Vistas. On each occasion, the boys from Bright Lights seem happy, and I see more of Derrick's artwork on the walls. A staff member pointed to one of Derrick's drawings and told me it was the house in Gardendale, Alabama, where Derrick and

Kyle had been held captive. Once a month, the top donor to the facility is awarded an original Derrick Portman picture.

Looking back, leaving Zaron at Open Vistas was the best thing I could have done for him. With each successive visit, I notice Zaron is a little more competent with language. He seems happy to spend time with me, but is no longer upset when I leave. I won't be seeing him for a while because it's difficult for me to travel now, but I like to think he misses me. I'll visit him in about three months when my daughter, Maya, who we plan to name after my mother, will be a month old.

ABOUT the Author

Fiction writer Deven Greene is a biochemist and pathologist who makes her home in the San Francisco Bay area. When writing fiction, the author usually incorporates elements of medicine or science. Deven has penned several short stories. *Unwitting* is the second novel the author has published and is the second book in the *Erica Rosen MD Trilogy*.

Note from the Author

Word-of-mouth is crucial for any author to succeed. If you enjoyed *Unwitting*, please leave a review online—anywhere you are able. Even if it's just a sentence or two. It would make all the difference and would be very much appreciated.

Thanks!
Deven

Acknowledgments

Once more, I find myself indebted to everyone who helped me with this project.

Feedback from others is indispensable. Again, kudos go to my little brother, Seth Greenberg, who has been immensely helpful. He is remarkably generous with his time when it comes to criticizing his sibling's painstaking work. I also appreciate the haranguing of my critique group members George Cramer, Jim Hasse, and John Schembra. Thank yous go to Rosalyn Jamison, Jen Petersen, Eric Petersen, and Suzanne Spradley for reading all or parts of the book and offering valuable feedback.

I am extremely grateful to my developmental editor, Nicole Ayers, who had invaluable suggestions and advice. I am also tremendously appreciative of Vi Moore, my copy editor, who humiliated me on every page with her much-needed corrections.

This book owes its life to Reagan Rothe and the staff at Black Rose Writing, who published *Unwitting*.

My biggest thanks again goes to my Amazing Husband, Glen Petersen, who not only read and offered suggestions on my work, but gave me encouragement at every turn and afforded me the time to write. Oh, and he brings me coffee in bed every morning.